D1738666

Regency Romance Books:

Scottish Scoundrels: Ensnared Hearts Series
Lady Guinevere and the Rogue with a Brogue, Book 1
Lady Lilias and the Devil in Plaid, Book 2
Lady Constantine and the Sins of Lord Kilgore, Book 3
Lady Frederica and the Scot Who Would Not, Book 4

A Whisper of Scandal Series
Bargaining with a Rake, Book 1
Conspiring with a Rogue, Book 2
Dancing with a Devil, Book 3
After Forever, Book 4
The Dangerous Duke of Dinnisfree, Book 5

A Once Upon A Rogue Series
My Fair Duchess, Book 1
My Seductive Innocent, Book 2
My Enchanting Hoyden, Book 3
My Daring Duchess, Book 4

Lords of Deception Series
What a Rogue Wants, Book 1

Danby Regency Christmas Novellas
The Redemption of a Dissolute Earl, Book 1
Season For Surrender, Book 2
It's in the Duke's Kiss, Book 3

Regency Anthologies
A Summons from the Duke of Danby (Regency Christmas Summons, Book 2)
Thwarting the Duke (When the Duke Comes to Town, Book 2)

Regency Romance Box Sets
A Very Regency Christmas
Three Wicked Rogues

Standalone Christmas Books
Christmas in the Duke's Arms

Paranormal Books:

The Siren Saga
Echoes in the Silence, Book 1

Highlanders Never Surrender

Wicked Willful Highlanders, Book 2

by
Julie Johnstone

The best way to stay in touch is to subscribe to my newsletter. Go to https://juliejohnstoneauthor.com and subscribe in the box at the top of the page that says Newsletter. If you don't hear from me once a month, please check your spam filter and set up your email to allow my messages through to you so you don't miss the opportunity to win great prizes or hear about appearances.

If you're interested in when my books go on sale or want to be one of the first to know about my new releases, please follow me on BookBub! You'll get quick book notifications every time there's a new pre-order, book on sale, or new release. You can follow me on BookBub here: www.bookbub.com/authors/julie-johnstone

Dedication

To James, Graham, Jules, and Davis. In years to come, if they happen to read this book, I do believe they'll know why it's dedicated to them.

Chapter One

The Year of Our Lord 1262
Highlands, Scotland

"Do ye willingly take Sinclair Ferguson to be yer husband?"

Brigid Campbell nearly snorted at Father Duncan's ridiculous question. The sliver of hope she'd been clinging to that the priest would act morally disappeared. He was the worst sort of coward—a cunning one. He knew very well she wasn't willingly taking Sinclair as anything, much less as her husband, but she knew better than to state that fact aloud with Ramsay standing where he could hear her. Her stepbrother had even less liking for her speaking her mind, or speaking at all for that matter, than her father had. Though it may have taken three painful backhanded smacks from Ramsay for that fact to sink in, it finally had. And she wasn't the only one who would suffer if she dared state the truth.

Brigid's heart pounded as she stole a glance to the left from under her lashes. Out the window, the iron cage that Martha had been put in swayed from the rampart over the inner courtyard of the castle under bright rays of sun. Her companion had no food or drink in that cage. How long could a body go without these things? She wasn't certain, but she suspected someone who had forty summers behind her as Martha did couldn't last long, and it had already been three days since Ramsay had placed Martha in the cage. Only someone with a black heart would use a soul as sweet as Martha to enforce his will.

The silence in the stuffy chapel was deafening. Everyone was waiting on her to answer the devil of a priest. Sweat trickled down her back in a slow, irritating slide. She bit her lip and wiped her damp palms against her skirt. 'Willingly' was such a laughable word for a woman. There wasn't much choice usually for her fairer sex. Either she wed Sinclair as Ramsay demanded or he'd leave Martha in the cage to die. And if she wed Sinclair, she didn't hold out much hope that she'd survive to see the end of the year given his first three wives had all met untimely demises before the dust had even settled on their wedding attire.

"Brigid," Ramsay hissed under his breath behind her. Whispers immediately commenced amongst the Fergusons and Campbells crammed into the chapel to witness her impending doom. Ramsay clamped his hand on her elbow and squeezed until she wanted to cry out, but she didn't. She refused to give him the satisfaction. Her nostrils flared searching for air to control the pain, and she forced herself to slowly turn to look at her intended.

She offered up a silent last plea to God, but for as long as she could remember He'd been deaf to her entreaties, and when her gaze met Sinclair's dark, hard one, she was certain this time would be no different. If only God were a woman, Brigid would have a much better chance of gaining an opportunity to save Martha and the two of them fleeing.

She forced herself to swallow again as Sinclair's grim stare held hers and she took a breath before speaking to link her fate with his, but a horn sounded out from the rampart, echoed by another and another and another.

"Someone has breached the castle!" Ramsay barked.

Almost as one, the men in the chapel surged out the door, leaving Brigid standing alone with a slack-jawed Father Duncan.

His bushy peppered brows dipped into a V as he frowned at her. "Why are ye grinning, lass?"

"Because it seems God may be a woman after all," she replied.

Yanking up her skirts, she bunched the material close to her stomach and turned toward the door to rescue Martha and escape. She didn't fear Father Duncan would try to stop her. He'd be too concerned about keeping himself safe. The parting glance over her shoulder when she stepped out of the chapel confirmed her belief. He'd wedged his bloated body under the sacrament table to hide.

Smoke and chaos reigned in the courtyard. Her eyes immediately began to water, and her throat became itchy, making her cough. Smoke billowed into the sky in all directions, surrounding her home. Fergusons and Campbells raced about, drawing weapons, manning horses, yelling orders. Servants darted out of the way of warriors thundering through gates, and no one took heed of her.

She winked up at the sky. God was most definitely a woman.

She bolted across the courtyard, reaching the stairs to the rampart just as a group of mounted warriors thundered past. She caught a glimpse of her stepbrother's bright red hair, impossible to miss in the daylight. He rode beside Sinclair. When the party the two men rode with disappeared from the inner bailey, she breathed a sigh of relief.

She took four steps up the stairs when someone grabbed her arm from behind. She yelped in surprise. Panicked, she yanked her arm as hard as she could. Retaliation was swift and brutal. Her captor jerked her back, causing her to lose her footing. She knocked into him, sending them both tumbling down the stairs as one; her bouncing on top of him all the way to the last hard, cold stone step. Momentarily dazed, she sat, dumbly gasping for air. Not so for the man.

"I'm going to kill my brother," he grumbled as he scrambled to his feet. He grabbed her, hauling her up as she fought to regain her senses. She struggled to suck in a gulp of air to scream, but hesitated. Calling attention to herself would not improve her overall predicament. The stranger took advantage of her uncertainty and shoved a piece of rough material between her lips, cutting off any chance of her bellowing. She flinched as the cloth scrubbed against the corners of her mouth. She could have sworn regret momentarily crossed his face, but it was gone in a flash, making her uncertain what she'd truly seen. A muscle jumped at his jaw line as if he worked to control his anger.

That hint of danger and the way his bright blue eyes darkened like a storm as he glared at her drove her into action once more. She swung to hit him, but he blocked her attempt with an easy flick of his hand. He spun her about and had the gag knotted behind her head and her turned back toward him to tie her wrists together before she even blinked twice. His adeptness stunned her, but before she could completely process that, he whistled, and a massive black war horse came galloping toward them at a startling pace. She would have hidden behind her would-be captor if he hadn't lifted her off her feet and tossed her onto the horse as if she were light as a feather.

The beast came to a shuddering halt, making her pitch forward since she lacked use of her hands to stop herself. Just as her nose grazed the scratchy mane, she was pulled backward against her captor's unyielding chest. He felt as if he were made of stone. Fear shot through her as his heavily muscled thighs settled on either side of hers, and his thick forearm slid across her belly to pull her even tighter against him. She screamed, a muffled, high-pitched sound that made the horse toss its head back and flail its front legs.

She almost jumped off, but with her hands tied she feared falling and being trampled by the horse. Her captor took the horse's reins and leaned forward so that his dark hair brushed her cheek, and his chest pushed her forward a bit.

"Contain yerself, Ailbert," the man's deep voice rumbled forward. "'Tis nae a way for a noble horse to behave."

The man was daft if he thought the beast was going to listen, but then, to her utter amazement, the *beast* did stop tossing his head.

"Ye," the man said, his tone no longer a gentle chide. She turned her head toward him just as he turned his to her. A piece of foolscap could not have been put between their noses.

Blue eyes were narrowed upon her. "Ye've caused me enough trouble this day, so do nae cause more."

There was no 'or' to his sentence, but there didn't need to be. The finality in his tone indicated he was a man used to giving orders that others knew better than to disobey. Her father had been such a man. Punishment for noncompliance had always been swift and harsh. She shivered as the stranger gave another whistle and flicked the horse's reins to send it galloping through the thick smoke of the inner courtyard.

Her eyes burned and watered, causing her to squeeze them shut in search of relief. She tried to open them when she felt like they had cleared the inner courtyard, but it was no use to do so. The smoke was so thick she could not see, so she closed them once more and struggled to find breath as her mind scrambled to come up with how she was going to escape her captor and return to save Martha without being caught. The horse galloped at a jarring pace. All around her, people called out to each other, and other horses' hooves thundered against the ground. Why was no one stopping this man from taking her? Of course, in a sense, he had saved her from a terrible fate, but what was in store for her if she didn't gain her freedom?

She opened her eyes once again and blinked in shock. They were riding away from her home, away from her father's men and Sinclair's men, and toward the woods that stood opposite all the burning fires. The air was finally clearing so she could see much better, and the first thing she noticed was that the man was wearing her family's plaid. No wonder no one had tried to stop him. They'd thought him one of them, but he wasn't, and likely in the heavy smoke they'd not even seen the gag in her mouth.

He sent the horse into the thick woods, and not more than twenty paces in, he pulled the beast to a halt. For a moment, she thought he'd changed his mind about taking her, but then another rider emerged from shadows beneath the thick canopy. This man was younger than the one who had taken her. He had an insolent look about him, but his blue eyes matched her captors in color and shape. *Brothers? Cousins?* They were somehow related. Of that, she was certain.

"Ye're a bloody fool," her captor growled, his tone harsh. His body behind her tightened with his words.

"Why did ye take her if ye think I'm a bloody fool?" the younger man demanded, his face turning red.

"I already told ye, Camden, that I did nae necessarily disagree with ye, but we needed to think things through!"

The man's tone became more forceful, more congested with anger, with each word he spoke. "Ye do nae ever think. Ye rush in without a plan."

"I had a plan," Camden protested.

The giant behind her made a derisive noise that rumbled from deep within his chest. "Did ye now? If I'd nae discovered ye had disobeyed me and come here, ye would have gotten yerself killed."

"I'd nae have. I—"

"Ye what?" the man bit out. "Ye started the fires to draw them out, but then what? Ye thought ye'd ride in pretty as ye please and pluck the lass right from the chapel without anyone taking notice of yer MacLean plaid?"

MacLean plaid? Why on earth would the MacLeans want her?

The younger man shoved a hand through his hair. "I admit I'd nae thought of that, but ye're here, and we have her, so let's take her. An eye for an eye, brother."

"'Tis nae her eyes I wish to remove from their skull," the man behind her grumbled. Brigid didn't know whether to be relieved or terrified. "Hear this, Camden, I only snatched her because I ken just what a mule-headed fool ye are, and I ken well ye would have refused to leave without her. Once ye are safely home, the lass will be sent back."

"We'll see," Camden replied, and he looked like he would indeed argue.

Listening to the exchange it occurred to her she could possibly use these men to free Martha, and then she and Martha could escape them, and the grumpy one would not have to worry about sending her back. She wiggled and grunted. As she'd hoped, her captor raised his hands to unknot her gag.

Suddenly, her brother's right-hand man appeared on the

forest trail. Momentarily shocked, she gaped as Oliver released an arrow toward her captor. Without thinking, she twisted toward her kidnapper, knocking his arm down with her own. A horrible pain shot through her as the arrow struck her upper arm. She cried out as the force of the hit toppled her to the left, but her captor caught her around the waist and pulled them both off the horse, shielding her, she realized in disbelief, with his own body.

Camden nocked his own bow and loosed two arrows toward Oliver.

"Stay put," her captor ordered. His sword slid from its sheath as he stood. He stalked toward Oliver and another warrior who had joined him.

She tried to focus on the fight between the men, but it was a blur of swords arcing through the air, and the pain in her arm had intensified tenfold. She glanced at her arm to judge how bad it was. Blood flowed from the arrow sticking out of the wound and nausea overcame her at the same time darkness did.

Chapter Two

Cormac MacLean stared down at the lass lying unconscious on the table in the healing room of his home. She'd woken once on the ride home, but only briefly to whimper in pain before her eyelashes had fluttered shut once more.

"Will she die?"

Tess turned from her worktable with a glass bottle clutched in her bony hand. "Maybe. Her heartbeat is verra weak and judging by all the blood on her and ye, she lost a great deal of it."

"I told ye we should nae have pulled the arrow out," Camden said.

Cormac glared at his younger brother who faced him from across the table the lass lay upon. They'd loss important time arguing about the arrow, but Cormac stood by his decision. If they'd left it in, they would have been unable to wrap her arm tight. Still, she had bled a great deal more than he'd ever seen an arrow wound bleed.

"I did nae intend for the lass to be injured!" Camden protested before Cormac voiced his displeasure. "How was I to ken she would be so foolish as to try to stop the arrow aimed at ye?"

His face had gone red, but Cormac suspected his brother's coloring was from anger at himself and not the lass.

"She tried to stop an arrow with her arm?" Tess asked,

arching her silver eyebrows at Cormac. "That does sound foolish. Then again, she's a Campbell, so I do nae ken why I'm surprised."

"She threw her arm up to keep the arrow from hitting me." Cormac still found it hard to believe that the lass had tried to protect him. It was bothersome that she had shown bravery. He didn't want to like anything about a woman who was stepsister to the man who had ravished his sister and killed his betrothed, but he couldn't just dismiss her actions either.

Tess set the potion bottle on the little table. She crossed the room to stand next to Cormac and looked at the lass. "Her color speaks to death."

"Aye," Cormac agreed, heaviness settling like stones in his chest at Tess's confirmation of what he judged to be the lass's fate. There didn't seem to be enough blood left in her body to offer her face any color. "Do what ye must to try to save her."

"Do ye care?" she asked him. "Her life for Elsie's and yer sister's?"

He clenched his teeth on the ache Elsie's name still caused him even after a year. The wave of anger for both his betrothed and his sister washed over him. His right hand curled into a fist.

"Maisie is nae dead," he managed to reply as he unclenched his fingers.

Tess clucked her tongue and shook her head. "Her spirit is dead, and I do nae see how we can get it back."

"'Tis why I went after the lass," Camden inserted. "I tell ye both that this—that she—" He motioned to the still lass, "is the way to healing Maisie."

"Nae if the lass is dead," Cormac snapped, his patience with his impetuous younger brother reaching its end. "If ye rushing off with yer half-arsed plan ends up with this lass dead, then ye've nae done a thing to aid Maisie. Think upon that," he growled.

"Enough squabbling," Tess said, her tone the stern one she had often used when she was their nanny as well as the healer. He let her ordering him go without comment, because she was Tess, and she was old, and he'd realized long ago, it didn't matter the years that passed, or that he was now laird, Tess would always see him as the boy she'd raised when his mama had died and his da had been busy ruling the clan.

"Cormac, get the lance from the fire," Tess added, "and Camden, ye hold the lass's ankles so she does nae kick me when I lance her arm. I'll hold her other arm as best I can."

"Nay," Cormac said, surprising himself with the word.

"Nay?" Tess asked, her own surprise evident in the lilt of the word.

"I'll hold her ankles, and Camden can hold her left arm down."

"What of yer vow?" Camden asked.

"What of it?" Cormac demanded in a way that would have shut most anyone up—except his brother. To Cormac's irritation Camden opened his mouth to say more, so Cormac turned away and started toward the fire to fetch the lance.

"Ye're gonna break yer vow now and touch the sister of the man ye hate more than anyone? The man who killed Elsie and ravished—"

"Ye do nae need to remind me what Ramsay Campbell did," Cormac said. He carefully retrieved the lance from the fire. When he turned back, Camden and Tess both gaped at him.

"That lass is near death because she risked herself for

me, and I've already touched her plenty. There is nae pleasure here in my hands upon this woman, so it does nae break my vow."

Camden gave him a look of disbelief, which irritated Cormac. "Ye think I gain pleasure from touching our enemy's stepsister?"

Camden shrugged. "She is bonny."

Cormac clenched his teeth. He would never break his vow, no matter how lovely the lass. And it wasn't even hard to keep. He didn't want another woman. He'd had one, and he'd failed to protect her, and his vow to never take another woman again remained. Not to his bed or heart.

"Enough talk," Tess said. "Come on then with ye, laird, and grasp her ankles and hold tight. If she's got any fight in her, this will bring it out."

He didn't doubt it would. A hot lance to the flesh to cauterize the wound would bring the fight out of most anyone. But the lass had shown bravery, and he suspected there was fight in there somewhere despite her fragile appearance.

He handed off the lance to Tess and moved to the end of the table, pushed up the lass's skirts to her calves, and stared at the slender legs displayed by his actions. Her ankles were delicate, her skin smooth and fair like a rare pearl. He moved to grasp her ankles, then hesitated for some reason. He didn't know why. He had a tug in his gut that he sometimes got that there was more to the moment than he realized. Camden and Tess stared at him, so he pushed the feeling aside and set his hands to the lass's ankles. Her skin was hot. Not just warm, but fiery.

"She's a fever."

"Aye," Tess said. "She'll get worse afore she gets better, if she does get better, that is. Ready?"

Tess spoke to them both, and Cormac nodded as Camden did. He set his gaze to the lass's face. The moment Tess touched the lance to the lass's wound, her eyes flew open. He startled at the brilliant color. He hadn't notice before in the chaos, but her eyes matched the bright green of the rolling hills that surrounded his home. They were full of fright, and they locked on him as she screamed and bucked. They held her tight and she let out a string of curses that rivaled any he'd heard by the roughest of his warriors. Camden chuckled and Cormac glared his brother to silence. There was nothing funny about the lass's pain.

"Let me go!" she bellowed, writhing on the table with a strength that surprised him and made Tess pull back for a moment.

"Hold her tighter," Tess ordered.

Cormac did as Tess bid, but when the lass whimpered, he instinctively lessened his grip. It was a mistake. She jerked her left foot from his grip and shot it back out to kick him squarely in the nose. Pain exploded and his nose immediately began to bleed, but he grasped her ankle and pushed her leg down.

"Cease yer kicking," he ordered above the amused howling of his brother.

The lass didn't cease at all but tried again to pull out the same leg. He held firm, though, and tears filled her eyes as her struggles lessened. Her despair made his chest tighten, surprising the devil out of him.

"Almost done," he said, trying to soothe her, not even understanding why, but feeling he needed to, as he nodded to Tess to finish. When Tess set the lance to the lass's flesh once more, her lashes fluttered shut on a moan and a pant, and her head lolled sideways before she went very still.

"Ye killed her," Camden announced to which Tess

made a derisive noise, finished with the lance, then set her fingers to the lass's neck.

"Nay. Her heart is thundering strong now."

Unsettling relief hit Cormac. Tess straightened, set the lance on the table beside her, and wiped a hand across her brow as she tilted her head and fixed her stare on him.

"She got to ye."

"Aye." He released the lass's ankles to touch his nose and wipe the blood away with the back of his hand.

"'Tis nae yer nose I was referring to." Tess studied him a moment longer before turning away and crossing the room to rummage at her medicine table.

"What the devil does Tess mean?" Camden asked.

"I do nae ken," Cormac lied. Tess was observant, and he knew she was referring to his offering soothing words to the lass and lessening his grip when he realized he was hurting her.

Tess marched back to them and handed him a rag for his nose. "Camden, go fetch me my henbane and hemlock. I forgot them on the table." The minute Camden was across the room, Tess whispered, "Do ye want to discuss it?"

"There's nae anything to discuss," he replied, hearing the bristle in his tone.

"I can nae find the hemlock," Camden bellowed.

"Keep looking," Tess called out, not removing her gaze from Cormac as a slow smile curled her lips, making her eyes twinkle. "So?" She arched her eyebrows. "Are ye certain there is nae anything ye wish to ponder aloud?"

He stared back at the woman who was like a mother to him. The day he'd realized he did not see Elsie as simply his younger sister's friend anymore, Tess had prodded him in this exact way to pursue Elsie. He narrowed his eyes at Tess, understanding fully now.

"Tess, there will ever only be one Elsie."

"I did nae say otherwise. But she's dead and yer alive still. And it seems to me ye just recalled that."

"There is nae anything to discuss about me *or* this woman or me *and* this woman. She's our enemy and only here because Camden is a clot-heid."

"If ye say so," she murmured. It was a phrase Tess often used when she thought there was more to be said. She was a stubborn woman, but if she thought he'd admit he felt more for the lass than basic human compassion, she'd be waiting the rest of her life. The only way the lass had struck him was with her foot to his nose. And it still smarted.

Tess's gaze continued to bore into him in that probing way she had.

"I did for her what I'd do for any lass in pain." The moment triumph lit Tess's eyes and lifted her eyebrows he wished he hadn't offered the words.

And then she snorted. "Ye did nae offer soft words for Alice a sennight ago when she was wailing after cutting her finger in the kitchen."

"A cut finger is nae as painful as a lance to the skin," he growled. The heat of irritation and embarrassment slid beneath his skin.

"I'd wager Alice thought it painful from her shrieks when I sewed her finger up, and ye told *her* to cease her hollering."

"Do ye have a point?" he demanded.

Tess grinned. "I've made it. I hope she lives."

"I'd think so," he said, "Ye are a healer, after all, dedicated to saving people."

"Aye," Tess nodded. "'Tis one of the reasons I hope she lives." Her eyes glowed with repressed mirth. She turned to her table and plucked up what he realized was the hemlock she'd told Camden to find.

"Ye're a wily old lass," he said, amused more than any-thing.

"Just ye do nae go forgetting that." She started to work on crushing the herbs to make her famous pain potion. She paused in mid motion and glanced up at him. "Ye can go. I'm certain ye've a great deal more important things to tend to than watching me treat her—like increasing the guards on patrol for when the Campbells try to take back the lass."

"I do nae believe they ken it was us who took her." Still, he did have a great deal to tend to since he'd had to rush off in the middle of his last clan council day. They'd not even been through half the clan members lined up to see him who wanted to lodge a complaint or a need before Quinn had returned with the message that his clot-heid younger brother had defied his order not to go after Ramsay's sister until they had time to logically think of the best course of action.

Upon hearing Ramsay was going to wed his stepsister to gain a powerful alliance, Cormac's initial gut reaction had also been to take the lass so the man would not get the alliance he sought. That was the least Ramsay Campbell deserved for his sins, but Cormac had wanted time to think carefully about things so they would obtain the vengeance they desired—destroy Ramsay for what he'd done to Maisie and Elsie.

"How did ye manage to get away from the Campbell stronghold without them kenning it was ye?" Tess asked as Camden strode back to them with a scowl on his face.

"Did ye send me across the room on purpose?" he de-manded.

"Aye," she replied, matter of fact. "Ye've big ears when it does nae concern ye."

Camden stared down at the lass on the table. "What does nae concern me?"

"If I wanted ye to ken that," Tess said, "I'd nae have sent ye across the room." She paused in grinding the herbs to study Camden. "Ye're staring like a cat in heat."

Cormac snapped his attention to his brother's face. He did have an odd, almost dazed expression.

"She's verra bonny, aye?" Camden said without his lifting his gaze from the lass, which annoyed Cormac.

"Ye've seen bonny lasses afore," Cormac growled, finding his own gaze inadvertently drawn back to the woman.

"Aye," Camden replied, sounding as dazed now as he looked, "but nae like this."

"She is uncommonly bonny," Tess agreed, which surprised Cormac. Tess rarely handed out compliments. "But that does nae mean ye should gawk."

"I'm nae gawking," Camden protested, "'tis just I did nae get a good look at her afore in the fray of the smoke, fight, and escape."

"What did happen?" Tess asked, catching Cormac's gaze as he forced himself to look up from the lass.

He felt he might be gawking like his brother, and he refused to do that. She was bonny, uncommonly so, as Tess had put it. He'd never seen hair as light as hers. It was like staring at the moon, it was that bright and shiny. And she did have ample curves in all the places a man might wish for a lass to—. He jerked with his own thoughts, cutting them ruthlessly off as heat coursed through him for his betrayal of Elsie's memory. He'd loved Elsie. He'd failed to protect Elsie, and for that, he would not take another in lust or love, which meant no thinking of a lass that way either. It hadn't been a problem until this moment.

"Did ye hear me, Cormac?" Tess asked again.

He'd heard her, and then he'd forgotten the question because of the lass. "Camden's grand plan was to start fires around the castle to draw the men out. Then he intended to ride in and magically come upon the woman."

"'Twas nae my plan," Camden protested. "I discovered her description first."

"Oh, aye," Cormac said, not bothering to disguise his sarcasm. "I forgot Camden got her description from a maid he encountered near the castle, but nae her name. He was going to enter the castle *in our plaid*—which would have alerted everyone to who had snatched the lass and bring them to our land for war. Oh, and he was going to do all this without studying the ground at all. He was just going to charge in."

Camden's face had turned red as a berry. "Ye make me sound like a clot-heid."

"Did I?" Cormac arched his eyebrows.

"So ye reached the young pup on time to stop him from getting himself caught or killed and then what?" Tess asked.

"I tried to get Camden to abandon his fool plan—"

"But he could nae," Camden said.

Cormac nodded. "I judged he'd get himself killed if I did nae go along with it then, and set it to rights after, so I *borrowed* a plaid from a guard who rode out to see to the fires, rode into the castle and straight into the inner courtyard that was in chaos."

"My plan worked," Camden crowed.

"It would nae have if ye'd been alone," Cormac snapped.

Camden slapped a hand on Cormac's shoulder and squeezed it. "I kenned ye'd come. Ye're my brother, and ye will always have my back."

Cormac shoved Camden's hand off his shoulder. "I'm

going to lay ye on yer back if ye ever do such a foolish thing again."

"How did ye two get away?" Tess asked.

"We killed the Campbell who tried to kill Cormac," Camden answered, "and we left the other one who was with him knocked out and trussed like the animal he undoubtedly is."

Tess's gaze once again probed Cormac. "And ye brought the lass here."

"We'll send her back when she's well." Cormac didn't want or need this lass around. They'd obtain their justice another way that would not surely bring the anger of the king down upon them.

"Nay!" Camden protested. "This is for the best. Ramsay ruined Maisie's life, and now we will ruin his sister's life; thereby hurting him. That's partial justice!"

"That makes ye nay better than him," Tess said. "The lass did nae ravish yer sister," she said, looking at them, but then her gaze was focused solely on Cormac, "or kill yer woman."

A muscle at the corner of his eye began to twitch as the memory of finding Elsie near death surfaced. He unclenched his jaw. "We will be sending her back."

"Nay," came an almost animalistic protest from the doorway.

Cormac's breath caught at the sight of Maisie standing in the doorway, looking nearly as wild as she sounded. Her red hair framed her pale face in a knotted disarray. She wore a soiled gown that he vowed didn't look like it had been washed in several sennights. Dirt smudged her face, her collarbones protruded, and she had a hollowed, haunted look about her. Her eyes burned bright with hatred, and though he didn't care to see his sister filled with anger, at least she had finally emerged from her bedchamber and did not seem to be a walking ghost. For the last year, she had refused to leave her room, and she'd not shown so much as a flicker of emotion since the day she'd been attacked.

"She's mine," Maisie said.

For a moment he had no notion what his sister meant by that until she let out a war cry and came charging toward the table, raising a dagger above her head.

"Maisie, stop!" he ordered, but she was in no mood to listen. She darted around Camden toward the table and plunged her dagger down. Camden grabbed her by the waist to jerk her back as Cormac lunged forward. He caught her wrist and plucked the dagger from her fingers. Camden lifted her bodily and dragged her back from the table, foiling her attempt to harm the other lass.

"Leave me go," she bellowed, thrashing wildly with her arms and legs. "Leave me go! Vengeance is mine! I deserve it. She will pay with her life!"

Maisie's screams were near deafening, and her efforts to escape Camden astonishing. She struggled like a trapped animal, pitching them both into a table near the one the lass lay upon. The work bench crashed to the floor sending bottles and herbs rolling and scattering a dark trail across the light wood of the floor. The lass on the table bolted upright, her eyes flying open, staring blankly.

There was no color to her skin and a sheen of sweat covered her brow.

"Please," she moaned, licking her lips. "I will nae speak again if ye'll just untie me." She slumped backward and she would have smacked her head against the table, but Cormac caught her by the shoulders and laid her gently back down. She was lost to the world of wakefulness once more, and he found himself relieved when her chest rose and fell in breath. He didn't want her death on his hands, was all.

And then her strange words hit him. *She'd nae speak again if they'd just untie her?* His gut told him the lass had been ill-treated, and as much as he wanted to ignore the instinct to protect her, he couldn't.

"Leave me go!" Maisie wailed again. "I want, I want, I want to kill her."

"Ye'll nae, though." Cormac pointed the dagger first at his sister then the lass. "This lass is under my protection, and ye'll nae so much as raise a hand to her. 'Tis her brother, ye want to kill. Nae her."

"I hate ye!" Maisie screamed at him, making him flinch. "I hate ye! Where were ye?" she demanded. Tears sprang forth as she jerked out of Camden's arms with a grunt and fled the room.

Chapter Three

*H*e sat in the healing room, listening to the labored breathing of the lass with only his guilt as company. The image of Maisie's face, twisted in pain, would not leave him. He was glad she'd finally broken her silence, but his shame at having failed her and Elsie knotted his heart. He stood then sat—then stood again, his tumbling thoughts a tangle in his head.

When he was once more in his seat, he glanced at the lass. His concern for her annoyed him. He didn't want to feel the slightest hint of compassion for Ramsay's sister, step or otherwise, but her earlier actions and her recent words left him helpless not to feel just a bit of kindness toward her.

He looked to the doorway. Tess's sleep potion had to be affecting Maisie now, so Tess and Camden should be returning, then Tess could take over with the lass in here, and he could go about his duties. He'd been foolish not to have taken Tess up on her offer to fetch a servant girl to sit with the lass. He still wasn't certain why he hadn't, except it somehow seemed his responsibility. He was laird, after all, and Camden's clot-heid plan was the thing that had put the lass in the path of danger and brought her to her current sorry state.

He swept his gaze over her and trailed his way down to her inner wrist. His heartbeat increased, and he frowned as he leaned forward close enough to inspect the delicate skin there. His frown gave way to a wave of anger when the distinct scar on her wrist became undeniable. He stood, reached over her, and took up her other wrist, not surprised now at what he saw—more faint lines of what looked to be rope scars. The woman's strange words now made sense. She'd been held captive before. Was it in her own home?

He couldn't simply send her back to her home if she was in danger there. His damned honor wouldn't let him. He shoved a hand through his hair as the tap of footsteps sounded behind him. He glanced over his shoulder to find Tess and Camden walking through the door. He arched his eyebrows at Tess.

"She's asleep," Tess said, answering his unspoken question.

"Ye can nae send Brigid back to her home," Camden said.

Cormac's brows dipped in a frown. "How do ye ken the lass's name?" He found himself wanting, for some inexplicable reason, to steal a quick glance at the lass, *Brigid*, but he didn't know why. Surely, no more than a curiosity to see if he thought her name fit her—not that it mattered. It did not, so he didn't look. He kept his gaze fixed on his brother.

"Maisie knew it," Camden answered. "Seems the lass was at Clan Donald's tourney where Ramsay..." Camden frowned now. "Well, ye ken."

Aye, he did. Camden was referring to the tourney where Maisie was ravished, and Elsie died from the burns she'd received trapped in the fiery cottage.

"Ye're nae the only one who should have ensured Maisie was protected, Cormac," Camden said. Tess made a sound of agreement.

Cormac scrubbed a hand over his face. His guilt must have been apparent for Camden to make the comment he had. "I'm the eldest and her brother. I should have kenned she was in trouble. And Elsie, too."

"Ye are just a man, Cormac," Tess said. "Ye can nae ken everything all the time and be everywhere at once, and ye were with the king and Laird Donald, as ye should have been, as winner of the tournament."

He had a flash of Ramsay calling him a cheater after Cormac had bested him on the field that day in the tourney. He could still clearly recall Ramsay's face red with rage when he'd tried to punch Cormac. Cormac had swept the man's legs out from under him, causing Ramsay to land on his arse in front of everyone.

Elsie and Maisie had laughed. They'd been standing to his right. Britta, the upstairs servant who was usually just as giggly as his sister and Elsie had surprisingly looked appalled by their behavior, and she'd shushed them both as Ramsay's father had approached. It hadn't worked, though. The lasses had gotten one of the giggling fits they often did when together, and they'd been unable to cease their laughter, so he'd shushed them before sending them to the cottage they'd been staying in during the tournament. Ramsay's father had snapped at the man to gain his feet just as the women were leaving. That was the last he'd seen Elsie alive, and that was the last he'd seen Maisie happy.

His chest ached, and he startled when Tess's hand squeezed his shoulder. He looked at her, and the sadness in her eyes only made his chest ache more.

She patted his arm. "Ye ken I do nae often agree with Camden's foolish plans—"

"Nay all my plans are foolish," Camden protested.

"Most are," Tess said, offering him an indulgent smile, "but yer impulsively going after Brigid Campbell may result in something verra good."

"'Tis what I was going to say!" Camden exclaimed. "Her being here brought Maisie out of her room!"

"Aye," Cormac agreed, allowing the sarcasm rising inside of him to flow over. "Maisie came out of her room to kill the lass." He motioned to Brigid.

"Anger is better than the lack of emotion Maisie has displayed!" Camden crossed his arms over his chest and jutted out his chin.

"Maisie said more words today than she's said since her attack," Tess added. "Mayhap she'll finally be able to tell us exactly what happened, and then the king will have to accept that Ramsay did as ye accused him."

Cormac shook his head. "The king will nae ever take Maisie's word over Ramsay's."

"Ye do nae ken that," Camden protested.

Cormac held up his hand. "I do, because he told me as much."

Camden frowned. "Why did ye nae tell me—"

"Us," Tess inserted.

"Sooner," Camden finished.

Cormac sighed. "Because of this."

He waved his hand at both their faces, which mirrored each other in the expressions of disappointed disbelief. "I ken how ye feel. I felt the same way when the king told me, but how ye feel will nae change it. That is why I said we must be clever in how we strike at Ramsay. He has the king's favor because of being the stepson of the king's eldest friend. The king thinks he honors the deceased Campbell laird by backing his stepson, and there is nae anything we can say or do to change his mind, unless we had proof of Ramsay's deeds that the king could nae deny. And Maisie's word will nae be proof enough for the king to believe that Ramsay ravished Maisie and killed Elsie because she witnessed it."

"Mayhap Laird Donald will back us if Maisie tells the laird from her own mouth? Then the king will be faced with two lairds who accuse Ramsay. Two is harder to deny than one," Camden said.

Cormac shook his head. "The king will say Laird Donald, in his grief over Elsie, will believe anything. And he would nae be wrong. We would need a confession from Ramsay himself in front of someone the king had to believe, and that, we will nae ever get, but I agree that the lass being here may help Maisie. We can use the lass to draw Maisie out, and hopefully Maisie's anger will give way to healing."

"What if the lass refuses to aid us?" Camden asked.

"If things are as I suspect," Cormac said, "then threatening to return the lass to her stepbrother may be the only thing we need to do to get her to aid us."

"I do nae understand," Camden said.

"I do nae either," Tess added.

Cormac faced the lass, and carefully turned over her wrist. She moaned in her sleep but did not awaken. "Do ye both recall when the lass said when she sat up?"

"Aye," Camden said.

"'Twas odd," Tess replied, and both Tess and Camden walked over to Cormac and Brigid Campbell as he motioned them close. "But likely it's the fever making her think she's tied up."

"Or it is because she's been tied up afore," Cormac said and pointed to the faint scars on her wrist.

"Oh," Tess said, anger and sadness in her tone as they stood beside him and traced a finger over the scar on Brigid's wrist.

"Do ye think mayhap Ramsay tied her up?"

"Mayhap," Cormac said. "Mayhap her da. I can nae say

for certain who."

"'Tis hard to keep a hatred of a lass who's been ill abused," Camden said, his voice begrudging.

"Aye," Cormac agreed. "'Tis difficult."

The lass whimpered suddenly and murmured, "Fine, fine, fine. I'll do as ye bid. Just do nae, just do nae put me in the dark again."

A fierce anger gripped Cormac. He didn't need another body to protect, to be responsible for, but it seemed he may have just inherited one. She turned her face toward them, and he was struck with how perfect it was. She had high cheekbones, and full lips, and her long lashes fanned her fair skin. His blood quickened, and he turned his gaze from her; only to collide with Tess's knowing stare.

"Call me when she's awake," he snapped and strode out of the room without a backward glance. If he had to find a place for this lass in his clan, it would be far from him. He didn't like that she was heating things in him he preferred to leave cold.

Chapter Four

$\mathscr{B}$ rigid came awake with a gasp and a wash of stark fear. Her eyes flew open to darkness everywhere.

"Nay!" She screamed, rolled over, thinking she was on the dungeon floor in her home, and promptly fell with a thud on to the cold, hard ground. She hit her shoulder and cried out in pain and confusion. Her head pounded against the sides of her skull, making her certain it was going to pop at any moment. Heat radiated down her arm, and when she tried to push up off the ground, the pain in her right arm intensified ten-fold.

She scrambled to her knees but nausea overcame her, causing her to double over, her hands on her hips as she gasped for breath. She tried to work through her confusion, but her thoughts were slippery and hard to hold. Had she spoken her mind to Ramsay? She frowned, trying to remember.

Footfalls brushed her ears, and her heart tripled its beat, sending her to her feet to prepare for her stepbrother. A door creaked, and a torch cast light in the room, illuminating the face of a man she did not recognize; but then a memory gripped her, and she screamed again. She tried to dart past the giant looming in the doorway, but he grabbed her by the waist and lifted her off her feet.

"Settle yerself." His warm breath washed over her neck as he set her to her feet once more and shoved the torch in the holder on the wall. She took a gulp of air to scream again, but he slapped a large hand over her mouth. "'Tis the middle of the night and everyone is asleep. Quit yer screaming. I do nae mean ye harm."

She'd never win a fight against him, so her only hope currently was to acquiesce. She nodded and was greatly relieved when he removed his hand from her mouth.

"Ye took me from my home," she blurted.

"Aye, albeit begrudgingly," the man replied.

She did grasp on to a thought then. There'd been another man, a younger one. He'd been the one to start the fires, and he'd been the one who had intended to take her.

"Where's the other man who was with ye?" The room tilted suddenly and caused her to slump toward the stranger. Her head knocked into his shoulder as he slipped his muscled arm around her waist. She immediately tried to push away but found herself uncommonly weak.

"What did ye do to me?" she asked, as the ground played tricks on her—tilting and then righting, only to do it again.

His fingers molded with a surprisingly gentle touch to her waist. "Ye've had a fever and been a bed for a sennight."

"A sennight!" Alarm slammed her in the chest. "I have to make my way home to get to Martha!" She tried to push upright once more, but this time she swayed on her feet, and the man gripped her more firmly.

"Ye'll nae be going anywhere in yer current state. Ye need food and drink, and then give yerself time to heal properly."

She wanted to argue with him, but the weakness she was experiencing told her his judgement was correct. "Who are ye?" she asked instead, "and why did ye take me?"

"Come, let me aid ye to sit first and get ye some mead."

Her mouth and throat did feel horribly dry, so she nodded. He held out his forearm for her to grip, which she did, and then with his other arm still around her waist, he led her over to the bed that she must have rolled off before. Beside the bed was a table littered with herbs, ointments, and bottles. "Well, I do nae suppose ye mean to kill me if ye've been working so hard to keep me alive."

"Nay, I do nae suppose we intend to kill ye." Wry amusement underlaid his words.

He guided her onto the bed with a care that surprised her as much as his gentle touch had. For a man who looked hardened and sounded gruff, the concern he showed for her person was unexpected. She scooted back from the edge of the bed to gain a comfortable sitting position, and the man presented his back to her to pick up a pitcher and a goblet that were on the table by the bed. He had a broad back, and his shoulders were massive. A strip of his clan's plaid crossed over his back, and she allowed her gaze to trail down his body, just as the strip did, to the braies he wore, which clung to his hips. He was well-proportioned without a smidge of fat, as far as she could tell, but a great deal of muscle, likely gained from hours of training with the sword. When he turned to her, she looked down, not wishing him to know she'd been staring at him.

"Drink this mead." Something in his tone sounded almost irritated.

She glanced to him, and he thrust the cup at her. When she grasped it, her fingers brushed his and he jerked his hand away like she was a hot log. She frowned at the odd reaction to her unintentional touch, but she took the goblet with a murmured thanks. She drank a large gulp of the wine, and then promptly began to cough as it heated her mouth, her throat, and her belly. It was stronger than any wine she'd ever had.

"Who are ye?" she asked again when the coughing finally stopped. She set the goblet on her leg, her hand still gripping it.

"Laird Cormac MacLean."

"And the other man who was with ye when ye took me was yer younger brother Camden?"

"Aye."

A memory stirred. "Do ye often want to kill him?"

"Aye." He cracked a smile that jolted her. "Almost every day."

"But this time it was because of his foolish plan?" she asked, noting his voice did not sound harsh when speaking of his brother.

"Aye."

"To take me?" she asked, seeing that her questions were making Cormac's jaw tense. The muscle on the right side of his jaw twitched. *Hmph.* If you were going to steal a person, it seemed to her he had no right being vexed about some questions.

"Aye," he replied, his word like a nip from an angry dog.

She scowled. "Are ye always this grumpy?"

"Aye."

"Do ye usually answer questions with one word?"

"If that's all the question is worth, aye."

Her back stiffened at his remark. "Ye're quite rude."

A smile tugged at his full lips. "Thank ye."

She gaped at him before finding the words to respond. "Why on earth would ye thank me for that? I insulted ye!"

"Nay, ye complimented me. Lairds must be strong and strong men do nae go about trying to please everyone; especially the sister of my enemy."

Of course, this was about Ramsay! A surge of relief filled her. If she could make this man understand she detested Ramsay, likely as much as he did, and that she wanted to flee him, except she needed to go back and retrieve Martha, then mayhap he'd help her.

"Ramsay is nae my true family." She didn't really have a family. She was certain a true family loved their members and made them feel worthy, as if they belonged. A true father, one who cared, would never tell his daughter she was nothing more than a commodity to be used. He would not lock her in the dungeon in the dark when she displeased him because she had spoken when not spoken to, or happened into his presence when he didn't bid her to do so.

She'd never been part of a real family, and she only knew what it should be because Martha had told her of what her own family had been like before they'd been wiped out in a Viking raid. She loved Martha, and she was like her family, but oh, how she longed to be part of a home where she could walk around freely, talk freely, be useful for a reason other than wedding her off to form an alliance. In her dreams at night, she wed for love to someone who adored her and would cherish her. Silly, silly dreams. It was no use thinking upon any of it now. An old familiar hollowness filled her.

"Are ye about to take ill?"

Laird MacLean's question snapped her out of her state of self-pity. She'd been utterly lost to it and likely staring at the man while she was. Her gaze clashed with his intense blue one. The probing way he studied her set her on edge. By the scowl on his face, she wagered he thought her a clot-heid.

Her cheeks heated and she looked down for a moment to pluck at an imaginary thread to give the blush time to cool, hoping Laird MacLean would not notice her embarrassment.

She worried her lip for a moment, trying to decide what to say. "I did feel momentarily ill," she lied, and that made the heat in her cheeks increase instead of lessening, but she pushed on.

She cleared her throat. "As I was saying, I do nae consider my stepbrother my true brother, so just because he's yer enemy, does nae mean I am."

"If ye say so," Laird MacLean replied, not sounding convinced at all.

The blasted man was going to make this conversation as difficult as possible for her.

"Why exactly did yer brother come to take me?"

"Because yer brother—"

"Stepbrother," she corrected.

"Stepbrother," Laird MacLean said, "ravished our sister and killed my betrothed at the Donald tourney."

Her stomach flipped at the news and her breath caught in her throat. She'd been at that tournament, though her father had mostly made her stay out of sight in the tent, as he preferred. She'd known Ramsay was not good, but these were evil acts.

"Are ye certain?"

A scowl settled on his face. "Do ye mean do I have proof?" The sudden anger in his tone was chilling.

"Aye, well, I suppose I do, though I do nae have a hard time believing my stepbrother could be capable of such things."

He leaned down toward her, so that their faces were only a hairbreadth apart. A faint trace of smoke lingered on him from a fire. "And why is that, Brigid Campbell?"

She thought of the nights in the dungeon when she'd

displeased Ramsay, and how he'd had her wrists tied together for her time in there, so that she could not even bat the rats away when they came out, and she thought of his tying her to the flogging poll to get her to agree to wed Sinclair. She didn't wish to share the particulars of the ways she'd been mistreated with a man she did not know, but she didn't think this man would hear her plea if she refused to share anything.

"My stepbrother is perfectly willing to wed me to a man whose first three wives died before their first year of marriage was complete, and he has caged my companion to compel me to do as he wishes, so it does nae take a great stretch of my imagination to believe he'd do other evil things. My companion Martha could die in that cage, and Ramsay does nae care as long as he gets what he wants."

"Let's make a deal," the man said suddenly, standing. "I'll nae send ye back to yer brother if ye'll aid my sister."

Brigid frowned. "The one that was ravished?"

"Aye."

"How could I possibly aid her?"

"I'm nae certain," he replied. "But she had nae come out of her bedchamber since the day we brought her home from the Donald tourney—"

"But that was a year ago!" Brigid said on a gasp.

"Aye." The word was heavy laden with sadness and anger. "She refused to leave her bedchamber, and she rarely washes, or keeps herself tidy, and the only word she said for a verra long stretch was yer brother's name. Actually, she screamed it for a good many months, and then one day, she called for her betrothed—"

"Who is that?"

"It was Ross MacLeod. She broke off the betrothal with four words, sent him away, and has nae spoken since until the night we brought ye to the castle."

"The night ye brought me?" she asked, surprised.

"Aye."

"What did she say?"

His head tilted to the right slightly, and he appeared to be weighing what to divulge. On an exhaled breath, he spoke. "She said that ye were hers. That she wanted to kill ye. That—well, the rest does nae matter as it does nae pertain to ye."

She wished to ask, but his unbending tone told her it would be pointless. "Let me see if I have this straight," she said, though she felt sure she did. "Ye want me to try to aid a woman that hates me and wants to kill me?"

He nodded. "Aye. Anger is a powerful motivator."

She agreed with that. "Why is it ye think it was my stepbrother who ravished yer sister?" She was assuming they had found her *after* the attack. It seemed far too personal to ask yet she had to.

"I'd bested him at the tourney that morning, and I do believe he was shamed when my sister and my betrothed—" He paused, and she suspected it was because he was struggling to suppress emotions, and that made her feel a little less fearful of him.

"They laughed at him, ye see. He tried to punch me after he accused me of cheating. I swept his legs out from under him, and he landed on his arse. The lasses got a giggling fit and yer father witnessed it all. Would that be something ye think that would shame yer stepbrother and mayhap send him into a rage?"

"Aye," she whispered. "My father was nae kind to Ramsay." And Ramsay had learned well not to be kind either. "He likely berated him for losing, and if Ramsay was shamed in front of him on top of the loss, well . . . ." She shivered. "It could have driven him to strike at yer sister and yer woman. I am sorry."

She felt somehow responsible simply because Ramsay was her stepbrother. "What was yer brother's plan for me?"

"To foil the union of yer clan with the Ferguson's. To slowly, but surely destroy yer stepbrother."

"Well," she said on a sigh, "yer brother unknowingly saved me."

"If ye aid my sister, ye can stay."

"Permanently?" she asked, merely to clarify.

"If ye wish it." He sounded so displeased by the notion that her feelings were injured. "But nae in the castle. Ye are nae family, and the castle is for my family."

It was like little cuts to her heart, though she knew logically it should not bother her. She was not this man's family. He had no obligations to her, but his words just reminded her how alone she was.

"I'd get a cottage?" she asked. What good was a cottage with a clan where no one would likely ever trust her or like her? It sounded dreadful, but currently she didn't have another choice.

"Aye, a cottage away from the castle."

"Aye," she replied, her injured feelings turning to sarcasm. "Ye've made that clear, and I'm nae a clot-heid."

"So?" He arched his dark brows at her.

"I'll try to aid yer sister to come out of her darkness, but I need ye to go back to my home with me to rescue my companion, Martha."

"Ye almost had me fooled," he said, his voice vibrating with sudden tension.

"How?" she asked, utterly confused.

He thrust a finger in her face. "*Ye're* nae going to lead me into a trap."

Her astonishment at his accusation turned quickly to hot anger. She poked him in his very hard chest. "Ye're right, I'm nae," she snapped. "How could I plan a trap when I did nae even ken I was going to be taken?"

"Ye're a Campbell, that's how, so ye're nae to be trusted." He crossed his arms over his chest and glared at her, which infuriated her even more.

Before she knew it, she was poking him in his chest again. "If I'm nae to be trusted, ye big clot-heid, then why in God's name would ye wish me to aid ye with yer sister?"

She couldn't believe her boldness. She didn't even know this man. He and his brother had taken her from her home, but even so, she was less fearful of him than her own stepbrother.

"I do nae need to trust ye to use ye. All I need is for my sister's hatred of ye to bring her fully out of her spell."

She was to be used yet again. She'd known it, but to hear him say it so casually and cruelly washed an enormous wave of sadness over her, and to her horror, her lip began to tremble as tears rose behind her eyes. She blinked furiously before they could spill over the boundaries of their confinements.

"If ye'll nae aid me in rescuing my companion, I'll simply go myself."

"Oh aye?" he growled. "Ye're so foolish that ye'd go back into yer stepbrother's clutches to use ye?"

"Nae foolish," she bit back, crossing her arms over her chest. "Determined. There's a difference."

"Well, determined or nae, lass, I can promise ye this," he said, turning on his heel away from her and toward the door. He paused at the torch and took it from its holder. "Ye'll nae get past my guards, so ye best settle yerself in to do as I bid, and if and when my sister is back to herself, I'll make a plan to aid ye with retrieving yer companion."

The door was closing at his back before she could respond, but it was just as well. She was hot with anger, and it wouldn't do to keep poking the wolf. She didn't need his aid! She threw herself back against the bed and cried out with pain as her arm hit the covers. With more care of her injured arm this time, she crossed both over her stomach, which was now growling something fierce, and she crossed her legs at her ankles to stare into the darkness.

This time when the tears filled her eyes, she let them slide down her cheeks in warm tracks. She had to save Martha, but the blasted Highlander was right. She could not march back into her home alone and think not to get caught. She'd be wed before she could blink and dead soon after. What was she going to do?

"Damn Ramsay. Damn Da, and damn Laird Cormac MacLean."

"'Tis an awful lot of men to be damning," a male voice drawled from the darkness, making her jerk upright and her heart jump. A torch cast sudden light in the room and illuminated the face of Camden MacLean. He was grinning, ear to ear.

"I was passing yer bedchamber and I heard ye cry out. I'm verra glad to see ye're finally awake. Now that my temper is cooled, I want ye to ken I feel terrible about taking ye as I did."

She wasn't one to give much to her appearance, but Ramsay had told her she was passable enough to get a good union for the family, and by the way Laird MacLean's younger brother stared at her with a look quite like a new puppy, she was inclined to agree with her stepbrother for the first time in her life, and it gave her an idea. If Laird MacLean would not aid her, then mayhap his brother would.

"Are ye hurt, lass?"

At least one brother had the decency to be concerned for her. That was the least they owed her after stealing her! Never mind being snatched had saved her, too. She didn't want to be generous to Laird MacLean in this moment. No matter how gentle his touch had been, his highhanded treatment of her had left bruises and prodded that voice inside of her that made her question if she was worthy to be loved.

Asking quick forgiveness for the deviousness she was about to commit, she took a deep breath and let out a sob. Once the man's hand was around her shoulder, she commenced her plan.

"I, I do nae ken what to do, and yer brother—" She paused to pretend hiccup. "Yer laird," she added. It was a good touch if she was judging correctly that Camden MacLean might well feel cast in the shadow of his older brother. Likely, it was hard not to feel thusly. Laird MacLean had a commanding air about him that swallowed up every bit of space in a room.

"My brother," Camden said, the words clipped like they'd had to wiggle out from between his teeth. She struggled not to grin.

"Aye, yer *older* brother." My, mayhap she had learned a thing or two about deception from her da and Ramsay. That made her frown, and she cast another prayer of forgiveness up toward God. "He's refused to aid me, and he told me plainly nae anyone here would aid me either, because everyone does as he says."

"Did he, now," the man replied, his irritation lacing his words.

Like milk to a bairn, that's what this was. It was entirely

vexing that guilt was shoving hard at her for the deception she was weaving. She shoved back. This was Laird MacLean's fault, after all. If he'd simply agreed to aid her, she would not have had to resort to trickery, but she was desperate to save Martha, and this was the only way available to her.

"What sort of aid do ye need, lass?"

"I need ye to go with me to rescue my companion."

"When?"

His quick response gave her hope. "Now," she said, looking to the darkness.

She had no doubt Laird MacLean meant what he said and come the light all the guards here would be alerted not to take their eyes off her. That's why she had to act now before Laird MacLean did.

When silence stretched, she added, "Unless ye fear the repercussions from yer brother. Then, I'll understand if ye're too scairt to—"

"I do nae fear my brother," Camden said, "Let's away afore—"

He stopped himself, but she knew what he'd been about to say. They needed to away before the beast woke up, and she couldn't agree more.

Chapter Five

Cormac willed sleep to come, but it refused. All he could think upon was Brigid Campbell, and that made him so irritated that his heartbeat throbbed in his ears, keeping him awake. He'd heard the tremble in her voice when she'd declared she'd rescue her companion herself, and the way his gut twisted had pushed him to be harsh. He didn't like that a lass he'd just met made his breath quicken and his belly ache, and he especially didn't like that she was the stepsister of the man he despised most in this world. He'd made a vow not to take a lass to his heart or bed again, and he did not intend to let lust cause him to break his vow.

He flipped to his right side, listened to his blood rush in his ears for as long as he could stand it, then flipped onto his back. Mayhap he should have gone back into Brigid's bedchamber when he'd heard her cry out right after he'd departed, but the fact that he'd wanted to rush in and ensure she was well had kept him from doing so. The lass had an odd effect on him he did not care for. He closed his eyes, determined to shove all thoughts of her out of his mind.

He listened to his breathing, and then to the wind, and then his heartbeat pounding against his eardrums once more, but his frustration only mounted. Finally, he gave himself over to contemplating vengeance against Ramsay, except his very thought led him straight back to the lass he was trying to forget. Still, he allowed himself one moment to consider the idea of using Brigid to draw her stepbrother out, and then cutting the man down like the animal he was.

Two things made him dismiss the idea out of hand. He was not a coward and only a coward would kill a man by luring him to his death. If he were to kill Ramsay, it would be face to face without any ploys. And he could not stomach the thought of using Brigid and putting her in harm's way.

He didn't owe her anything—unless she became part of his clan. Even if she wasn't, his sense of honor would not let him do anything other than protect her. Devil take his brother. His unthinking actions may aid their sister, but they also added a burden to Cormac he'd not wanted.

Want it or not, he now had it, and that's why, when the sun finally split the darkness, he got out of bed and started toward the lass's room to immediately check on her. Halfway down the passageway, he encountered Britta and another upstairs servant arguing over who was to take on Brigid's bedchamber to clean. A glance down the hall toward Brigid's bedchamber door showed it standing open.

"Is the lass nae in her chamber?" he asked.

"Nay, now, laird," Britta said, "but Tess was in there when I knocked."

"Where's Tess?" he inquired, impatient to discover where Brigid had gone.

"She was called to the McCormac stronghold. The laird's wife was delivering her bairn."

"Did ye see if she had the lass with her when she departed?"

Both the women shook their heads. He went from there to his sister's bedchamber, thinking mayhap Tess had taken Brigid there. He knocked on the door, and when he got no answer, he slowly opened it to give Maisie time to make herself descent if she wasn't so.

She sat in her chair in the same gown she'd been wearing for weeks. Her hair hung down on either side of her thighs in knotted waves of fiery disarray. Dirt smudged her right cheek, and there looked to be a streak of some sort of blackberry juice on the left cheek.

"Where is she?" Maisie demanded.

He was glad for the three words, even if venomous hatred did underline each syllable. They were much more than she'd spoken before Brigid had been brought here.

"I do nae ken," he replied. He pushed the door open and walked slowly toward his sister. She did not scramble out of her chair to a corner as she'd most often done when he or Camden approached her in the year since her attack, but she did noticeably stiffen the closer he got, and her fingers curled so tight over the wooden edges of the arms of the chair that her knuckles turned white and the bones there protruded.

He lowered himself to his haunches in front of her, allowing enough distance that he hoped he didn't spook her. "I suppose then, given yer question, ye have nae seen Brigid Campbell this morning?"

Before her inner fire had been snuffed out, Maisie had been stubborn as the Highland winter was long. He had to bite back his grin when her jaw thrust forward, even it was only a glimmer of her former spark.

"Where is she?" Maisie asked again, instead of answering his question.

"I do nae ken," he said once more. "I'm off to find her. Do ye wish me to bring her to ye?"

"Bring the green-eyed *ban-druidh* to me," Maisie said in a velvet-edged voice.

"She's nae a witch, Maisie."

His sister simply stared at him. As he watched, her eyes dulled and then the light went right out of them. He sighed, but he had hope.

"I'll bring her to ye as soon as I find her."

He waited, but Maisie seemed to have slipped back into whatever darkness had held her for so long. She stared past him now, but not in total silence. She was humming. At first it made him smile, but then after a moment of listening, he flinched. It was the tune their mother used to sing when trying to soothe one of them.

He stood slowly, stepped toward her, and the humming stopped, but he proceeded with the hope that she'd allow him to give her a measure of comfort. He set his hand to the top of her head, wanting her to know he'd never fail to protect her again, but she began to keen like a wild animal, so he dropped his hand away. The moment he did, silence fell.

"I'm sorry," he whispered as he'd done so many times before, but there was once again no response.

He left and made his way to the great hall in search of Brigid, and when he didn't find her, he went to the kitchens, stopping servants along the way. No one had seen her. A disquieting tension stirred in him. He should have already appointed guards to watch her every movement. Surely, the lass was not so foolish as to try to make her way back to her home to save her companion herself. Not only was she weakened from her injury that wasn't totally healed, but she was also unarmed, and he doubted she had any notion how to sneak into her home without getting caught.

He made his way to the banks by the loch where the men trained every morning. He'd get Camden and pull together a group of men to aid him in searching for her, and if they didn't find her, they'd have to go after her, all the way to her home, if necessary. He couldn't just abandon her to the fate she'd told him her brother had in store for her, and it wasn't because he didn't want Ramsay to gain the union with the Ferguson Clan. That was true enough. It was because the idea of doing nothing while the lass was married off to a man whose other wives had met untimely questionable deaths set a coldness in his chest.

He reached the banks to find his men in clusters working on offensive and defensive moves, and he scanned the warriors for his brother, who should have been leading the exercises in Cormac's absence, but Camden was nowhere to be seen.

He called out to the captain of the guards. "Quinn, have ye seen Camden?"

"Nay today," Quinn replied, lowering his sword.

"I—" Quinn's younger brother started to speak, then clamped his jaw shut.

The uneasiness that had plagued Cormac earlier gripped him now. "Ye what?" He leaned over to look the lad of ten summers in his eyes.

The boy shifted from foot to foot. "I can nae recall, laird."

"Do nae lie to me, lad. Ye'll nae ever be a member of this guard if ye lie. Ye must have honor."

The boy flushed red and puffed his chest out. "I've honor! I gave my word nae to tell."

"Ye gave yer word to who?" Cormac asked.

"If I tell ye, is that nae me breaking my word?"

Cormac shook his head. "Telling me who ye gave yer word to is nae the same as revealing what it is yer nae supposed to tell." Cormac wagered his life this had something to do with his brother and Brigid, and the uneasiness he'd been feeling was rapidly giving way to anger.

The boy shot his gaze to his older brother who nodded. "Tell, yer laird. 'Tis where yer first loyalty should always lie, nae matter yer word or nae."

The boy's shoulders fell. "Yer brother, laird. I gave my word to yer brother nae to say anything."

His nostrils flared with his irritation. "I'll nae make yer break yer word, as I can see it's important to ye, as it rightly should be, but I want ye to nod yer head for anything I guess correctly. Does that suit ye?"

"Aye," the lad croaked.

"I take it ye saw my brother somewhere?"

The boy nodded.

Cormac looked to Quinn. "Was yer brother with ye on guard duty last night?"

"Aye, laird. And he was alone in the tower when I went to relieve myself."

Cormac caught the boy's gaze once more. "Did ye see Camden leaving the castle?"

Another nod came.

"With a woman?"

Again, a nod.

"Did she have hair the color of the sun?"

The boy's face got a dreamy look about it. He didn't even have to answer Cormac's question. He knew Brigid had been with Camden. She was a bonny lass. Mayhap, the bonniest Cormac had ever seen, and the boy clearly had gotten the same impression.

"Did my brother say where they were going?"

The lad shook his head.

Cormac thought for a moment. "Did the lass say where they were going?" The boy hesitated, but finally shook his head, but it was the lad's hesitation that made Cormac believe the lad knew where Camden and Brigid had been heading, even if she did not say so to him directly.

He racked his mind, thinking how the boy possibly might know where his brother and Brigid were going. "Did ye overhear the lass say something to Camden?"

The boy nodded, and Cormac smiled. Now, they were getting somewhere, but he needed answers faster. He had a hunch Brigid Campbell had somehow talked his witless brother into aiding her, and he'd learned with Maisie's attack and Elsie's murder not to ignore his instincts. He'd had a strange feeling that day when he'd been with the king and the other lairds, but, to his everlasting regret, he'd dismissed the feeling.

"Did ye overhear the lass say they were going to her home?"

The boy bit his lip but nodded. Cormac clamped a hand on the boy's shoulder. "Ye've kept yer word to my brother and kept yer allegiance to me as laird. Good job."

Cormac looked to Quinn. "Gather five men. We're off to the Campbell stronghold, and I've nary a doubt we'll have to save my brother's arse—and likely the Campbell lass's as well."

Chapter Six

She noticed the vibration first. It increased tenfold in the air. No longer was it the steady low noise of the horses' hooves striking the ground as the two beasts galloped toward her home. This was the deafening thrum of a dozen horses charging. She glanced to Camden to warn him, but there wasn't a need. The concern on his face showed he'd heard and felt the noise as well.

He looked up the trail in the woods and she followed his line of attention with a gasp. Coming around the sharp turn of the descending hill was her betrothed, and fast behind him were four men. She and Camden were still hidden by the brush, but they'd not be in another five breaths. They'd never outrun them without a distraction. Something had to be done.

"Go!" she cried, and before he could argue, she slapped his destrier on the hind quarter. But instead of leaping forward, the beast just gave her a steady look.

"If they catch us both, ye can nae save me and Martha."

She saw his understanding in the darkening of his gaze.

"I'll come back for ye," he replied, regret resounding in his words.

She knew it was the right decision, but when he turned his horse from her and galloped away, she had never felt more alone or scared. Sinclair spotted her the moment he was high enough over the brush, and she'd no more than gripped her reins tight before he was upon her, taking her reins in his own hands.

"Brigid, we've been searching for ye! Where have ye been?" he demanded. Nothing in his countenance spoke of concern, only anger.

"Bandits snatched me," she lied. "I . . . I got away."

"From what clan?" Sinclair said, glowering at her, as if it were her fault bandits had snatched her.

"I do nae ken," she said, hoping she didn't sound as desperate as she felt. "They only said it was for crimes my brother committed against them." That should be easy enough to believe, and when Ramsay nodded, she barely contained her sigh of relief.

"How did ye get away?" he asked, as his men surrounded her.

"I was injured." She held up her arm to show him the bandaged limb. "I believe they thought me too weak to escape."

That wasn't totally without truth. Laird MacLean had thought her too weak-willed to defy him. *Blast the man.* If only he'd agreed to aid her, she'd likely not be in this predicament now. Laird MacLean did not strike her as the sort of man to ever be caught unaware of an enemy's approach like his brother had been. Of course, she'd been caught unaware as well, so she could hardly fault Camden, nor could she fault him for how quickly he'd abandoned her. Obviously, it was the wisest choice. She'd suggested it, after all, but it would be nice to have a man by her side that would protect her with his last breath because he loved her that much.

"How far back is the enemy?" Sinclair asked, looking past her now.

"Oh, a day away. I've been riding home since yesterday.

If they are anywhere behind me, I'd be surprised."

The man focused his hard stare on her, and the coldness *there*, made her shiver.

"They'll be pursuing ye," he said. "The stronghold that comes with yer hand makes ye too valuable to nae pursue."

"What stronghold?" she asked with confusion.

"Ye do nae ken of yer birthright?" he said, his shock evident in his tone.

"Nay," she admitted with a shake of her head.

"Well, 'tis nae surprising, I suppose. Ye are only a woman after all."

Only a woman. She gritted her teeth on the desire to respond. She didn't doubt that she'd get a slap in the face from Sinclair if she said something to displease him. It was funny she'd not had that same feeling from Laird MacLean.

"Ye're grandad was a weak man."

She felt her brows dip together. "Are ye speaking of my mother's da?" The man was long dead, and his younger brother now ruled the McPherson Clan.

"Aye. Laird McPherson allowed himself to be swayed by his wife, likely because she was *ban-druidh*.

Brigid had to clench her teeth again on the desire to set Sinclair straight. Why was it men always assumed a woman was a witch if she was intelligent, or assumed if a man listened to a woman's counsel, then the woman was surely a *ban-druidh* who had swayed him?

"How was my granda swayed by my grandmama?"

"She convinced him to leave Clooney castle to yer mama, since she was his only legitimate heir. Upon his death, she inherited the castle, but at least yer granda was nae a complete clot-heid, and he stipulated that though yer mama inherited the castle upon his death, whoever she wed would control the castle. When they had an heir, ye inherited the castle. But when ye and I wed, I control it and all the warriors who serve there."

Her pulse beat furiously against her neck. Her da had nae ever told her about her inheritance nor had Ramsay. But she did know she'd not been wanted. Her da had not wished for a girl. He'd desired a boy. Martha had told her so. She knew many men felt this way, but now she could not help but wonder if it had been about Clooney Castle as well. She knew *of* the castle. She knew it held a strategic position to guard against Viking Raids that had long made the king beholden to who owned it.

"And if I die after we are wed?" she said, barely able to get her voice above a whisper.

Sinclair narrowed his dark gaze upon her. He slowly raised his hand and ran one long, thin finger down her cheek. It was not a loving gesture and it made her shiver.

"Well then, if we do nae have a bairn, I inherit it."

Ramsay had known all of this and traded her for something to Sinclair. She knew it as certain as the sun was shining this day.

"What does Ramsay get if ye wed me?"

Sinclair slowly arched his eyebrows as he grabbed her chin. "Do ye nae mean when, Brigid?"

She forced herself to nod.

"He gets my fighting arm against his enemies, of course."

She had no doubt Ramsay had a specific enemy in mind, and she suspected that enemy was Laird MacLean. Ramsay would give her over to a man who almost certainly intended for her to meet an untimely death so he'd inherit her castle, and her step-brother likely had the man's word that he'd stand against the MacLean Clan with him. With Sinclair's first three wives having died before the first year of marriage and without bairns being born, she could not help but think that perhaps Sinclair sought out lasses who had inheritances such as she did—ones he would get all for himself if the wives died without producing an heir.

"Come," he said, releasing her chin to take hold of her reins once more. "We've a half day's ride left afore we reach yer home, but when we do, we'll wed immediately."

She had to escape before she stood in front of the priest once more. Her fate would be sealed if Sinclair wed her. Her mind scrambled to think how she could possibly get away, but even if she did, where would she go? If she went back to the MacLean stronghold, Laird MacLean would certainly not let her out of his sight again to try to rescue Martha, and he'd already made clear he'd not aid her until his sister was herself again. It could be that Maisie MacLean would never be right again. God above knew the horror locked in the woman's mind.

Despair gripped her as Sinclair clicked his heels against his beast and her horse followed his destrier's lead and began to move. She was being led to her death and there didn't seem to be anything to do about it. But what she *could* do was free Martha. She needed to be cannier than she had been before. If she could convince him that she now wanted to wed Sinclair, and that she'd like Martha to help her prepare for the wedding, mayhap he'd free Martha, and then at least Martha could escape.

It was near twilight when Cormac spotted Camden riding toward them like the Devil himself was chasing him. The fact that Brigid was nowhere to be seen didn't bode well. Cormac urged his horse into a gallop and met Camden halfway up the steep, winding trail. The first thing out of Camden's mouth was, "I'm sorry."

Hot anger flushed Cormac. "Ye always are," he snapped. "Where's Brigid?"

"I had to leave her because Sinclair Ferguson had too many men with him to fight alone."

Cormac's anger rose, a scalding fury that singed his veins with his boiling blood. "Ye should have stayed and fought to the death, then."

"Oh, aye?" Camden snapped.

Cormac's men rode up behind him and stopped in silence. They knew not to interrupt.

"If I'd died defending her, what good would that have done the lass? She'd still be caught! She knew it, and I knew it when she urged me to go!"

The news that it was Brigid's urging that had encouraged Camden to flee surprised Cormac momentarily, though after a breath, he didn't know why. Since he'd met her, she'd proven herself to be shockingly selfless, brave, and foolish. He opened his mouth to blast his brother once more, but then snapped it shut. They were wasting precious time. It would soon be too late, for she'd be wed and long gone into the safety of the Sinclair holding, a fortress much more difficult to breach than her fool stepbrothers.

Or she could be dead. That thought set a chill in him.

Cormac moved his horse close to his brother so that he was face to face with him. "We ride to the Campbell stronghold to rescue her."

"And her companion," Camden added. "She'll nae leave without her. 'Tis the reason we—"

"I ken well why she left!" Cormac exploded. "What I do nae ken is why ye were such a fool to let her talk ye into accompanying her!"

Camden opened his mouth then clamped it shut, lips a thin tight line. After a pause, he grunted. "She's verra persuasive."

Cormac snorted. "Let this be a lesson about agreeing to a foolish plan simply because a bonnie lass asks ye to."

Camden's forehead scrunched as if he wanted to argue, but he finally jerked his head in a nod. "What's our plan?"

"To get in and out alive with the two women. That's our plan," Cormac snapped. He urged his horse past his brother's beast to start the journey to save the woman who he was certain was nothing but trouble.

They rode in stony silence—or rather, he refused to acknowledge Camden—the rest of the day. He didn't quite know why he was so angry. He was used to his brother making impulsive decisions. Camden had done so for as long as Cormac could recall, but those decisions usually only put his brother in danger. This one had also put the lass in danger, and now Cormac and his men too, but it was the lass he was mostly concerned about.

As they galloped through the woods back toward her home, he couldn't help but wonder if she was worried no one would come to her aid and what foolish decisions that might lead her to. She certainly had no way of knowing he would come for her as he would any member of his clan in danger. Though, technically, she was not a member of his clan.

Still, she was now his responsibility, and he felt it in his chest—a tightening—greater than familial love for his brother, Maisie, Tess—or even Elsie, when she'd been alive.

In fact, as they rode through the ever-darkening day and thickening forest, the weight of what might be happening to the lass grew heavier until he found himself rubbing at his chest to ease the pain. He called a stop at the edge of the forest and they dismounted in the shadows of the impending night. In the distance, the rampart of the Campbell castle glowed with torches, and upon the rampart, a torch seemed to sway in the air. He frowned, unsure what that might be.

Camden stepped close. "Brigid told me her companion Martha had been caged by Ramsay when Brigid refused to wed Sinclair Ferguson. Ramsay put the companion in the cage without food or drink and she was nae to be released until after Brigid did as bid. 'Tis why the lass agreed to wed the bastard in the first place. She told me she did nae want to."

"I ken that," Cormac growled, a strange feeling running through him. He was irritated with his brother, speaking as if he knew the lass's mind intimately, but he didn't know why that should bother him. It shouldn't, therefore he would ignore the feeling. Instead, he focused on Castle Glowm in the distance. It was surrounded by a moat they hadn't had to worry about when they'd come last time, because, as much as he was loathe to admit it, his brother's plan to draw Sinclair and his men out with fires had worked. But it would not work twice. Sinclair was a clot-heid, but he was not so foolish as to make the same mistake again. That error had been one of an unseasoned laird overly confidant in his abilities.

The Campbells were not going to lower the drawbridge to let them pass to the inner courtyard and gain access to the castle, and even if the bridge was lowered, they'd have to somehow get passage through both gates. Even from here, he could see each gate was manned by two guards, and the gates themselves looked to be made of thick wood and iron.

The way in was the moat, an unpleasant thought at

best. Cormac shuddered to consider the filth emptied into the moat from the castle. He didn't relish the idea of becoming an easy target for arrows, either. An arrow in the back or neck would do more than hamper his ability to cross the stagnant sewer.

They could not simply all take to the moat together. In fact, it was likely best if two of them went and the others stayed back, hidden in the woods, to spirit the women away. Brigid and her companion would be protected by himself and Quinn.

Once inside the castle, they'd have to find Brigid, and, assuming the companion was still hanging in the cage, they'd have to release her. He was heartily glad now that he'd thought to bring the Campbell plaid he'd taken when he was last at this castle, but they'd need to secure another one for Quinn to move freely about as well.

He turned toward the men behind him and glanced at his brother. "Quinn and I will go into the moat."

"Quinn and ye?" Camden sputtered; the three words jerked from his mouth in outrage.

"Aye," Cormac said, ensuring his tone was as unbending as he currently felt. "Quinn and I will find the lass, release the companion if necessary, then swim them both to freedom. Ye will stay here in case I do nae make it out of the water because ye are next in line to be laird. And by God, Camden, if ye argue, or if ye do nae do as I say, I may just kill ye myself."

A long, tense silence commenced, broken only by the steady breathing of the men gathered around him and the sounds of the creatures beginning to stir in the forest for the night. Somewhere, a chirping commenced, and croaking floated from the water. Something buzzed by his ear. He raised his hand and swatted it away.

"Fine," Camden said with all the reluctance of a petulant younger brother. "I'll stay, but only because if ye get yerself killed, I'll need to lead the clan."

"God help us," Quinn said.

"What's that supposed to mean?" Camden demanded.

"That," Quinn said, "means ye're impetuous, and the last thing we need is an impetuous laird."

Cormac could not have said it better and maybe Camden would listen to his oldest friend better than he had his older brother.

"If I die, ye will nae be impetuous any longer. Think afore ye act."

Grunts of agreement came from the circle of men.

After a pause, Camden said, "I vow it, but I do nae wish yer death on my mind so do nae die."

"'Tis that yer way of admitting ye made a mistake?" Cormac asked, allowing one moment of lighthearted teasing with his brother, because it could be the last, and he knew well what it was like to have the death of someone ye'd loved on yer shoulders. He did not want that for Camden, so he wished to depart with his brother understanding he forgave him.

"Aye," he said reluctantly.

Cormac gripped his brother's forearm. "From here, what I do is my decision, nae yers. Remember that. I could turn back—"

"But MacLeans do nae ever surrender what is ours," Camden said, inserting the statement their father had hammered into them. "And the lass is yers."

"Nay," Cormac corrected his brother. "The lass is my responsibility as part of our clan. 'Tis all."

"If ye say so, but the last time ye were so surly about a lass's well-being—"

"Enough," Cormac said cutting him off abruptly. He didn't need his brother to remind him. Elsie had been the last lass he'd been so surly over regarding her safety, and why Brigid Campbell, why now, he could not say, nor did he want to examine it. Now or ever.

Chapter Seven

$\mathcal{M}$artha stood by Brigid at the window of her bedchamber overlooking the moat. "I do nae ken if I should be pleased with ye or dismayed that ye've become such a good liar in the short time we've been parted," Martha said.

Brigid stared down at the dark waters as an idea, mayhap a foolish one, began to form. She turned to Martha, glancing at the locked door to her bedchamber. Any moment now, Ramsay would come for her to take her to the chapel to wed Sinclair. Convincing Ramsay that being snatched had made her most agreeable to wedding Sinclair had been much easier than she'd anticipated, and finding Martha already released from the cage had been most unexpected. But upon further thought, she understood that Ramsay freeing Martha had everything to do with him wanting the woman still alive in case he needed to use her further for persuasion purposes and nothing to indicate he'd suddenly become compassionate about others. Martha was no good to him dead.

"What are ye thinking?" Martha asked.

Brigid squeezed Martha's bony hand. The woman had lost a great deal of weight in the cage. "I had thought originally to send ye to freedom by simply letting ye beg to get flowers in the outer courtyard to dress my hair. But since Ramsay has locked us in the bedchamber until the wedding...."

"I'd nae have left ye behind anyway," Martha said, a stubborn lilt to her statement.

"Aye, well...." Brigid met Martha's faded gray gaze. "We do nae have to quarrel about it now, because the only hope left for escape is the moat."

"But ye can nae swim!" Martha exclaimed.

"I can swim a little," she reminded her friend.

"Bah, ye sink like a stone 'cause ye take a fright. The darkness of the night will nae help yer fears."

The hairs on the back of Brigid's neck and her arms prickled upward in silent agreement with Martha's statement. Brigid rubbed her arms for a moment, then marched over to her bed and tugged the coverlet free.

"If I stay, I will be wed, and then I will surely be killed soon. Do nae forget all Sinclair wants from me is my inheritance, and he'll nae get that with me alive."

"Aye," Martha agreed, her voice ripe with fear. "He's a wily bastard to build his power through poor lasses he's wed." Martha moved to stand next to Brigid. "So, we will jump into the moat." Her frail hand grabbed the coverlet in a show of support.

"Aye." Brigid eyed Martha whose head barely came to Brigid's shoulder. "Do ye think ye can withstand the plunge into the water?"

The woman scowled, making her wrinkles on her skin deepen. "Bah." Martha waved a hand. "Do ye think *ye* can withstand the plunge? I will try to aid ye, but—"

"Nay!" Brigid said, more sharply than she'd intended. She grabbed Martha by the shoulders. "Do nae get close to me in the water."

A memory of Sinclair holding her beneath the water when she'd been no more than a lass and he'd boasted he could teach her to swim, swept through her in cold panic. She'd nearly drowned a young stable lad she'd later asked to help her overcome her fear, and almost killed Martha as well in her terror. "Ye ken I forget myself and will take ye under if my fears grip me."

Martha pressed her lips together and stood silent for a moment before speaking. "I ken, but what do ye propose I do? Watch ye drown? Ye're like the daughter I did nae ever have."

Brigid pulled Martha into a fierce hug. "Ye're like the mother I did nae have, Martha, and that is why I'm begging ye to let me go under if it comes to that. We'll both drown, otherwise."

The woman pursed her lips and stood for a moment before speaking. "There has to be another way!"

"There's nae. I've accomplished swimming short distances in the last year—" It was more like she'd paddled like a pup than swam, but it had been sufficient, and she'd been proud to be able to keep her head somewhat above water and not go into a black fright. "We'll tie up the bedcovers and lower ourselves as far as we can to the water, then drop the rest of the way down. Then we'll swim across the moat and flee."

"Assuming we survive, where will we go?" Martha inquired, resuming the task of pulling the bed linens off Brigid's bed.

"To the MacLean stronghold," Brigid immediately replied, and her lack of hesitation surprised her.

"Ye're certain?"

"Aye. Laird MacLean is stubborn, but any man so concerned for the welfare of his sister must be a good one at heart, and as I said, he offered me a place in the clan—"

"Aye, on the edge of his land like a cast off," Martha

muttered.

Martha's outrage on Brigid's behalf made her smile. It was true she'd never been part of an actual home, and she'd been made to feel her only worth was what she could bring a man, but Martha had always given her love, and that was more than some people had.

"We will be outcast together, until we convince them to truly trust us."

"Hmph. Highlanders have long memories and hold grudges, Brigid. Given what ye told me about them accusing Ramsay of ravishing the laird's sister and killing his woman, it's unlikely any MacLean will ever accept us as one of their own."

"Aye, I ken," Brigid said, ignoring the tug of forlornness threatening to bring her down, "but we've nae a choice."

"For now. Ye've an inheritance, so we can make ye a choice if we're canny."

"We'll discuss it when we're safe," Brigid said.

They worked in silence for a bit pulling all the linens off the bed and tying them end to end. When they were finished, they secured one end of the linens to one of the bed's legs, then threw the other end out the window.

They both stuck their heads out the window at the same time, nearly colliding in their haste. Brigid looked down the castle wall, but the night had been swallowed by darkness, and it was impossible to see how far down the linens reached.

"Can ye see how close to the water we are?" Brigid asked.

"Nay. The moon is dull tonight, which bodes well for us nae being seen when we drop into the water and swim the moat, but the lack of light does nae help to ken just how far we'll have to drop."

Worry blossomed in Brigid's chest. Martha was hearty for her forty-five summers, but she was also less hearty than she had been before her time in the cage. "Will ye be able to climb down the material and withstand the drop?"

Martha made a derisive noise. "Do nae worry about me, missy. Worry about yerself and nae drowning." As the words left Martha's mouth, the distinct rattle of the door handle caught their attention.

Brigid's gaze locked with Martha's and the fright in the woman's eyes matched the fear hollowing out Brigid's gut. "Hurry!" Brigid shoved Martha toward the window. The woman didn't hesitate. She launched herself up onto the ledge, pulling on the linens as Brigid aided her. Martha scrambled out the window with surprising agility for one her age, and she was swallowed by the darkness.

Brigid turned back toward the door, trepidation trembling her limbs at the thought of Ramsay on the other side of the portal. She had to gain time for them.

She rushed to the door, put a palm against it, and sent up a silent plea to God. "I'm nae ready," she said, her tone desperate, but hopefully Ramsay would think she was upset to be rushed. "Please, brother, I wish to look perfect for my wedding."

"Nay. Ye'll come now and—"

"Laird," came a voice from the other side of the doorway. "One of the drawbridge guards was found attacked."

"Stay here and guard this door," Ramsay said. "Do nae let anyone in."

Brigid didn't hesitate. Something amiss in the castle was her chance to escape. She raced to the window, scrambled over the ledge, then paused, momentarily surprised with how strong the wind was. It flapped her gown about her legs and slapped her hair against her face. Horns announcing possible intruders rang through the night as she gripped the linens and pressed first one foot against the castle wall and then the other.

Fear spiked her pulse and lodged a knot in her throat. She wiggled her other leg off the ledge of the window and her weight tugged her immediately backward. She clamped her teeth against the scream which rose in her throat. Her wounded arm protested her weight but held her. The linens cut into her palms as she pressed both feet firmly against the stone wall of the castle and began the slow decline into blackness. She glanced over her shoulder, hoping to see Martha in the water waiting for her, but she could see nothing. One hand over the other, she went for what seemed like an eternity, and her heartbeat increased with each motion until it thudded near deafeningly in her ears.

Sweat trickled down her spine and down her scalp to sting her eyes. The harsh scrape of the linen against her palms warmed them. *Blood*. The linens had worn the skin off her hands.

She took another step down, and another, and another, and the closer she suspected she drew to the end of the linens the greater her fear became until it was an all-consuming vine that writhed through every part of her body.

Saliva pooled in her mouth no matter how hard she tried to swallow. Her breath grew shallow as she struggled for air, and her heart skipped a beat. Nothing mattered beyond not falling, not dropping into the stygian darkness below. The pain in her hands was nothing, the wind a foe seeking to batter her against the stone of the tower.

She was going to die.

What had she been thinking? She tried to recall how she had doggie paddled the few times she had managed to keep herself afloat in the water, but every time the image popped in her mind, it was swallowed almost immediately by the image of water covering her head, of gasping for air, of fighting and failing to find the surface of the water.

She finally moved her left hand under her right, but there was no more linen to grab.

She screamed.

The sound ripped from her before she could stifle it, but the raw desperate notes rang in her ears as she grasped in terror at nothing but air.

For a single moment, she held on with her right hand, her arm throbbing at the use. Her grip slipped. Air rushed at her for one horror-filled breath. Her back struck the water first and she sank under like a stone tossed into the dark bowels of hell.

Her scream was lost as water filled her mouth and lungs. She kicked and flailed at the water with a desperation that consumed her. She didn't want to die. She tried again, but the water stretched around her. With no moon, no light, she could not orient herself. There was no up, no down, only a watery death.

Suddenly, the sensation of drifting ceased. The need to breathe set coals in her lungs. She burned with the desire to inhale one last time. Images filled her mind. Curiously happy images of racing through tall grass with Martha, the sun warm on her face as she laughed. Her arms drifted outward as if to embrace the memory and the pressure in her lungs eased.

Someone grabbed her.

Black terror sliced through her lethargy. The will to live flooded her. She clutched the arm that gripped her, giving no thought to who her rescuer might be. She clawed and kicked, using the person to climb upward, oblivious to the harm she inflicted. Suddenly, a forearm slid around her waist, pinning her flailing arms to her sides. She screamed, but she only succeeded in gaining a mouth full of water. In one last desperate attempt to free herself, she threw her head back. Stars shot through her vision as she struck something solid, but the arm around her did not so much as loosen one bit.

Then there was air. Blessed air. The shock of it, cool upon her face, stole the life breath she so desperately needed.

"I've got ye, lass, and I vow to ye, I'm nae going to let ye die."

The words registered just as the warmth of Laird MacLean's breath hit her cheek and her neck. She gasped, sucking in a greedy breath, the sob wrenched from her lost to the deafening horns blowing. The darkness that had consumed her was awash suddenly in fiery light as burning torches fell around them in a circle meant to trap them.

She was flipped onto her side, face to face with Laird MacLean, and for one instant, she could see his face. Determination and conviction etched into the set line of his square jaw. Calmness descended over her.

"Do nae fight me," he said, the strong strokes of his arms drawing them through the water toward the other side of the moat. Brigid gripped him tight about his waist, doing her best to keep her legs from tangling with his.

Something whistled past her.

"What is that?" she gasped.

"Arrows. Yer stepbrother means to kill me."

She looked then to the rampart. Archers lined the walls, aiming arrows down on the water. "We'll nae make it."

"We will," he said with a certainty that sounded unbreakable.

She met his gaze, a bit of hope rising. His lips thinned. "Take a breath."

"What?" she cried out, fear resurfacing and scattering her wits.

"Take a breath and hold it now."

The harsh command startled her into doing as told. She scarcely had a chance to suck air into her lungs before she was pulled under the water. Panic stiffened her limbs. She tried to push away from Laird MacLean, but his arm drew tight as a band around her. The strength of his grip and the solidness of his body as he held her against his chest acted as a counterweight to her terror, and a strange calm descended as he pulled them through the water. A moment later, they once again broke the surface.

She gulped a grateful breath, and as she looked back, she realized he had swum them beneath the fiery circle of torches to the edge of the moat. He shoved her toward the embankment, then hoisted her, as if she weighed nothing, out of the water toward the shore.

"Do ye see the rope?" he asked.

The roughness of it brushed against her fingers before she saw it. "Aye."

Grasping it, she began to climb, wincing as the coarse fibers bit into her already raw hands. Cold air hit her like a wave and seeped through her sodden gown to set her teeth on edge. Her hair lay plastered to her face, against her neck, and down her back, and gooseflesh peppered her from scalp to foot. But she was alive.

Laird MacLean climbed toward her, inching his way out of the water. She dropped to her knees onto the soft dirt, then leaned down to aid him.

"Get back!" he barked. "Yer brother's fool guards may hit ye in their haste to kill me."

"I've got ye just as ye had me," she insisted, extending her hand further.

He made a derisive noise but grasped her hand with his right and tugged on the rope with his left. He then heaved himself onto the steep embankment but slipped and he fell atop her with a thud. For one moment, she was trapped under the weight of him, and their faces were so close their noses touched. The quick intakes of his breath resounded between them, and the thudding of his heartbeat into her chest was a fast, steady rhythm.

"Ye're either the bravest lass I've ever met or the fool-hardiest." Each word washed his warm breath over her face. He rolled off her, sprang to his feet, then pulled her up.

"Why?" she asked.

Against her protest, he shoved her before him. A new wave of arrows hurtled toward them. He was shielding her. Shock and gratitude washed over her as arrows rained down, barely missing her. Did Ramsay know his guards shot at her? As the question filled her head, a shrill whistle split the cacophony, and the arrows stopped just as suddenly as they'd begun.

Laird MacLean shoved her upward as she climbed out of the ditch and finally reached level ground. He scrambled up next to her and grabbed her hand. "Yer companion told me ye could nae swim."

"Martha!" Brigid exclaimed, shamed that in the chaos and fear, she had utterly forgotten Martha.

Before she could say more, Laird MacLean bolted toward the trees, dragging her along with him. She nearly tripped trying to keep up with his pace. When they reached the woods, men materialized out of thin air, as did Martha. The woman ran toward her, but Brigid got no more than a quick hug before she was swung up and onto Laird

MacLean's horse. He came up behind her, tugged her back and between his thighs, slid his arm around her waist, and set his horse to an immediate, dizzying pace straight into the darkness of the forest.

Normally, she would have feared that he'd run the horse or them into a fallen log or tree branch, or down a steep incline, but Laird MacLean rode with the surety of a warrior who refused to fail. The jarring ride rattled her teeth and made her bottom ache, but she welcomed the pain, having come so close to death. With every turn, she looked back to the darkness, expecting to see a torch illuminating the night, heralding the approach of Ramsay, Sinclair, and their men.

And she knew Laird MacLean expected it too, because he looked back as well at every turn, and spoke to his horse, urging him faster. He jumped the beast over a log, and rode him across a stream, splashing water up around them as they crossed the water. They took a steep embankment she knew well, and at the top he paused. In the burgeoning light of the new day, she could now see far below them. Riding fast on their heels were two dozen of Ramsay's men and what looked to be a handful of Sinclair's.

Laird MacLean's brother and his warriors gained the embankment with Martha on Camden's horse.

"They're gaining," Camden said.

"Aye," Laird MacLean agreed. "We'll take the Pass of Death."

"Nay!" She protested, knowing enough to understand the pass was a narrow passageway around the mountain where one misstep of the horse would plunge them to their demise over the ledge of the steep mountain.

"There is nae a choice," Laird MacLean said from behind her. "We'll take it and reach MacLean land and safety afore they reach us. Even Ramsay and Sinclair are nae foolish enough to come after us on our own land without a plan and a great deal more men. Trust me, lass," he said, as he had in the water. "I'll nae let ye die."

"Ye best nae," Martha pipped up, breaking the tension, "or ye'll have to deal with me."

"I've nary a doubt yer a formidable foe," he replied, then set them off into a dizzying pace once more. They reached the pass of the mountain in no time, and as he guided his horse to the opening, he paused before entering it.

He leaned forward, his mouth next to her ear. "Do nae close yer eyes, aye. 'Tis better to ken what's coming but do nae look down either."

She nodded, almost too afraid to speak as he guided his destrier onto the path that didn't seem wide enough for a person, let alone a horse. She was tempted to look over the edge but recalled Laird MacLean's words and instead stared straight ahead into the white mist. A cold knot formed in her stomach and breathing became difficult. She squirmed, and the horse neighed in response, kicking a few stones over the ledge. Her stomach gave a queasy lurch.

"I can nae," she whispered. She squeezed her eyes shut and turned her face so that her right cheek pressed up against Laird MacLean's chest. His heart thumped solidly, comfortingly in her ear.

"Did ye know," he said, his deep voice calm and steady, "that my horse is a Kelpie?"

"'Tis nae," she replied, not moving her face. "Kelpies are nae real."

"Ailbert is real. Ye're riding on him, lass, and he's a Kelpie."

She opened her eyes a sliver and glanced up at Laird

MacLean, surprised to find him smiling. He had, she realized, lovely full lips, and for a shocking moment, she wondered what his lips might feel like on hers. A hot blush stole over her for her sinful thoughts. Never had she wondered such a thing. She swallowed hard against the unfamiliar rush of heat but forced herself to speak.

"Why do ye think yer horse—"

"He prefers to be called by his given name Ailbert."

His tone was so serious, and the statement so preposterous, that she laughed. "Did he tell ye this?"

"Horses do nae talk, lass," he said in that same serious tone that made her laugh again. "But he neighed when I asked him."

"Ye talk to yer horse?"

"Aye. He's a verra good listener."

He sounded so earnest that she realized he meant it. The gruff laird had a soft side!

"Why do ye believe he's a Kelpie?" she asked, thinking about what she knew of the legend of the Kelpies. "Did yer horse appear to ye as a woman or did ye see it change into a woman?" she teased.

"Nay a woman. I once saw him change into a bird, though, afore he was injured, and he lost his powers."

"Ye're serious?" she said, finding she wanted to hear the story and be proven wrong and discover magical horses did truly exist.

"Aye, I am. I had hit my head that day though, so if I'm to be totally honest, I could have imagined it, but my betrothed Elsie—" He paused, his grip tightening around her, and then he continued. "Elsie swore she saw him change into a bird as well. We were at Falkirk for a tournament, and she went to the stream to fetch water. I was cleaning my sword when Ailbert appeared as a bird and pecked at me, until I followed him to the stream and found Elsie clinging to a rock. She'd fallen in and the current was fierce strong, so she could not make it back to the embankment. She'd gone into the stream when she'd seen Ailbert as a horse to try to pet him."

Brigid frowned. "Did she believe him to be a Kelpie when she tried to pet him?"

"Oh aye. 'Tis why she tried. She had seen him transform from bird to horse, and she wanted to touch him."

"But legend says Kelpies are dangerous."

"Aye, but Elsie was brave that day and foolish, too. Much like ye today."

Laird MacLean both complimented her and criticized her in the same breath, but given the man had saved her, she decided to let the critical part go.

"And ye also saw Ailbert transform back into a horse?"

"Aye," he said in so matter of fact a tone, that it left no room not to believe him.

"Poof? Like this?" she snapped, only realizing she'd been clutching his thighs when she released him. The blush that had warmed her face moments ago spread down her chest.

"There was nae a *poof*," he said. "Elsie's fool brother shot Ailbert down when he was in bird form and he fell into the water with the arrow in him. When he emerged, he was a horse."

"So ye did nae see him transform afore yer eyes?" she said, unable to disguise the skepticism she felt.

"Nay," he replied, "but I chose to believe it's what happened."

She felt her brows dip into a frown. "Why?" she asked.

"Because," he said slowly as if thinking on his answer. "Things like magic and such are unexplainable."

"What other sorts of things are unexplainable beyond

magic?"

"I . . . I do nae recall." The words were hedged, indicating he was not being truthful.

"I did nae take ye for a liar," she said, deciding to be bold and confront him, because she found she was very curious to know what else he considered unexplainable.

"Ye question my honor?" he growled.

"Aye," she shot back. "I do. I do nae believe ye do nae recall what other sort of things are unexplainable in yer opinion, but if I'm wrong, please take my apologies for questioning yer word."

A long silence stretched, and she waited, breath held, with an odd sort of hope that he'd answer.

He let out a long sigh and said, "Matters of the heart." All four words sounded as if they had been yanked from him.

She felt her brows dipping even further with her confusion. "Matters of the heart?"

"Aye. Ye ken."

She shook her head, which elicited another, longer sigh from him.

"Are ye jesting with me?" he demanded, sounding a tad irritated.

"Nay." Embarrassment heated her. She did not understand what he meant about matters of the heart, but based on his tone, she did realize that he thought she should know.

"Have ye nae ever been in love?"

The words held a tinge of incredulity in them, and her embarrassment became acute, driving her reaction.

"Who was I to be in love with?" she demanded. "The only man presented to me to ken has been Sinclair. Am I to give my heart to a man who has had three wives afore me all deceased questionably early? That's foolish. Is love foolish then? Is that what ye're telling me?"

"I did nae mean to tell ye anything," he grumbled. "I do nae normally speak of these things."

"Well, ye started it," she muttered, crossing her arms over her stomach, feeling suddenly somehow more exposed than she ever had in her life.

"Aye," he replied, the word begrudging. "I suppose I did."

A long pause ensued where the only sound was the clopping of the horse's hooves against the ground, and then Laird MacLean said, "In my experience, ye can nae explain who takes ye."

"Takes ye?" Brigid didn't understand why the man spoke in confusing circles.

"Love, Brigid. I speak of love. Though for the life of me, I can nae say how I happen to be, and I wish to quit."

"Oh." Her face burned with embarrassment. "Ye're saying love is unexplainable."

"Aye. To me. Can we speak of something else now?"

"Might I ask one more question, Laird MacLean?"

"Why do I get the feeling ye'll ask it whether I agree to it or nae?"

"I probably will, but 'tis yer fault."

"How?" he demanded.

"Well, ye're the first man I've felt I could ask a question of without suffering consequences."

"Ah, damnation. Now I have to let ye ask. Go on then and ask it afore I change my mind. And I suppose ye should call me Cormac. If we're having such an intimate conversation, it seems silly to have it on a formal basis."

"What is it about love that makes it unexplainable?"

"Ah, lass, so many things. But here's the one ye need to

ken the most. 'Twas my experience that I did nae *give* my heart, as ye said afore. It was *taken*, and then I realized it, and there was nae *a* choice but to go along with it, because to fight it, to try *nae* to love her, would have been impossible."

Brigid sighed. She wanted to be loved like that by a man someday. "Ye still love her then?" she asked quietly. He stiffened behind her.

"Aye." The word sounded a bit choked. "Love does nae depart just because someone leaves ye. 'Tis another thing ye need to remember. Love is dangerous and foolish and once lodged inside of ye, damn near impossible to get rid of."

"Are ye suggesting it's to be avoided?"

"Most assuredly."

"But ye said ye did nae give yer heart, it was taken."

"Aye, but now I ken to guard against it, ye see."

"So ye did nae enjoy being in love?"

"Ye've asked a lot more than one question."

"Aye," she agreed. "I'm sorry. As I said, ye're the first man I have ever known who I did nae fear asking questions of."

"I'm fearful!" he said, the words an amusing protest.

"Oh, certainly!" She'd injured the man's pride. "Most fearful, indeed. But I also can see ye're honorable and would nae ever purposely hurt me. Though ye will use me."

"Mayhap ye are *ban-druidh* after all," he grumbled, moving the horse, to her shock, off the narrow path, and onto wide land.

"We made it across, and I did nae even realize how far we'd gone!" she exclaimed.

"Aye," he agreed. "'Tis why I was talking to ye. To distract ye."

Cormac MacLean was a good man. Or at least he seemed to be. He was outwardly gruff and inwardly considerate. She suspected he was guarding that heart that had been taken against his will before. The thought almost made her laugh, but then she had another. Would he guard himself against love the rest of his life? That seemed sad, but she shouldn't see why she should care what he did with his heart. It was not her business or place to care, so she'd not, and that was that.

When he pulled Ailbert to a halt, she turned to look behind her, passing his bright gaze, fixed on her, to focus on the trail. Once she saw Martha and Camden and ascertained that Martha was ok, Brigid allowed her attention to return to Cormac.

His burning gaze held hers, and she had to fight the urge to look away for fear he'd see something about her she didn't want revealed.

"Why did ye say I may be *ban-druidh* after all?"

His eyes brightened with merriment, and a smile graced his lips, transforming him from stern laird to approachable man. "Ye've a way of saying things to convince someone of what ye wish—"

She opened her mouth to protest, but he held up a silencing hand, so she waited to hear the rest of what he was going to say.

"But I do nae think ye do it purposely, which may make ye even more dangerous."

"Dangerous?"

He nodded. "Someone who is nae purposely deceiving but can get what they wish by merely being themself, is dangerous."

"Then ye're dangerous, too," she blurted.

He grinned at that, and the two dimples that appeared

in his cheeks fascinated her. For a hardened warrior, he certainly had some endearing things about him. She had the urge to run her fingertips down the dark stubble that covered his cheeks and chin and trace a path to his dimples, but she didn't. Of course, she didn't. She was not so foolish, after all.

"I thank ye for the compliment."

"Ye've the strangest sense of what a compliment is," she muttered.

"Nay. 'Tis just I'm a man, and ye're a woman—"

"My, my I did nae ken ye were so observant."

He served her a mock scowl before he smiled once more. "If ye'll let me finish...."

"By all means." She flourished her hand in the air to indicate he should continue.

On a chuckle that was lovely, low, and shocked her by making her belly tighten, he said, "I'm a leader, and therefore need to be seen as dangerous."

"I'd think that was for yer enemies, nae yer family."

"Well, ye're nae my family, are ye?"

His words, though nothing but truthful, hurt for some reason, and she sucked in a breath.

"Ah, lass, I'm sorry. I can say unthinking things at times."

She turned slowly toward the front, away from him, and shrugged. "'Tis fine. Ye spoke the truth."

"I use ye only to aid my sister. If it was nae for her—"

"I ken," she said. She swallowed strange emotions down that were clogging her throat. She was tired, so tired, and it was making her feel odd, she was certain. "I will do my best to aid her, but if I can nae bring her from her darkness, are ye . . . will ye send Martha and me away?"

"Nay. Ye can stay."

"I'm growing on ye, am I?" she teased.

"Nay," he replied so quickly she frowned. "But giving ye safe haven prevents yer stepbrother from using ye to make himself stronger, and that benefits me."

"I'm glad I can be of use to ye," she snapped. Aghast at how quickly her emotions changed. She didn't care why he allowed her to stay. Did she?

"I'm glad ye can, too," he replied. Was he truly that insensitive to her vexation with him?

Mayhap the man was a clot-heid, after all.

Chapter Eight

The day after returning home from rescuing Brigid and Martha, Cormac stared down at the sketch of the inside of the Campbell castle he was working on. A knock sounded at the door to his solar. Before he could give permission to enter, the door creaked open, and he knew that it had to be either Tess or Camden. No one else would dare to come into his space without being granted leave to do so first. Well, Maisie once would have dared, but that had not occurred in over a year. Sure enough, in the doorway with his arms crossed over his chest and a mutinous expression on his face, stood Camden.

Without waiting for permission, his brother strode in and did not stop until he stood in front of the hand-carved desk. He slapped both palms on the desk, the sound shattering what little peace Cormac had managed this morning. His pulse spiked with irritation, but he inhaled a slow, steadying breath to keep his temper under control. Instead of blasting Camden for his belligerent actions, he set down the quill he'd been using to sketch what he could recall of the Campbell inner courtyard, and he arched his eyebrows. He leaned back in his chair to regard his young, foolhardy brother.

"Do ye need something?"

"I just encountered Quinn aiding Brigid and Martha in their move to their cottage," his brother said, his tone short.

Cormac knew better than to rise to his brother's bait. He sat silent and patient, waiting for Camden to say whatever was bothering him. A long pause ensued, then Camden said, "Why have ye moved the lass and her companion out of the castle?"

Cormac slid his teeth back and forth, thinking on how to answer that. He'd made the final decision this morning after a night where he'd done nothing but dream about the lass—and they had not been innocent dreams. He'd woken hard as a stone with the images of Brigid still lingering in his mind. He'd never seen her without clothing, but he'd dreamed of it—in detail. He had no intention of breaking his vow, and so it seemed to him that the farther away the lass was, the less likely he'd see her. And that was for the best.

"The castle is for family."

Camden frowned. "Servants live in the castle, and they are nae family."

"They serve us," Cormac replied, trying to keep his tone even, though his irritation was rising despite his efforts to keep it tamped down. He didn't like Camden questioning his decision mainly because he didn't care for Camden to know Brigid had invaded his head.

"Quinn lives in the castle, and he's nae family nor a servant," Camden said.

"Quinn is like family."

Camden's eyebrows dipped even further. "I do nae like Brigid being away from the castle where she is nae within arm's reach."

"Why?" Cormac snapped. "Do ye wish to reach her?" The knowing smirk of Camden's face told Cormac he'd made a grave error with his words and lack of control of his temper.

Camden leaned a thigh against the desk, picked up

Cormac's goblet of wine and took a sip, merriment lighting his eyes. After a moment, he set the goblet in front of Cormac and grinned.

"I would certainly nae mind reaching her." Camden's tone was suggestive, and Cormac's body went rigid. "Touching her," Camden added. Cormac's fingers curled into fists under his desk. "Bedding her, even."

Cormac shoved his chair back and rose to tower over his brother. "Do nae even think of it."

"Why, brother?" Camden asked. "She's brave. She's bonny. She's honest. I could see taking her to wife or at the verra least to my bed."

For one beat, Cormac envisioned his fist meeting his brother's smirking mouth, but he gave himself a good shake and unclenched his hands. "She is here to aid Maisie."

Camden winked. "She can aid me, too."

"Do nae even say such things. Do nae think them. In fact, keep an arm's length between ye and the lass."

"Why?" Camden demanded. "It may be that we suit and I take her to wife. Were ye nae telling me recently that I needed to think of taking a wife?"

Damnation. He had. The family needed an heir for the future, and since it was not going to be coming from him, the duty fell to Camden. "I was, but nae her."

"Because she's a Campbell?" Camden asked.

"Aye," Cormac immediately replied, grasping the excuse his brother had given him.

"Ha!"

"Ha?"

"Yer eye is twitching!" Camden said, pointing at Cormac's right eye. "It does that when ye are nae being truthful."

Cormac had to force himself not to press his fingertip to

the vein. He could feel it beating furiously.

"Ye want the lass for yerself," Camden accused.

"Nay." And that was the truth.

Camden studied Cormac for long minute. "Ye want the lass, but ye do nae want to want her."

"Have ye always been this eloquent?" Cormac snapped.

Camden chuckled. "Ye're just irritated because ye desire the lass, but ye made that clot-heid vow to nae ever take another lass again."

"'Twas nae a clot-heid vow," Cormac bit out. He shoved past his brother and started toward the door, intent on going down to the shore to train and rid himself of some of his anger. He didn't get more than four steps before Camden grabbed his arm from behind. He swung toward his brother, temper full flared. "What?"

"I misspoke. 'Twas nae a clot-heid vow."

His brother's unusually serious look and apologetic tone cooled Cormac's anger. He nodded. "Thank ye."

"It was a vow given out of grief and guilt."

"Camden," Cormac warned.

Camden held up his hands. "Hear me out, aye?"

"Fine."

"I ken ye think ye failed Maisie and Elsie, but ye did nae fail them anymore than any of us did, or any of Elsie's family did. Ye could nae have kenned what evil Ramsay would get up to. Nae any of us could. And ye can nae punish yerself for the rest of yer life by making yerself spend yer life alone and miserable."

"I am nae miserable."

"Well, ye are nae happy."

Cormac frowned. His brother's words were true, but only lately had he realized he generally went around in a grumpy state. He hadn't quite figured out why, but he was suspecting he was lonely. He missed a woman's touch. Her laugh. Her eyes upon him. Her smile just for him. Her listening and understanding. But he deserved no less than to miss these things.

Frustrated, he shoved a hand through his hair. There had been plenty of lasses at the castle in the last year since Elsie's death to extend offers of comfort that included joining their bodies, but his interest had not been piqued in the least. Keeping his vow had not been a question. Why Brigid now captured his interest, he couldn't say.

"I'm happy enough," he finally said.

"Elsie would nae have wanted ye to stay alone forever," Camden replied.

"Elsie can nae say what she would have wanted because she's dead." Before his brother could say more, Cormac forced himself to address the situation with Camden and Brigid.

"If ye want the lass, pursue her, but do so with honor."

Camden shook his head. "Ye're a stubborn fool, but I'm nae a fool, too, so I will pursue the lass—with honor—if she shows any interest."

Cormac wanted to take back his words. His body rejected the possibility of Camden with Brigid, but he accepted it with the iron will forged from being born and raised to lead a clan. He jerked his head in a nod.

"I do nae like her nae under our roof, given Ramsay and Sinclair now ken she's here with us. I'm going to move her back into the castle where she and Martha will be most protected," Camden said.

Cormac didn't relish the notion of running into Brigid constantly, but he also didn't want to give Camden more reason to question him, so he shrugged and said, "If ye think it will be best, then I'll acquiesce to ye in this. Now, I'm going to train."

He didn't wait for Camden's reply. He was halfway out the door when Camden called out, "Do ye wish to go to Maisie's room with me to see how Brigid is doing with her?"

Cormac swung back toward his brother. "I thought ye said ye encountered Quinn aiding the lass and her companion with their move. If she's moving, how can she be with Maisie?"

"Because I told Quinn nae to move her," came Tess's voice from behind Cormac. He swiveled round to face Tess, and damned if the vein by his eye was not beating so furiously that his eye was twitching.

"Why the devil did ye do that?"

Tess gave him a patient look. "Because I believed that once ye thought upon it, ye'd see that the lass would be much safer here at the castle, and I ken ye well enough to realize ye'd want to keep her safe, nae matter yer personal feelings."

"I do nae have any personal feelings for the lass," he bellowed.

"I meant yer dislike of her as a Campbell," Tess said, sounding innocent, but he saw her exchange a look with Camden.

He narrowed his eyes, looked between the two of them, and then settled his attention on Tess.

"Did ye send Camden to come talk to me?"

"Why would I do that? she asked, her attempt to sound innocent failing miserably.

He gritted his teeth then unclenched them enough to speak. "Because ye meddle."

"'Tis a rude accusation," she retorted, but he noted she did not deny it.

"Rude or nae, 'tis the truth."

Her lips pressed into a line "Well, yer decision was foolish. If anything were to happen to that lass while staying at that cottage, ye would have added that guilt to what ye already carry, and a body can only cart so much afore it gives."

A bit of his irritation abated. Tess cared for him as a son, and she was merely doing what she thought was right to aid him.

"'Tis likely a sounder decision for the lass and her companion to stay within the walls of the inner courtyard, given her stepbrother and betrothed will undoubtedly try to come for her."

Tess and Camden exchanged another quick look, this time triumphant. He'd not put it past the two to have hatched up even more of a scheme, perhaps one in which they thought to make Cormac jealous by Camden showing interest in pursuing the lass and thereby hoping to inspire Cormac to pursue her. Well, they were mistaken.

"Well then," Camden said, "why do ye nae join us to see how Brigid is fairing with Maisie?"

"Nay," he replied, enjoying for a moment the surprise on both of their faces. It was confirmation that they had conspired to set him on a certain course, and he had foiled their foolish attempt. "I feel certain that between the two of ye, ye can keep a watchful eye on how things are progressing with Maisie and keep me updated."

"But—" Tess protested. He held up a silencing hand.

"Brother—" Camden added, but Cormac glowered him into silence, deciding subtleness would not work.

"That's all I'll discuss on the subject." He turned on his heel and strode way away from them, away from the castle, and away from the ghosts, both living and dead, that haunted him.

Chapter Nine

*B*rigid stood just inside the doorway of Maisie MacLean's bedchamber.

"Maisie," Brigid tried again, but the woman did not respond. Perhaps it was because Maisie was embarrassed? After all, Tess had told Brigid that Maisie had threatened to kill her, which was why Tess had insisted a guard stay with Brigid when Tess had brought Brigid to Maisie's bedchamber. But having the man here was hampering her efforts to get Maisie to engage. Brigid was certain of it.

"Ye can go," Brigid said in the strongest voice she could muster.

"But my lady—"

She'd forgotten the brown-headed man's name, and she certainly didn't want to admit that now. It might somehow make her appear weak to Maisie, and she knew she needed to appear confident and in control.

"Yer laird gave me authority over his sister." That was a truth of sorts. "And I need to be alone with her."

Uncertainty fell across the man's face, but he finally nodded. "As ye wish."

That was the first time a man had ever said those words to her. It gave her a sense of accomplishment and bolstered her confidence. Once the guard was gone, Brigid swept her gaze around the room, looking for anything Maisie could use as a weapon. Though Tess had assured her they had taken anything away the woman might use to try to injure her, double checking seemed wise, especially since she'd dismissed the guard.

"Maisie," Brigid called again to no response. She wished Martha was in here with her, but they did need clothes, as Martha had pointed out, so she had gone with Tess to the sewing room to procure cloth to start making them clothes and find some gowns that they could borrow in the meantime, as well as personal items they would need.

Brigid stood there trying to decide what to do as Maisie hummed to herself as she had been since Brigid had arrived at her bedchamber. She wanted to help the woman. She could not fathom the horrid memories that haunted Maisie, but she did understand a hatred for Ramsay. Mayhap, that was where she should start now that they were alone and she could talk freely?

She cleared her throat, hoping Maisie would look up, but when she didn't, Brigid took a few tentative steps toward her. Maisie's head remained down, red, tangled hair cascading on either side of her face to obscure Brigid from seeing the woman's expression.

"I'm going to come sit beside ye, so we can talk."

Maisie did stop humming, but her face remained tilted down. Brigid continued to move forward, and as she did, and she got a better look at the sad state of Cormac's sister, a hot ball of anger lodged in her chest. The woman's gown was in tatters, indicating she had not put a fresh one on in a good long time. And there was a rather bad smell coming from her. Plus, Maisie's feet were filthy and so were her hands. She had clearly not washed in quite a while. Whyever did they not make her?

Brigid inhaled a steadying breath as she moved forward. The reality of what Cormac had been facing with his sister, hit Brigid and made it hard to stay irritated with him. Aye, she was vexed to be used yet again by a man, and if she was truthful, Cormac had also injured her feelings with his comments about her not being family. They were true and should not have bothered her, and yet, they had. It was foolish, but she could not change it. And she also should not have gotten upset when he'd bluntly told her she was not growing on him. What had she expected? That simply because she'd suddenly realized the man was rather handsome that he might think her bonny?

She bit down hard on her lower lip. She had feathers in her brain. She needed to set her mind to the task at hand and forget all about Cormac MacLean and his dimples.

She approached Maisie and knelt in front of her, keeping enough distance between them to be safe. She recalled Martha telling her when she was younger that anytime she approached a dog who did not know her, she should get down on their level so as not to scare them and show them she was friendly and meant no harm, and it seemed to her that Maisie was acting much as a skittish hound would. Not that she blamed the woman one bit.

"Maisie," she said softly. "I ken ye know who I am. And I ken ye stated a wish to kill me, and I understand it. I do. Ye hate Ramsay, and because I am Ramsay's stepsister, ye hate me as well. But I want ye to ken that I despise him, too, and what he did to ye."

The woman's hands curled into fists in her lap and ever so slowly she raised her head. Despite the gauntness and the shadows beneath her golden-brown eyes, Maisie's face was one of startling beauty. Her gaze smoldered with vitriol Brigid was certain was aimed at her. Maisie MacLean's stare was so intense, so filled with loathing, that Brigid's scalp prickled a warning. Mayhap, she should not have dismissed the guard.

"What ken ye of hatred?" The question was soft, but the woman's eyes narrowed into slits. Brigid wanted to retreat, but she did not. She was certain she'd not get through to Maisie if she backed down.

"I—"

"Have ye been used against yer will by a man?" Each word was hard and cold as the thick icicles that hung from the caves at her home in the dead of winter.

Brigid swallowed the sudden lump in her throat. "Nae as ye have, but, aye, I have been used. Bartered for what I might bring my stepbrother with nay concern that he would wed me to a man whose first three wives all died questionable, untimely deaths."

She waited uneasily beneath Maisie's unearthly stare, but when Maisie did not speak, she wiped her nerve-damp palms against her skirts, and said, "And my da made it verra clear that my only use to him was for what I could do for him."

Maisie leaned forward suddenly, her bright hair tumbling over her shoulders. She set her hands on her knees and a sudden lethal calmness almost worse than the burning hatred came into her eyes.

"Do nae talk to me of being used." Each word dripped with heart wrenching pain. Brigid realized they were even more alike than she'd thought. They had both been used. Yes, in vastly different ways, but men had used them, and if they banded together, mayhap they could find healing and strength together, and carve a path of their choice out for their lives.

"Ye do nae ken what I mean," Maisie continued. "Until a man—"

She broke off with a shudder. Ever so slowly, her gaze

roamed over Brigid. The woman was plotting and calculating, it was clear. "Ye smell of heather and spice."

Brigid blinked in confusion. Maisie touched Brigid's hair, further surprising her.

"Yer hair feels like silk." Maisie touched her own hair and grimaced. She then lifted her arm sniffed and gave her head a shake.

"I wish to bathe. I have nae washed in . . . ." The woman's words trailed off, and she shrugged. "Will ye come with me to the loch?" Her voice dropped to a whisper. "I'm . . . I'm scairt to go alone."

"Aye," Brigid said, suspicion nagging at her that the woman was plotting, but she'd be watchful.

They rose together and made their way out the door and down the passage. As they passed startled servants, Maisie kept her head down and fell into very close step behind Brigid. It occurred to her she had no idea which way the loch was, so she had to stop at the top of the stairs to ask Maisie.

"Which way?"

Maisie looked up long enough to point, but her gaze darted past Brigid when voices drifted to them, and she scuttled behind Brigid with a quick intake of breath. Brigid looked down the stairs. Two warriors headed toward them, laughing and talking. Maisie huddled so close that Brigid felt her trembling. Brigid nodded at the warriors as they passed, but one of them, a man she recognized from the group that was with Cormac to rescue her and Martha, paused in front of her, looking with obvious surprise between Brigid and Maisie.

"Maisie," the blonde-headed man said, "'tis good to see ye out of yer bedchambers."

Maisie did no more than grunt at the man.

His friendly brown gaze settled on Brigid. "I'm Quinn. I did nae get to formally meet ye yesterday."

"Thank ye for coming to aid me," Brigid replied.

"Do ye need me to guide ye somewhere?" he asked, darting his attention to Maisie for one moment before settling his focus back on Brigid.

"Aye, the loch."

"Oh, 'tis easy. Take these stairs to the first floor. They put ye at the main castle entrance. In the inner courtyard, ye'll take a right to the outer courtyard, and then from there ye'll take the pebbled path to the sea gate stairs. Those stairs will lead ye to the shore below that juts up next to the loch. Careful on the stairs, aye. They are slippery, narrow, and steep."

She nodded, deciding she'd have Maisie walk in front of her. Until the woman came out of her darkness and back to herself, Brigid would take a care.

"Thank ye," she said, then started down the stairs the way Quinn had told her to. They passed servants on the way out of the castle, and each time someone spoke to Maisie, the woman only grunted in response. Brigid considered saying something to her, but in the end, she decided to start with a gentle approach, and only become firm if she absolutely felt there was no choice.

As she went through the inner and then outer court-yard, she found herself scanning faces for Cormac, but she didn't see him. Disappointment filled her chest. It vexed her that thoughts of him invaded her head yet again. She shoved them away, then made her way across the outer courtyard—which was surprisingly empty—and toward the pebbled path. The tiny stones crunched beneath their shoes as she and Maisie approached the gate. She grasped the thick black iron, which opened with some effort and a loud creak.

Her breath stuttered in her chest as she viewed the steep, winding staircase. It seemed barely wide enough for one person—certainly not two abreast—and the ground beneath it was naught but sharp rocks.

She moved back, heart pounding, and motioned to Maisie. "Ye first."

The woman smirked. "Scairt of me, are ye?"

It was the first thing Maisie had said since they'd left the bedchamber. Brigid felt it was some sort of test. She could scarcely deny she was afraid when it was likely obvious from the expression on her face that she was apprehensive about what Maisie might do. Brigid might be perceived as weak if she admitted it, but she'd also be perceived as truthful by the woman and that seemed much more important in this moment.

"Aye," she replied. "I am, so until I trust ye nae to try to kill me, ye go first."

The woman let out a cackle that made Brigid's spine curl. She passed Brigid, eyebrows arched challengingly as she did, and started down the stairs. The strength of the wind at this height pushed against her body. She found brief respite from the wind if she stayed to the left, near the rock the stairs were carved from. A desire to keep from a misstep and not plunge to her death kept her gaze fixed on her feet as she carefully placed them one in front of the other. It wasn't until they were close to the foot of the stairs that she dared to look to her right.

She gasped at the blue, sun-glistening water. The day was uncommonly warm, the sky clear, and she could swear she could see through the water. A small vessel was docked near the water at the edge of the loch, but it was the only thing on the shore. There were no warriors training, or castle servants milling about, or children playing upon the shore, and when she looked at the position of the sun, she realized everyone was probably at the nooning meal. Her stomach growled then; a reminder that she had not eaten.

Maisie marched across the sandy, rocky shore with the surefootedness of one who had taken this path many times. Maisie stripped off her clothes to nothing but her chemise, and her gauntness was painfully apparent. She paused at the edge of the shore, took off her shoes, and moved far enough in the water that her toes were covered. Brigid hung back, thinking to allow the woman some privacy. The woman's ribs and spine protruded painfully beneath her pale skin, and her arms and legs appeared like twigs.

Brigid winced.

Maisie's knotted hair hung in heavy clumps down her back to graze past her narrow hips. The woman turned then and speared Brigid with a look. "Why are ye nae undressing. I do nae wish to swim alone."

"I can nae swim," Brigid admitted which elicited a look of irritation from Maisie.

The woman glanced over at the small boat. She crossed the rocky shore and climbed inside where she knelt and did something Brigid could not see. Then she stood and motioned to the dinghy. "Ye can take this. That way, I'll nae be alone."

Brigid nodded, though after yesterday's occurrence in the water, uneasiness coursed through her. Maisie walked into the water to her waist then dove under, disappearing. Brigid forced her legs to move, though they did not want to. She leaned over, push the dingy all the way into the water, then carefully stepped in. She gasped as the little boat rocked atop the shallow waves. She lurched to the small bench seat and sat, and the boat steadied.

A paddle lay beneath the seat. She picked it up and dipped the flat end into the water. Maisie bobbed some distance from the shore. It seemed to Brigid that every time she drew near to the woman, Maisie moved further away. Frustrated, Brigid shouted, "Maisie, can ye stay still?"

Maisie's response was to flip onto her back and swim even further away from Brigid.

"Irritating woman," Brigid growled, but she was determined to get close enough for the two of them to talk. She was so concentrated on that task, that it wasn't until she paused to take a breath from all the paddling and give her aching still healing arm a chance to rest, that she noticed the water in the bottom of the dingy. Her heart lurched and she scrambled off the seat, hands in the water, searching for the plug. In her haste, she dropped her paddle into the water, and it drifted infuriatingly just out of reach. She knelt on the seat and leaned over the side, stretching her arm as far as she dared. But the paddle danced atop the waves carrying it farther and farther away.

"Maisie!"

The woman did not respond. She treaded water so far away that Brigid could not even see the woman's expression. Even if Maisie could not hear her, surely, she could see her.

"Maisie!" Brigid called louder, waving her arms so the woman would know she was in distress. "The dingy is filling with water."

It was to her ankles now, and nauseating despair gripped her.

"Maisie!" Brigid screamed. "I've lost my paddle and need yer aid."

"'Tis awful to feel helpless, is it nae?" Maisie called back, and the vindictive tone knotted fresh fear in Brigid's chest.

The woman swam toward Brigid in rapid, sure strokes, halting when she was close enough that Brigid could clearly see her, and she knew Maisie could view her clearly as well.

"Is yer plan to watch me drown, then?" Brigid said, her voice catching.

"Mayhap," Maisie said. "Yer life for mine seems fair. May Ramsay rot in misery at yer loss."

"He'll nae," Brigid said, matter of fact. "He does nae love me let alone care for me. I was nae lying about that fact."

"Ye expect me to believe anything that comes out of yer mouth?" Maisie snarled.

"Nay," Brigid replied, the thought of drowning, tearing her insides. Could she reach the shore? She glanced to it, and seeing how far it was, her heart sank. The water was at her calves now. She had precious little time to convince Maisie to aid her by swimming the boat to shore.

"Please, Maisie," Brigid said. "The only way killing me will hurt Ramsay is that it will ensure he does nae ever get a beneficial union by wedding me off, but yer brothers have already ensured that will nae occur by taking me. Ye do nae need to kill me. It will nae erase yer pain. It will nae change what Ramsay did to ye."

"Shut up!" Maisie screamed, and then dove under the water, leaving Brigid alone on the sinking dinghy. She leaned over the side, trying to see if she could move the vessel toward shore. When it was obvious she could not, she glanced around the empty shore in growing panic. A lone figure appeared very far away on the seagate stairs, and she started to scream for help.

Chapter Ten

*H*alfway down the seagate stairs to go train in peace, what sounded like a scream reached Cormac. Frowning, he swept his gaze over the empty shore and then to the water. There in the vast array of blue bobbed the little dingy they used to get to the caves on the other side of the loch. And in it was a woman with pale hair waving her arms madly.

Brigid.

He bolted down the stairs. To his surprise, Maisie bobbed up from the water. Her unmistakable flaming hair floated about her pale shoulders as she treaded water, staring at the boat. Brigid was in trouble and Maisie was not moving to aid her.

As he ran down the steep stairs, he cast a look toward the dinghy. It tilted oddly, as if the front of it were sinking. A band tightened around his chest. He increased his pace further, his gaze on Brigid.

She seemed to be kneeling and trying to paddle with her hands, and the shocking truth hit him. The dinghy was sinking with Brigid in it. God above, was his sister trying to kill Brigid?

The clearer Brigid's voice became as he drew toward the end of the stairs, the surer he was that she was in immediate danger. He sprinted toward the water, blood rushing through him, blocking any sound but the throbbing in his ears. He dropped his weapons as he ran so he'd not have to pause to do so once he reached water, and he had all but his braies off by the time he gained the loch.

The dinghy had sunk further, and he searched for his sister. She was nearer to the vessel now, but still did not seem to be doing anything to aid Brigid. He raced into the water, ignoring the bite of the cold, and when he was deep enough to dive, he did so. The loch swallowed him up, and he cut through the water with quick sure strokes, glad for his years of constant swimming. As he propelled himself forward, one question after another came to him.

Why the devil did Brigid Campbell not know how to swim? Why the devil had the foolish lass allowed Maisie to talk her into going into the loch, and what in the name of God was Maisie thinking? She'd watch the woman drown? God, above, it was exactly what she was likely thinking. In her current dark state, she had no doubt justified it—an eye for an eye—and he, he would never forgive himself if Brigid died.

He broke the surface of the water, blinded for a moment by the sun, located the dinghy—roughly twenty strokes away and nearly under water now—and pinpointed Brigid clinging to the bit of the vessel that was the highest above water. He swam with a desperation that nearly choked him. Five strokes in, the vessel sank all the way. Brigid flailed her arms and cried out as the weight of her dress pulled her under. Finally, Maisie was there, swimming as if to aid Brigid.

But he knew his sister's strength was no match for the desperation that Brigid would bring because of her fear of drowning. With a shriek, Brigid climbed atop Maisie, trying to escape the water. They both sank beneath the surface.

Five strokes. Four. Three. Two. He dove under just as a

foot came at his face and connected with his lip, splitting it. Pain lanced up his jaw, but it didn't stop him. He grabbed the ankle that belonged to the offending foot and gave it a tug, praying to God he had hold of Brigid. He could save her, and Maisie could damn well save herself.

Hands reached from behind a mass of blonde hair. Brigid grabbed his hair in a death grip, and he'd wager she'd rip out a chunk as she fought for her life. He managed to grasp first one of her wrists and then the other and he pinned her arms to her sides. Freeing one arm, he stroked toward the surface, Brigid in tow. As they broke the surface, he flipped Brigid onto her back and pressed his lips to her ear, ducking once as she continued to fight him. "I have ye, but if ye hit me in the face again, I may decide to let ye drown, *ban-druidh.*"

He didn't know if it was his attempt at humor or his threat, but she stilled suddenly, and her body went limp.

"Ye have me?" Her voice was tentative and full of fear.

Maisie broke the surface then, and he glared at his sister who went from looking momentarily fearful to mutinous.

"Aye, I've got ye, and I vow to ye I'll nae let Maisie drown ye."

There was a long stretch of silence before Brigid said, "She did nae try to drown me."

He darted his gaze to Maisie, saw the shock on her face before she hid it, and he knew Brigid was lying to protect his sister. In that moment, heat flooded him, and he was consumed with admiration for the lass.

"Nay?" he said as he swam them toward shore with Maisie following a wise distance behind him. He was vexed at her to a simmer.

When he reached shallow water, he did not release Brigid. Instead, he scooped her against his chest and waded to the shore with her cradled in his arms. He was acutely aware of her soft curves beneath his hands and pressed to his body. When he glanced down, the first thing he noted was that the bodice of her gown was molded to her. Her lush curves flaunted a body made to be loved. His blood coursed hot through him.

"I can walk, laird."

"Call me Cormac, remember?" he asked, wincing at the huskiness of his tone. This woman had the ability to affect him like no other since Elsie, and the way Brigid moved him was very different than the way Elsie had. He'd grown up with Elsie and come to love her for her sweet disposition and loyalty to him—once he'd seen her for more than his sister's friend—and he'd loved her for the fact that she had known him almost as well as he had known himself. It had been an attraction that had been slow to grow, going from friendship to something more, until it had been love.

Brigid was the sun, bright with promise, blinding with beauty, and dangerous if you stared too long. Yet one was compelled to gape, to linger, to bask in the rays that would heat your skin and then burn you if you were not careful. Taking care was so hard to remember because nothing made you feel alive in quite the same way.

"Cormac, I can walk now."

"I'll set ye down when we're clear of the water."

"But we *are* clear of the water."

He looked down and frowned. The lass was correct. He was indeed standing on the shore with the grains of the earth between his toes. He set her down and she turned to him, her gaze going past him for one moment. A frown creased her forehead. Behind him, the splash of Maisie's progress to shore brushed against his ear.

"Do nae fear that I'll leave ye alone with her again." He

studied Brigid's face as she watched his sister approach the shore. Her long lashes swept upward. Skin as smooth as silk boasted a smattering of freckles across the bridge of her upturned nose. Her full, ruby lips begged the touch of his own. He growled at the desire that would not abate. She brought her gaze to him, a question in her eyes, but it was one he would not, could not answer.

"I was nae left alone with her," she said, guilt in her tone as she nibbled her lip.

"What?" he asked frowning.

Her chin jutted out. "Tess left a guard with yer sister and me, and I dismissed him."

"Why the devil would ye do that?"

Hard determination filled Brigid's eyes. "I want to aid her. The guard's presence hampered that. And I do nae fear her." Her tone was firm. "She did nae do anything wrong," Brigid added. "I . . . I forgot to ensure the plug was properly fitted in the vessel."

"Did Maisie check it?" he asked.

She shifted from foot to foot and worried her lower lip before finally shrugging. "I do nae recall seeing her go to the vessel."

The woman was a terrible liar, and he took a breath to tell her so, but Maisie caught his attention as she marched past him, slowing ever so slightly to send Brigid a glare of utter dislike. His temper snapped. She could have killed the lass. He grabbed his sister's arm, thinking to stop her and make her listen to reason. Maisie recoiled as if he'd struck her. He released her immediately and watched her run away, her sodden garment flapping at her left thigh as she went. His anger gave way to worry for his sister.

"Is this the first she's been out of her bedchamber since the incident?"

Cormac drew his gaze to Brigid, noting her shivering, and moved toward her. "Come," he said. "We will talk as we make our way back to the castle. We both need dry clothes."

"And some food," Brigid added.

He laughed at her unexpected candor. "Aye," he agreed as they fell into step together, "and some food."

As they made their way across the rocky terrain toward the seagate stairs, he was struck with the fact that this was the first woman he had been alone with, other than Tess or his sister, since Elsie's death. Being alone with Brigid wasn't the same, however, as being alone with Elsie. Brigid looked nothing like Elise, for one thing, being taller and slighter than his former betrothed. And Elsie would have carried on spectacularly had she nearly drowned, weeping and clinging to him.

He found himself filled with admiration for Brigid's bravery once more, but also guilt, because as he walked with Brigid, he realized he thought her much braver than Elsie. Elsie had been sweet, yes. Loving, most surely. But fearful of almost everything. Snakes. Wolves. Spiders. Strong winds. Full moons. He had always blamed it on her parents for coddling her and doing everything for her.

Elsie would have never ridden into enemy territory to rescue someone, but she would have cared for them once they'd been rescued. And, certainly, Elsie would not have jumped from her bedchamber window into dark waters to escape capture. She would have prayed for divine intervention. And she would have never agreed to go out on the water in a vessel by herself—and she had known how to swim. But she'd not liked being alone, mayhap because she never had been, nor had she ever had to rely on herself.

He stole a side look at Brigid, curious what her life had

been like thus far to make her so brave and resourceful. Guilt tightened his chest at his curiosity and the comparisons he'd been making between the two women. He'd not spend one more moment on thoughts of her, and yet, he should ask her of her past, shouldn't he? It was wise to know her since he was giving her such access to his sister. It had nothing to do with attraction to her, or her bravery, or—

She slipped and careened into him at just exactly the right—or mayhap the wrong—moment. His ankle caught the rock to his right and threw him off balance. He grabbed her, dragging them both down to the dirt. Somehow, she ended up half on top of him, soft womanly flesh pressed along the length of his body in dangerous places. Her locks fell forward on either side of her face, and the wet ends brushed his chest. Their eyes locked, and she sucked in a sharp breath as his own body hardened with need. He was in peril of losing control.

"I'm sorry," she rasped. Her cheeks turned the most beguiling shade of pink with her embarrassment. She leaned forward, sliding her hands from his chest to the ground, and he knew she intended to push off him, but the movement of her hands across his body made him groan. Her eyes widened.

"Am I hurting ye?" She shoved upward; her groin crushed tight to his.

God's blood she was hurting him, but not in the way she thought.

"Nay." The word was a hoarse croak of lust. He cleared his throat and tried again. "If ye could just raise up a bit more, I'll slip out from under ye."

"Oh, I'll just—" She attempted to roll off him, got tangled in her gown, and plopped back down against him once more. This time, her face pressed against the side of his neck, and her lips brushed the tender skin there.

Lust gripped him in an iron hold. He had to get her off him now. He set his hands to either side of her waist, his fingers curling over the nicely rounded flesh, and every drop of blood in his body seemed to travel from his brain to his groin.

He froze in place, grasping her, as vivid images pelted his brain. Her above him. Her beneath him. Her thighs spread and her hair fanned out around her lovely face as they came together in a violent storm of passion. He squeezed his eyes shut just as she wiggled once more, muttering about annoying skirts. He throbbed everywhere.

Inhaling a breath, he lifted her up and rolled to his side to lay her on the ground. She gave a startled yelp as he gained his feet. He held out a hand, intent only on helping her up. But his gaze caught the picture laid at his feet. Even completely disheveled and wet, she was innocent temptation. Rosy cheeks, wide eyes, and curves on display beneath her wet garment filled him with awe for how lovely she was.

"Take my hand."

Her slender fingers curled about his hand, and he was struck with another realization. He'd never held the hand of any woman but Elsie. It was intimate and unsettling.

She gained her feet and faced him, frowning.

Before he could stop her, she released his right hand, reached up, and brushed her fingers across his busted lip. Her touch was gentle as a feather and made his gut tighten. When she brought her fingers away, blood stained them. Without a word, she pulled up the edge of her wet gown. Unable to make himself look away, he watched her, mesmerized by the determination in her movements.

She sucked her lower lip between her teeth and her brows dipped together. She proceeded to rip a strip off the edge of her gown, wiped her fingers against the swath of material, then held it up to him. The look upon her face had transformed yet again to concern and slight amusement.

"For yer lip. 'Tis bleeding."

He took the offering and pressed the material to the injury, which he just noticed was throbbing.

"Ye've a habit of busting things," she said, amusement in her sparkling eyes and slightly upturned lips lacing her words.

He served her a mock scowl. "Actually, ye've a habit of busting things on my body."

Her eyes popped wide at that. "I busted yer lip?"

"Aye, under the water ye kicked me in the face."

The rosiness in her cheeks spread across her flesh in a manner that was nothing but enticing. He jerked his gaze back to her eyes; glad she didn't seem to notice the effect she had upon him.

"I'm so sorry!" She squeezed his shoulder.

It was an innocent gesture, but his body responded as if she'd slowly stroked his chest. His blood turned thick and hot in his veins. He needed to think upon something other than how fetching she looked in her wet gown and how her touch heated him.

"We should return to the castle."

"Aye. I'm certain Martha must be in the cottage wondering where I am," she said.

He motioned for her to get moving. She turned away from him and started walking. He raised his hand right above her back, so if she were to lose her footing on the stairs, he'd catch her.

But he did not touch her.

The simple movements of her hips swaying back and forth was torture enough to his brain and body. If he touched her, he was certain his desire for her would be an ache that would keep him up well into the night.

As they started the long climb to the top of the stairs, he said, "Ye and Martha have been moved back to the castle."

"Oh?"

"Aye. Camden suggested the two of ye would be safer there and easier to protect should yer brother or Sinclair try to snatch ye away. I agreed, so ye have been moved."

"I appreciate the sacrifice ye're making to see to my safety."

"'Tis nae a sacrifice," he replied, hearing a wobble in her tone he thought might be a slight hurt.

"Hmph," she replied. "Ye sounded as if it was a great inconvenience to have us there."

The inconvenience was that he would see her regularly and lust after her, but he could not say that.

"'Tis nae. We've plenty of unused bedchambers, and Camden was right. 'Tis much safer for ye to be in the sanctuary of the castle."

She stopped and turned toward him slowly, looking down at him from two steps above. Fright danced in her eyes. "Ye do nae really think my brother or Sinclair would dare to try to breach yer castle to retrieve me, do ye?"

"I think," he said slowly, trying to order his thoughts but finding it nearly impossible as she peered at him with her golden hair drying in a halo of wisps and pale moon curls around her face, "that desperate men will do foolish things nae to lose what they want."

"Oh, neither of them really want me," she said in such a matter of fact manner that his heart lurched in pain for her. It was clear that what she knew of men so far was that they did not want her for herself. And he and his brother were now two more men who had proven this to her.

Brigid shrugged. "My brother wants my union with Sinclair to gain his fighting arm, likely in hopes that he can crush ye once and for all."

He thought about telling her she was a treasure to be prized, but that was a statement that could only lead to trouble in this moment. So instead, he said, "Yer assessment of the situation is undoubtedly correct."

"Of course, it is," she said as she resumed her climb. "I've lived with the devil long enough to ken his mind."

"But ye've nae lived with Sinclair, so why is it ye do nae think he wants ye?"

"Because," she said, the word drawn out and giving him no information. The pause that followed made him believe she was trying to decide whether to say more or not.

"I've a castle."

His brows dipped together in confusion. "Ye've a castle?"

"Aye. I admit I was confused why Sinclair wanted to wed me, because I did nae believe my brother would be generous at all with what he offered to entice a man to do so."

"Why in God's blood do ye think yer brother would need to offer anything more than simply ye for a man to want to wed ye?"

The minute the words left his mouth, he regretted them, but there was no taking them back. Nor could he avoid Brigid's sudden stop that told him his question startled her. Hell, it startled him. Not only did the lass heat his blood, but she also made his tongue loose and his private thoughts fly out of his uncontrolled mouth.

"Well, because I'm nae so bonny and men like bonny

lasses. They do nae appreciate what I have to offer."

The astonishing declaration was said in an embarrassed whisper. He knew, God above, he did, that he should leave it alone. Hadn't he decided that a mere breath ago? And yet, he could not mind his own business and allow her to think such a grievously wrong thing about herself. It would be more than wrong. It would be dishonorable.

When they reached the top of the stairs, she opened the creaky gate, and he followed her through. But before she could take another step, he grasped her by the arm and gently turned her toward him. They stood so close he could see that her smooth skin glowed with pale gold undertones. Her generously curved lips parted in surprise, and her lashes swept downward for a moment before she raised them once more, and her clear green eyes met his.

Her head tilted back just a bit as she met his gaze, exposing the slender column of her neck and the pulse that hammered there. He wanted to kiss her in that shadowy space where her life force was strong, and then along her neck up to her—

"Did ye wish to say something?" she asked, snapping him out of his lustful thoughts.

It wasn't wise to say anything, but he could not seem to get a grip on his sensible side. He had to make her see what he did.

"Ye are quite possibly the bonniest woman I've ever laid eyes upon." He winced at the low growl in his words. Her lips parted further, and then ever so slowly the corners turned up into the faintest smile.

"I," she said in a soft voice, "thank ye."

He wanted to say more, but by the mercy of God, he kept the words in his mouth. He wanted to tell her she was like a fresh field of heather after a rain when the sun breaks through the clouds to part the darkness and shines its warm rays down up the field made clean from the storm. She was possibility and hope with her quick smile and bright eyes.

He kept it to himself. He'd overstepped his boundaries already, no need to leap over them.

He nodded then searched for something to say to change the subject, because it felt awkward, and he felt the fool. And then he recalled she'd said she had a castle.

"How is it that ye come to have a castle?"

Her expression transformed before him from welcoming and smiling to one of such suspicion that he could not help but laugh, despite knowing it would do nothing to alleviate her obvious worries.

"I do nae want yer castle," he finally managed to say when the look she served him went from suspicious to downright hostile.

She snorted at that, set her hands on her hips, tossed her hair, and glared at him from underneath a lock that had fallen over her right eye. She was vexed, he knew, but God's blood, when she was vexed, she was enticing enough to convert the devil to a saint.

"Ye're a man," she said, each word ringing with her ire, "and all men want from women is what they can gain from them in land, coin, or warriors."

"Ye're wrong." Somewhere in the last breath his pulse had spiked, and his blood was rushing through his veins. He had swum into dangerous territory with this conversation, but he could not seem to turn toward shore and escape.

Her brows dipped together. "I'm wrong?"

Her chest heaved with the question. "Aye," he replied, drinking in the way her eyes now flashed with her growing vexation.

"What else do men possibly want from women?" she

demanded, the question so very innocent yet so enticing. He wanted so badly to show her what else men wanted. What little control he had on his raging desire for her snapped. Before he comprehended what he intended, he closed the space between them and brought her to him in one forward motion. He had never been under the grip of such strong yearning, such stormy wanting as in this moment. Horns of warning rang in his head, but his gaze fell to her lips, and he was lost to the anticipation of their touch.

He brought his hands to her face, reveling in the fact that her skin was every bit as silky as he'd thought it would be, then slid one hand into her damp locks until his fingers splayed against the curve of her skull. A dull ache sprang up in his chest, shocking him, and as they stood there, heart to pounding heart, he knew he was venturing to a place he could not stay, a thing he could not have. But he could not turn away. Not yet.

He lowered his lips to hers and brushed them across the delicate surface. The contact of her skin to his sparked lightning though his veins. He wanted to taste her, and beyond that he could think of nothing else. He claimed her mouth and gave himself to the moment.

Chapter Eleven

*E*verything about him consumed her all at once. His large, rough hand caressed her cheek and his other cradled her head with so much tenderness that her belly clenched. His closeness to her was so bracing it sent shivers of delight through her. When his lips brushed hers, her heartbeat tripled, sending her blood through her veins like an awakened river.

She had never been kissed, was unsure how to respond, but her body knew instinctually what to do. Her hands slid about his neck, her fingers twining through the soft curls of his hair, as his tongue traced her lips. She was unsure what he wanted, but she knew she wanted more. She wanted more of the tingly feeling his kiss was producing, to open her mouth and allow his tongue to twine with hers. The thoughts were shocking, and yet she could not make herself care enough to pull away and end the kiss.

Instead, she parted her lips and he slipped his tongue inside her mouth. She tentatively twined hers with his, causing a quiver to surge through her veins. His hand on her cheek trailed down her neck as they kissed, and then he broke the kiss to feather new ones down her skin.

Gooseflesh raced across her neck and chest, and she tightened at her core in a way she had never experienced before. His breath on her neck was warm and moist, and her flesh now burned where his lips touched. Her heart jolted. He trailed his kisses back up her neck in the same way he'd gone down it, and then his mouth covered hers with a hunger her body happily responded to.

The whimper of pleasure that came from her shocked her. It must have shocked him as well because he broke the kiss immediately, sending her senses crashing. They stood face to face, both panting, the surprised look of his face mirroring how she felt. She did not miss the curse he muttered under his breath.

His blue eyes showed the tortured dullness of disbelief. Silence engulfed them, and he scrubbed his hand first over his face, then tugged it through his hair. It was obvious he didn't know what to say. All her loneliness and wishing for someone to love her, a place to belong, a family to be part of, melded together in one upsurge of devouring yearning that she understood was misplaced, but she simply couldn't help it.

"Is that what else men want from women?" She blinked in surprise at her bold words. Out of fear of punishment, she'd learned well not to speak her mind to her da or Ramsay. It was startling that she was perfectly comfortable doing so with this stubborn man she'd known for such a short time. Why was that? The question repeated itself in her head, as she watched uneasiness creep over him. The answer came to her just as quick as the question had. She did not fear him one bit. He had proven she did not need to, not just with the way he treated her, but with his actions with his sister.

"Aye," he finally replied, the word gruff, his stare drilling into her.

"And ye want that from me?" God's blood she could hardly believe the things she was saying.

"Nay." He shoved his hand back through his hair, a look

of misery settling on his face. "Aye," he added, sounding as miserable as he looked.

"Ye do nae wish to want me?" she guessed. Her stepbrother was his enemy, after all.

"Aye. I do nae wish it. It can nae lead to anything."

"Because of my stepbrother?"

He nodded. "Because of him, because I made a vow, because of my sister."

She did not know what vow he made, and he'd not offered to tell her, so she'd not ask. She understood he felt it disloyal to his sister to desire the stepsister of the man who so grievously hurt Maisie. He was a complex, brave man. One, she realized, she could possibly fall in love with, but that was foolish, because he'd plainly told her he would never allow what simmered between them—because something clearly did—to go anywhere.

She wanted to be loved and to be part of a family, and it would be imprudent to become attached to this man. Unless he were to change his mind about his vow, and his sister somehow miraculously came out of her darkness and stopped hating Brigid simply by her association with Ramsay. Those were enormous exceptions that would likely not be met, and yet she found herself unable to totally let go of hope. She'd keep it at the outer edges of her heart. That's what she'd do. Likely, he'd show her she was a fool to have hope at all. And if she didn't let him all the way in, he could not break her heart. She'd concentrate on aiding his sister and making a place for herself in this clan.

Decision made, she stuck out her hand for him to shake. "Then we shall be friends and nothing more," she announced.

"We can nae be friends." The incredulity in his tone matched his expression. "Please do nae take offense to this, but I'll be keeping clear of ye from here on out. If ye need something, if ye have a problem, see Tess or Camden."

She clenched her jaw. Well, that had not taken long at all for him to show her she was a clot-heid to have any sort of hope.

"Fine," she snapped and shoved past him. "We will nae be friends," she bellowed. "And rest assured I'll nae have any problems that I need ye for!"

Cormac's harsh words to Brigid haunted him all morning as well as her wounded look when he'd told her not to seek him out with her problems or needs. But he was also hounded by guilt that made his training go poorly once again and put him in a devil of a mood. He could not believe he'd kissed her, nor could he believe how much he had enjoyed it. What sort of man was he to make a vow to never take a woman to his bed or heart again, and then go kissing a lass?

He was not a weak man who would break his vow, and that was why he would set Brigid out of his mind from here on out. But near the nooning meal a knock came at his solar door, and Tess entered with a troubled look upon her face.

"I need ye to come speak to the women in the kitchen."

"Why?" he asked, sitting back in his chair.

"I brought Brigid in there to allow her to help and Aila cut her."

He was halfway out of his chair full of anger and worry when he caught himself and paused, standing all the way up, but not yet making a move to leave the room.

"What do ye mean Aila cut her?"

"Well, Aila said she accidentally dropped her knife, but

ye ken as well as I do that given a chance, Aila would plunge a knife in Brigid's back in an attempt to avenge Elsie."

Tess was right; Elsie's cousin would do such a thing. The two of them had been like sisters.

"Is Brigid hurt?" If the woman had been badly injured, Tess would have led with that the moment she entered the room.

"Nay. It skimmed her big toe and cut it a wee bit, but she's fine. She's still in the kitchen helping to cook."

He got an image of Brigid with a defiant look upon her face staying put in the kitchen and refusing to be run off.

"Tell Quinn I said to speak to his wife."

"Quinn has gone to the MacLeod clan."

"Why?" Cormac asked, frowning.

"Because Brigid asked him to go and bring Ross back."

"Why the devil would Brigid have Ross MacLeod come here? Does the lass nae ken that Maisie broke off the betrothal?"

"Aye, she kens it. I told her so, but Brigid seems to think Ross can have an impact on Maisie's recovery."

"She should have asked me first afore she sent Quinn after Ross," Cormac said, starting around his desk, but Tess grabbed hold of his forearm as he moved past her.

"I told her the same thing, but she said ye told her nae to bother ye. Did ye tell her that?" Tess asked.

"Nae those words exactly," he admitted begrudgingly, "but aye. I told her to see ye or Camden if she needed something or had a problem."

"Well then, seeing as how she spoke with me about it, I suppose the lass did follow yer order. 'Tis unlike ye to pass off the responsibilities of being laird."

"I'm nae passing off the responsibilities," he snapped. "Did ye tell her she could send Quinn to fetch Ross?"

"Aye," Tess said, glaring at him. "I did after she told me what ye said. I agree with her assessment that Ross may be able to aid Maisie."

"Fine, then the decision has been made. Have Camden speak to Aila about her trying to injure Brigid."

"Do ye nae think ye should see to it yerself?"

He couldn't shake the memory of his kiss with Brigid and the guilt gnawing at him for enjoying the moment. "Nay," he said, "Camden can handle it."

"If ye say so," Tess muttered and left the room.

He stared down at the drawing of the Campbell holding, determined to finish it, but his mind instead replayed his kiss with Brigid, driving him to leave the solar and go back down to the loch for more training. He didn't return until he was dripping with sweat and Brigid's image was mercifully not in his head. But the moment he sat in his chair once more to finish his sketching Tess appeared in his doorway again. He let out a growl, and she held up her palms in peace.

"I would nae have come to ye again, but I do nae think this is something Camden can handle. The bedchamber servants are refusing to put fresh rushes in Brigid's bedchamber and linens on her bed."

"Let me guess," he snapped, "Britta convinced the upstairs servants nae to tend to Brigid's bedchamber."

"Aye," Tess confirmed, crossing her arms over her chest, and giving him an 'I told ye so' look. "I did say I did nae think it was a good idea to keep both of Elsie's cousins here after Elsie's death."

He remembered. Tess had argued after Elsie had died that they had to obviously let Aila stay, because she was Quinn's wife, but they should send Britta back to the Donald holding because the two cousins together would stir trouble for the next mistress of the MacLean Castle because of their loyalty and love for Elsie. And he recalled now how he had responded, which had seemed perfectly reasonable at the time.

"Do ye recall what you said?" Tess asked, and he suspected the woman thought he was now doubting his decision, but he wasn't.

"Aye," he replied. "I told ye I would nae be taking a wife, so there was nae a call to worry how Elsie's cousins would treat a woman who would nae ever exist."

A smug smile came to Tess's face. "Are ye regretting that now?"

"Nay, Tess, I am nae. Brigid is nae my wife, nor will she ever be, nor will I have another as my wife, so my decision stands. And I have every faith that Camden can handle Britta and the rest of the upstairs servants."

Tess's skeptical look prompted him to ask, "Did Camden speak to Aila?"

"Aye," Tess said.

"And I'm assuming Brigid worked in the kitchen with her after?"

"Aye," Tess said again, but scowled at him.

"Then I do nae see yer concern about Camden handling Britta if he handled Aila."

"'Tis how he handled Aila that makes me concerned."

Cormac was fast losing his patience. He inhaled a long breath, hoping to hold onto the few remaining threads of patience long enough to finish this conversation without snapping at Tess.

"Was he mean to Aila?"

"Nay."

"Then what in God's name is the problem, Tess?"

Tess's scowl told him he'd failed to hold onto his patience until the end of the conversation.

"Brigid was right," Tess grumbled. "Ye are a high-handed man, and I'm certain when the whole situation catches fire under yer nose ye'll discover for yerself what the problem is with how yer brother handled Aila and dealt with Britta."

"Fine," he agreed, refusing to comment on the fact that Brigid had called him high-handed. "That is acceptable to me."

"Fine!" Tess snapped. "Rest assured I'll nae be coming to ye again for yer aid."

After Tess stormed out of the room, he realized it was the second time that day an angry woman had told him to 'rest assured'.

Funny, he felt anything but assured.

Chapter Twelve

Cormac had been seated at his place on the dais scarcely long enough to nod to the person to his left when a single shrill scream ripped through the normal suppertime chaos in the Great Hall. As he lifted a hand for one of his guards to see what had happened, there was a flurry of movement at the entrance. To his amazement, Maisie stood on the other side of the threshold with Brigid on one side of her and Quinn and Ross MacLeod on the other. Maisie still looked like a feral animal, but the fact that she was entering the Great Hall was progress.

Of course, she didn't exactly appear happy. She had her arms crossed over her chest, her eyes narrowed, and she marched to the dais, not stopping for anyone who tried to talk to her. Right before she reached the dais, Aila stepped into her path, and Cormac held his breath, half afraid of what Maisie might do, but she paused and seemed to be listening to what the woman said. Then Maisie continued forward, ascended the dais without speaking, and took her seat, which had been unoccupied since before they'd left for the ill-fated tourney. Her hair hung on either side of her face so her expression could not be seen.

"I'm glad to have ye with us once again at supper, sister," Cormac said. Camden, who sat to Cormac's immediate right, made a sound of agreement. Maisie growled at him in response then attacked the trencher before her like a wild animal. But as Brigid approached, Quinn and Ross at her heels, Maisie sat up, wiped her mouth, and folded her hands in her lap. Cormac resisted smiling at her sudden change. He understood now why Brigid had wanted Ross to come here. Ross might possibly be the only person whose opinions Maisie still cared about. It was clear she was trying to act civilized in his presence, even though what had happened to her had stripped her of her desire to be part of the world.

Brigid, Quinn, and Ross stopped in front of the dais, and Cormac's chest tightened at how lovely Brigid looked. She had white flowers tucked behind her ear and a lovely green gown on that fit her in a way that stirred his imagination toward kissing her once more, touching her, and—.

He willed himself to cease the line of thought.

He inclined his head to the youngest son of the Mac-Leod laird. "Ross, 'Tis good to have ye amongst us once again." He did not ask Ross what brought him to them, because he knew well it was Brigid's doing. He motioned to the seat, he suspected, had been left open by Maisie. "Will ye take yer supper upon the dais with us?"

"Aye," the man said, his hungry gaze barely leaving Maisie. Cormac understood and did not begrudge the man for drinking his sister in. Ross had truly cared for Maisie and obviously still held those feelings.

"Ye can take the seat beside Maisie."

Maisie whipped her gaze to Cormac, and if she could have shot fire out of her eyes, he would have been incinerated. But as Ross started up the shallow steps, unmistakable longing filled his sister's brown gaze before she lowered her lashes to veil her feelings.

Cormac turned his attention back to Brigid and Quinn who both still stood waiting for him to address them. He addressed Quinn first because that would be simple. The man was merely waiting to be given his leave to go find his seat at the table where his men were.

Cormac waved the man toward his table. "Thank ye for yer service today. Enjoy yer supper."

Quinn gave a nod and departed. Cormac reflected upon the situation with Aila. He should ask his brother how he had handled it and determine if Quinn needed to speak with Aila. But he would wait for privacy to question Camden.

It was time to focus on Brigid, and when he set his attention back to her, he did not care for the fact that merely looking at the lass made his blood heat. "Ye may sit with us if ye wish it. There's a seat beside Camden or ye may find yer way to an empty seat at one of the tables with the other clansmen and women." The fight against the unmistakable pull made his words harsher than he intended.

She flinched and he instantly regretted his tone. He wanted to change his words, the scowl dragging his lips and brow downward. But to do so would be dangerous for him. Each interaction with her tempted him to abandon his vow, and that, he could not do. Maisie would never forgive him, and he'd not forgive himself.

Her eyebrows rose in a challenging arc. "I do nae ken how I can possibly resist such a heartfelt invitation, but, alas, I must." Sarcasm dripped from her every word. "I could nae possibly leave Martha to dine alone with strangers. I'm certain a man as concerned about the feelings of others can understand that."

Why the devil did the lass have to be so bonny even when she was mocking him?

"Well, if ye must—"

Camden interrupted. "Father Gordon is nae joining us for supper tonight."

Cormac kicked his brother under the table. Camden glanced at him, and Cormac gave a subtle shake of his head. Camden scowled but turned his attention right back to Brigid.

"Martha can join us as well. I'm certain everyone at the dais will agree with me when I say, we'd all like to have the two of ye dine with us."

"I'd nae," Maisie said without looking up.

Her saying anything at all surprised Cormac and everyone else on the dais. It appeared her unmistakable dislike for Brigid was just the thing to get her speaking. With only a slight pang of conscience, Cormac resolved to keep putting Brigid near his sister to force her out of her darkness and join the world again.

"I'd be happy to have ye join us," Cormac said, and it was both the truth and a lie. There was most assuredly a part of him that wanted her near, but it was a part he needed to quiet. The smirk that quirked her lovely lips up told him she knew he was not telling the truth, but her gaze darted to Maisie, and Brigid let out a sigh of submission. She was utterly selfless. She did not want to join him on the dais, and who could blame her? He'd kissed her. Then, told her not only did he only lust after her, but he did not want to, and they could not be friends. Then, he'd all but commanded her to sit somewhere else other than near him.

"Take my seat," Camden said, standing before Cormac could even think to stop him. "That way ye and Martha can sit beside each other. I'll go fetch her for ye." Camden bounded down the steps.

Beside Cormac, Tess chuckled. Next to Tess, Maisie banged her dishes around. He half wondered if Maisie's obvious hostility would scare Brigid off, but after she made her way onto the dais, she paused at the back of her seat, her hip so close to his shoulder that she grazed him for a moment before she scooted back. Her startled intake of breath reached him, and God's blood, he understood what gripped her. Contact with her, even a simple quick accidental brush, was like a punch to his gut, an attack to his system.

He'd never felt anything like it.

"I did nae get the chance to properly introduce myself to ye outside earlier." Brigid glanced toward Ross MacLeod. "I'm Brigid Campbell."

"I ken who ye are," Ross growled.

Cormac leapt to his feet. He pushed between Brigid and Ross, his legs braced apart, his entire stance one of challenge. Brigid gasped. Tess grinned at him, and Maisie and Ross gaped in clear astonishment.

"Brigid is a member of my clan now, so ye will treat her with respect and nae disdain."

"She's a filthy, rotten, Campbell!" Maisie screamed. She slammed her goblet onto the tableland and shoved out of her chair. Without another word, she stormed from the dais.

When he started to command her to stop Brigid placed her hand on his arm. He wrenched his gaze from his sister to the silent woman beside him. She shook her head. He scowled, but she crooked her finger, giving him little choice but to lean down so she could whisper in his ear. The heady scent of honeysuckle drifted from her hair, and he knew he'd never smell the fragrant vine again without thinking of Brigid. Her warm breath against his ear and neck filled him with desire and hardened him to stone. He clenched his teeth and forced himself to concentrate on her words.

"If ye command her to return, she'll be shamed and only dig into her stubbornness to continue to hate me. 'Tis good she's getting her anger out. I can handle the ire that she directs at me."

She had a determined set to her jaw, so he knew she would not willingly cede her request. Silence filled the Great Hall, and a stolen sideway glance confirmed that his entire clan watched what was transpiring. If Ross MacLeod was so hostile to Brigid, and Aila and Britta were as well, he did not want to add to her difficulty being accepted by his clan. He knew well it wasn't something he could command them to do.

Finally, he nodded his agreement then waved a general hand toward the clan for them to return to what they had been doing. It took a moment of people looking at him and between each other, and then a hushed whisper started which became a dull hum of chatter. After a brief interlude, the noise returned to the normal boisterous one of the clan supper.

Satisfied, he turned to deal with Ross. His lips pressed thin as he glowered at Brigid. To Cormac's surprise, Aila climbed the dais and set a trencher of food before Brigid's seat, then another on the table where Martha, who now approached the dais with Camden at her side, would sit to eat her supper. Aila curtsied to him, glared at Brigid, curtsied to Tess and Ross, and then departed the dais, nearly tripping down the last step as she craned her neck to look back at them. When, she was out of earshot, he inhaled a breath to speak to Ross, but Brigid interrupted.

"I would hate me too if I were ye," she said, her voice gentle and her expression even more so. "What my stepbrother did to Maisie was unspeakably evil, and I can assure ye, just because he is my stepbrother does nae mean I condone his behavior. I loathe it and him. If ye will give me a chance, I want to try to help Maisie and ye."

"How can ye help me?" Ross asked, his rigid posture relaxing slightly.

"Well," Brigid began as she moved to sit, so he did as well. They sat at the same moment, hips touching, then her knee grazing his thigh before she moved it. Her attention settled on him for a moment, and he found himself wanting to lean toward her. Instead, he held his distance, but not without strain.

Brigid returned her gaze to Ross. "If her hatred of me can draw her out of the darkness she has been dwelling in, then I think with time, patience, and a great amount of love, ye can make her feel safe, and bring her back to life fully. Then, I pray, she will open herself to ye once more."

"Just tell me what I need to do," he said, his words choked, and his posture totally softening now. Cormac watched in amazement at how she handled this man with ease and a new-found confidence he'd not seen before. That same wave of admiration for her as he had before washed over him.

"We'll discover what to do together," Brigid responded, "but I suspect just being there for her, reassuring her what happened to her has nae changed yer feelings for her—"

"It has nae. I only agreed to go along with the breaking of our betrothal because she threatened to disappear if I did nae agree to it," Ross said.

"Why did ye nae tell us that?" Cormac demanded.

"Maisie made me promise I would nae speak of our agreement for me to go along with breaking the betrothal, and I did nae want to break my vow to her."

Cormac had a flash of holding Elsie in his arms as she struggled to survive. She was so badly injured and keening with pain, but he could see she wanted to live for him, despite how much she suffered. He wanted her to survive, but not if she was going to live a life of pain. So, he'd told her if she wished to depart this life, if she was holding on for him, she could go in peace. And when she heaved what seemed a sigh of relief, and her breath rattled in her chest, he assured her that he'd never take another woman into his bed or heart.

"Then why are ye breaking the vow now?" he demanded, the words coming out much harsher than he intended. Tess's eyes popped wide at him, as did Ross's. He was glad that everyone else was behind him, and he could not see their expressions.

"I break it now, because I realized the vow, though given for the right reasons, was going to ultimately cost me yer sister if I kept it. And how can that be good?"

"'Tis nae," Tess said. "To keep a vow that strips ye of all hope for happiness is nae good, and if breaking it does nae harm anyone, does nae put yer honor into question, I do nae see any reason ye should nae rethink it."

"Aye," Camden agreed, holding up his goblet. "To breaking vows that are breaking *ye*."

Cormac knew the toast was aimed at him, but he did not join in the toast. He scowled at Tess and Camden. He didn't like that they were trying to goad him. Brigid took a long swig of her mead, then turned her head ever so slightly toward him as the others at the table began talking amongst themselves.

"I'm sorry," Brigid whispered.

He frowned. "For what?"

"For no one understanding that whatever vow ye gave, 'tis nae something ye can break."

The woman was too astute for her own good. He leaned so close to her their heads nearly touched. "What makes ye think I can nae break my vow?"

She set her fingertip to his temple, but she might as well have set her lips to his for the reaction to her simple touch that his body had. "Yer eyes," she said, her voice low. "They burn bright with desperation to keep it."

She dropped her hand from his face, reached for her goblet, and took a long draw of her wine. He watched as it slid down her throat. She licked her lips, and though desire did flare once more, it was not the strongest emotion that gripped him—curiosity was. He wanted to ask about her scars, her past, what made her the strong, outspoken, woman she was, but those were personal things. Those were questions a man who had vowed to never allow another woman into his heart dare not ask. So instead, he settled on the mundane.

"Tell me of yer day," he said, thinking she'd relay the trouble she'd encountered in the kitchen, and with her bedchamber, and even what she had done while with Maisie. He was curious how she had managed to get his sister to come into the great hall for supper tonight.

"'Tis nae much to tell," she replied and took a hearty bite of meat.

He frowned, and it occurred to him then that Brigid had no notion that Tess had come to him throughout the day to tell him of Brigid's troubles. But that did not explain why she was avoiding telling him herself, unless she was trying to protect his clan members from what she thought might be repercussions for how they had treated her. If so, that would be one of the most selfless acts he'd ever been privy to.

"So," he began after she took another bite of her meat and another swig of her wine, "the women welcomed ye into the kitchen to work with them?"

She paused in her motion of running a hunk of bread

through the gravy filling her platter and glanced at him from beneath her lashes. Her cheeks pinked and she nibbled on her lower lip. He'd learned that meant she was about to lie. He had to swallow repeatedly not to laugh.

"How did ye ken I worked in the kitchens today?"

It was his turn to be less than forthright, but he refused to feel even the slightest measure of guilt for it. "I happened to glance into the courtyard when ye were making yer way into the kitchens, and I assumed ye meant to offer aid. Or were ye just hungry?" he teased as she consumed the entire chunk of bread she'd been holding.

After she finished chewing and swallowing, she smirked. "This is the first proper meal I have had in days."

"Umm-hmm," he teased. "'Tis good for a woman to have a large appetite."

She smacked him on the arm. "I do nae have a 'large' appetite.

"If ye say so," he said, feeling suddenly lighter than he could remember in ages. "So did ye make friends in the kitchens today?"

"Oh aye," she replied, her cheeks now red.

"Aye?" he prodded.

"Aye," she said, glancing down. He was positive it was to hide a guilty expression.

"Who did ye make friends with?" he asked, positively enthralled as she worried her lower lip.

"Aila," she finally replied. "She let me borrow her knife."

Behind him, Tess barked suddenly with laughter, and he turned to determine the cause. Clearly listening freely to their conversation, she leaned both her elbows on the table, an expression of rapt attention on her face.

He turned back to Brigid to find her tugging the bodice

of her gown open a bit. A sheen of sweat was on her forehead. So, lying also made her perspire, did it? But the lass was lying to protect Aila. He was certain of it. To protect someone who had injured ye, treated ye with open hostility you did not earn, was a significant display of loyalty. He would make sure Aila knew it in case whatever Camden had said to her had not banished all her ill will toward Brigid, knowing this might.

"And how do ye find yer room?" he asked, wondering if the situation with Britta had been taken care of.

She set her goblet down, but he noticed as she did that her hand trembled slightly. Alarm coursed through him as he saw her face, which had suddenly lost all color.

"Do ye feel well?"

Instead of answering, she slapped a hand to her mouth, grabbed her side with the other, and shoving back from the table, she doubled over with her head between her knees.

Apprehension raced through him as Brigid began to retch right there upon the dais. He shoved out of his chair as did everyone, but he was the first to reach her just as she slumped over with a moan. He scooped her up and to his chest with little effort.

He turned to Tess. "Follow me."

"'Twill be fine, lass," he said, not certain if he lied for her sake or his. Her eyes stared through him, glassy and distant. His apprehension increased tenfold. "Brigid?"

"I'm sorry, Da," she mumbled, then her eyelids fluttered shut.

Panic gripped him as a disturbing thought hit him. Had his sister followed through on her threat to try to kill Brigid?

"Cormac?" Camden called out.

He saw Aila out of the corner of his eye, hovering by the door that led to the kitchens. Rage took hold of him.

"How did ye handle Aila?" he demanded as he strode down the center of the great hall. A hush fell as he made his way toward the door.

"I ordered her to accept Brigid," Camden answered.

Cormac clenched his jaw. Ordering a mule-headed lass like Aila to do anything was the worst way to handle her. "And Britta?"

"The same," Camden replied, sounding uneasy. "Is that nae what ye would do?"

"Nay," Cormac replied as he made his way out of the great hall door and a fresh wave of anger hit him. But he was not vexed with his brother. He was livid with himself. He'd been so focused on avoiding Brigid, he'd failed in his duties to protect her. He just hoped the price was not her life.

He took the stairs to her bedchamber three at a time. Multiple footsteps followed him, but he didn't pause to ascertain who it was. He guessed it was Tess and Martha, and when he and Camden entered Brigid's bedchamber, it was indeed Martha and Tess who came after him.

He started toward Brigid's bed and paused, letting out a string of expletives he normally would not have ever said in front of a lass, let alone three. A snake, albeit not a poisonous one, slithered across her bed. Behind him, Martha gasped.

Tess said, "I'll go fetch Aila and Britta."

"Fetch Maisie as well," he ordered as he shifted Brigid's weight, grasped the snake, went to the window that overlooked the garden, and slung it into the night.

"But Cormac," Tess began but he shook his head.

"I do nae care if ye must drag her kicking and screaming. Bring her to me. I do nae doubt she has a part in this."

"I'll fetch her," Tess said.

He lowered Brigid to the bed as her eyes fluttered open once more.

"Da, I promise nae to speak when nae spoken to. I—"

She jolted upright and rolled off the bed before he could react. She hit the floor with a thud, scrambled to her knees, and began to vomit.

Martha came beside her and drew her hair back while whispering soothing words.

"What can I do?" he asked, feeling completely helpless.

"If ye could fetch a cool rag and water. She's burning up."

"I'm on fire!" Brigid said, as if hearing the words from her companion's lips had reminded her of the state she was in. She retched yet again, and then, shoving out of Martha's grasp, she rolled to her side on the hardwood floor.

His chest squeezed so tight it felt hard to breathe as he watched.

She drew her knees up and hugged them to her body, displaying a great amount of flesh from her ankles all the way up to her creamy upper thigh.

"Fetch a rag and wash basin," he commanded his brother, not wishing Camden to be standing there gaping at Brigid's half-exposed state.

Cormac came to his knees beside her as Camden did as bid, and she opened her eyes once more, her cloudy gaze locking on him.

"I'm dying," she whispered.

"Nay," he said with more reassurance than he felt. He got to his knees before her and took her small hand in his. "I'll nae allow it." He squeezed her hand as her eyes closed on a moan of pain.

"My side," she whimpered. "It hurts. I—" She sucked in a sharp breath, wrenched her hand out of his, scrambled to her knees yet again, and heaved once more. She slumped backward, and he moved behind her to catch her. She collapsed against him panting. He slid his legs on either side of hers to cradle her and drew her firmly against his chest.

"I can do that," Martha protested, wringing her hands.

Tess entered the room with Aila and Britta on either side of her. He glanced behind them, expecting Maisie's presence, but Tess shook her head.

"She is holding onto her bed screaming," Tess said. "I left her with Ross and told him I'd be back to aid him in prying her loose."

Cormac shook his head as Camden set the wash basin down beside Martha. She took the rag from him, dipped it, wrung it, and handed it back to him. With great care, he patted Brigid's neck, then her head, then gave the rag back to Martha to dip again. Brigid snored softly, and he was glad she was out for the moment. From his position behind her, he could see her pulse beating furiously at the side of her neck, and her pale locks curling against her chest to fall to her waist. He forced himself to look away from her, and he turned his gaze and his anger on the women before him, who he was certain had caused this.

"Tell me."

Britta blanched, but Aila, who had been closest to Elsie, stared back at him, chin lifted and a defiant look on her face. Aila took Britta's hand in hers, and he knew it was a silent message not to give him the answers he sought.

"Aila, I want retribution for Elsie as much as ye," he said, "but Brigid is nae to blame for her stepbrother's crimes."

Aila bit her lip, but the defiant look remained. Britta was frowning something fierce now. He inhaled a deep breath for patience and his temper.

"Brigid's death would nae bring Elsie back, and then ye have killed an innocent woman. Ye will have a black sin against yer soul and will nae enter God's kingdom." He wasn't one to normally use fear, but he was not above it in this moment to save Brigid.

"We did nae give her a deadly dose," Britta murmured.

"Britta!" Aila cried out, snatching her hand away.

"I'm sorry!" Britta said, reaching for Aila who stepped away from Britta and glared at her.

Britta sighed but continued. "We put just enough in her food to make her ill."

He resisted the urge to yell at them. "What did ye give her?"

"Do nae ye dare say!" Aila cried out. "She's a Campbell. She deserves to be ill."

"Oh, ye're a wee wicked one," Martha bit out, scrambling to her feet with her fists clenched.

Tess stepped between the women who looked like they might come to blows.

"Brigid has nae done anything to ye, Aila. In fact, she lied for ye to protect ye tonight."

Aila frowned. "What do ye mean?"

"She means," Cormac said, "when I asked Brigid about her time in the kitchen today, she did nae tell me that ye purposely dropped yer knife so it would cut her. Instead, she told me that ye let her borrow yer knife, and that the two of ye had made friends."

In that moment, Brigid moaned in his arms and mumbled, "Let me out. Let me out of this dungeon, please. I beg ye. I'll be quiet. I'll be obedient."

The room fell silent as they all looked to Brigid who shuddered in his arms, her eyes still shut. He didn't know who was more responsible for her pain, Ramsay or her da, but her da was dead, so that left Ramsay to pay for what he'd done to Brigid—and for what the man had done to Elsie and Maisie. If it was the last thing he did, Cormac intended to find a way to make the man do that.

"I . . . I would nae ever kill anyone," Aila said in a near whisper. "We did nae give her enough to kill her, just make her ill. We hoped she'd leave then."

"What did ye give her?" he asked once more.

"'Tis a mushroom in the forest outside the boundaries of the castle known to give cramps of the stomach and make ye empty it."

"It makes ye see things that are nae there as well," Britta added.

"Fly agaric," Tess said.

The women nodded their confirmation.

"Wicked, wicked creatures," Tess hissed and clucked her tongue. She looked to Cormac. "I can make a potion to counter the effect, but it will likely take all night to work. She'll be getting sicker afore she gets better, and she should nae be left alone because she could die of her own retching if it did nae come out properly."

"I'll stay with her," Martha said. "If ye'll create the potion," she said, looking to Tess who nodded, "then the rest of ye do nae need to stay."

"Nay," Cormac replied. "I need to stay." He could have added that it was because it was his duty, but that wasn't the only reason he was staying. He felt compelled to. His need to protect her in this moment was stronger than his desire to avoid her.

"As ye wish it," Martha said.

"Tomorrow," he said, focusing on Aila and Britta as Tess departed the room, "Camden will take Britta back to the Donald holding."

"Laird, nay, please!" Britta cried out. "I'll do anything! I . . . please, give me another chance."

"Brigid would nae want this, laird," Martha said in a quiet voice beside him.

He looked down at Brigid. She was whiter now than she had been earlier, and it renewed his anger, but he thought Martha was probably right, and since it was Brigid who had been harmed, he would let her decide.

"When Brigid is better, I'll let her hand down the punishments to both of ye."

"Like she's mistress of the castle?" Aila spat. "Are ye replacing Elsie so easily then? With the sister of her murderer?"

"Woman," he bit out, his anger making the vein in his head pulse, "I am nae replacing Elsie with anyone."

He would not surrender to his desire for Brigid, but he wasn't going to avoid her and anything to do with her. That clearly sent a message to the clan that they could treat her poorly.

"Now out with ye."

They both immediately turned to leave, and it occurred to him that he had not asked about his sister's involvement.

"Hold," he commanded. They paused and faced him. "Did Maisie ken what ye were about with the poison?"

"I told her that we had struck against the woman for her stepbrother's sins, but she did nae even seem to hear me. Her only response was that she had surrendered."

He frowned at that. "Ye may leave." After they had departed, he looked to Camden. "Why do ye think Maisie said that?"

Camden shrugged. "I do nae ken. Da said it to us often that MacLeans do nae surrender that the notion is engrained in all of us."

That was true enough. The notion of not surrendering to one's enemies, fears, and weaknesses was one their da had repeated to them all the time growing up, but why would Maisie say that? It seemed very important to discover how she felt she had surrendered, but as Brigid was jerked away once more by another bout of retching, he shoved the questions aside and concentrated on the woman he was determined not to fail to protect again.

Chapter Thirteen

$\mathcal{B}$ rigid woke with a horrid taste in her mouth and a ravenous hunger. She opened her eyes to sunlight streaming into the room, and it took her a moment to remember she was in her new bedchamber at the MacLean stronghold. She lay there, trying to recall how she'd gotten into bed, but the only memories she could pull up of the night before were of Cormac teasing her about her appetite, a warm, fuzzy feeling consuming her when he smiled and two dimples appeared on his handsome face, and then her feeling ill and retching. Other than that, there was only blank space where her memories should have been. How had she gotten to her bedchamber and into her bed for that matter? On that thought, she lifted her coverlet and gasped at the site of her *in* nightclothes. Who had undressed her?

"It's good to see ye awake finally."

She yelped at the sound of Cormac's voice from the doorway. He leaned into the door with his hands above him, gripping the ledge. He had nothing on but braies which clung to his hip bones. His chest and stomach, bands of muscle, glistened with sweat, and his dark hair was wet as if he'd just bathed and curled at the nape of his neck. His eyes appeared startlingly blue against his sun-kissed skin, and they held what looked like concern to her.

"What do ye mean *finally?*"

"'Tis late in the afternoon."

She had never slept to late in the afternoon in her life. "How did I get to my bedchamber from the great hall?" she asked, her voice a peculiar raspy sound which must have come from her sickness.

"I carried ye," he said, shifting ever so slightly forward as if he were stretching out his muscles, which, she could not help but notice, were exceptionally well formed. His upper arms curved nicely, and as her gaze trailed downward with a will of its own, she noted that his stance emphasized the slimness of his hips and the force of his thighs.

Her throat went suddenly dry, but she did not think it had a thing to do with the fact that she had been ill. She had never felt desire, but her instincts told her this tightening in her belly all the way to her core, this ache between her legs, this spike in her heartbeat, was desire for this man before her. And then his words hit her, and she gawked.

"Ye carried me?"

"Aye." The corners of his mouth tugged up into a smile.

"Did ye . . . did ye undress me?"

"Nay, lass, friends do nae undress friends."

Good heaven, she was on fire. His gaze held a sensuality she was certain he did not wish it to, but nevertheless, it was there. She pulled her coverlet up to her chin, feeling wanton and exposed at the same moment.

"So, we're friends now, are we?"

He nodded, a serious look settling on his handsome face. "It was nae well-done of me to tell ye we could nae be friends. I am perfectly capable of controlling my, er, desires."

She wasn't certain she could say the same, and the thought was shocking. Despite how tired and ravenous and stuffy headed she was, she wouldn't at all mind if he strode over to her bed, gathered her in his arms, and kissed her as he had done before. Well, except she imagined her breath smelled horrid. On that thought, she glanced to her side and saw a pitcher of mead on the table as well as a goblet. She started to reach for it, but Cormac was across the room, whisking the pitcher and goblet up to serve her before she could even fully twist her body to do so.

"I see ye've returned," came Martha's voice from the doorway.

Brigid glanced to her companion who breezed into the room and came to stand alongside Cormac at Brigid's bedside. The two of them exchanged a surprising look that could only be described as one of comradery. Cormac handed Brigid the goblet, which she drank slowly from while Martha and Cormac smiled at each other as if they had become fast friends in one night.

"This one," Martha said, hooking her thumb in Cormac's direction, slept on the floor beside yer bed until I forced him to leave this morning. And he's been back five times since then. I told ye," Martha said, scowling at him, but Brigid could tell it was playful by the tip of Martha's lips upward, "that ye would see the lass at supper if she felt up to it."

Brigid gaped at Cormac, and she could not seem to make herself stop.

"Ye slept by my bed?" she asked, wincing at the amazement that underlined her question. She did not think anything could embarrass the gruff Highlander standing before her, but her question seemed to do just that. He flushed and tugged a hand through his hair.

"Aye, well, I felt it my fault that ye were ill, and I wanted to ensure ye were watched over every moment."

Martha clucked her tongue as she motioned for Brigid to sit up. Brigid did so and Martha fluffed the pillows behind her.

"I told him I was perfectly capable of seeing to yer welfare. I've been doing it all yer life. Tell him," Martha commanded in her motherly way as she set a gentle hand to Brigid's shoulder to guide her back against her now fluffed pillows.

They both peered at her with so much concern, it touched her and made her want to laugh.

"Aye, Martha is like a mother to me."

"I can see it," Cormac said, "And I do nae doubt it, but a mother can nae protect a lass like a man can."

"And ye think I need protecting?" she asked, surprised at the warmth that infused her that he would want to safeguard her.

"Well, aye. My sister is down the hall and what with ye ill and—"

"It's nae as if Maisie poisoned me," Brigid said. When Cormac and Martha exchanged a glance, Brigid sucked in a sharp breath. "Did yer sister poison me?"

"Nay, but Aila and Britta did," he said, making her exhale in disbelief. "And Maisie was told of their actions afore ye ate the meat and drank yer wine, so technically, she could have stopped ye."

"I do nae think the poor lass's mind is all there," Martha added, patting Brigid's hand. "I'd nae be so vexed with her."

"I'm getting used to Maisie trying to harm me," Brigid said dryly.

Cormac scowled at her. "I have failed to protect ye twice now, but I vow it will nae happen again."

And there was the real reason he was standing here hovering over her and why he had slept by her bed last night. The man clearly harbored some immense guilt regarding his dead betrothed and he was transferring the need to make up for it to her. Did he believe he had somehow failed to protect his betrothed and therefore it was his fault that she was dead? Brigid wagered he did, and she intended to ask Tess that very question the moment she got the woman alone.

She had no idea who Britta was, but she had met Aila, who Tess had told her had been Elsie's cousin, so had an instant and vitriolic dislike of Brigid.

"Let me guess, this Britta person was also yer betrothed's cousin?"

"Aye," he confirmed on a sigh.

Her feelings were injured even though she knew it was ridiculous to allow them to be. Still . . . . Maybe trying to be a part of this clan *would* be impossible. Maybe she would never have a chance at really belonging.

"Does everyone in this castle despise me simply because I'm Ramsay's stepsister?"

"Nay everyone," he assured her. "My brother likes ye just fine now, and Tess as well."

He cocked his head, as if trying to come up with another person which made her want to laugh. It was better than tears, she supposed.

He snapped his fingers. "Quinn has decided ye're nae horrid."

"Well, that's a compliment if ever I heard one," she grumbled.

For a moment, when his gaze met hers, she could have sworn she saw real tenderness in his eyes, but it was just wishful thinking, she was certain, and it was gone in a breath.

"Give it time. Once they ken ye, they will see ye're nae bad."

"Like ye?" she couldn't help but ask.

"Aye," he said, smiling. "Like me."

"Still," she said, "It seems extreme that Aila and the Britta lass would poison me simply because I'm Ramsay's stepsister. Should I be worried that others will try to poison me or that they will strike again?"

Tess breezed into the room at that exact moment with a trencher laden with food. She paused at the bed with the trencher, and said, "Those two clot-heided lasses will nae try anything else. They're both afraid of being banished from the clan now since Cormac threatened he might, and he also assured them he did nae have any intention of replacing Elsie with ye."

Cormac shot Tess a murderous look to which she grinned. Brigid inhaled a long breath, considering what she'd just heard. She understood a bit better now. The women were loyal to Elsie's memory, and they did not want her forgotten by Cormac, but most especially they did not want her forgotten by Cormac for Ramsay Campbell's stepsister.

"I'm glad ye set them straight," she said, meaning it, though it did sting a bit. She would dismiss her disappointment because there was naught else she could do. He had made it clear there would be no going forward for the two of them, and she would accept that.

A distinctly uncomfortable look settled on his face. "'Tis nae . . . well," he said, tugging a hand through his hair, "'tis just that—"

"Though I am enjoying watching ye stumble around for words, I'm also ravenous, so I assure ye, 'tis fine."

He gave a curt nod. "I plan to send Britta back to the Donald clan today as punishment for—"

"Please, nay," she said, cutting him off. "The women of yer clan certainly will nae accept me as one of their own if

I'm the cause of one of them being sent away. I'll speak with Britta and Aila personally."

"Well, they must be punished," he said.

"I do nae think that's the best course," she replied. "They will only resent me more, and as Tess said, ye have put the fear of being banished in them. I imagine that ought to do the trick."

"I do nae like it," he grumbled. "It makes me look soft."

She smiled at that. "It makes ye look understanding, and to comprehend what it is that drives people to make the choices they do, means ye can better react to them."

He gave her an uneasy look that she had to fight not to smile in reaction to.

"Nay everyone wants their actions to be understood, lass."

"I disagree," she said, truthfully. "I think some people are afraid to be understood, because then they have nowhere to hide from the person that understands them, so they must either choose to change or remain as they are."

He went from looking uneasy to downright uncomfortable, and he said, "I've got to go train."

"Did ye nae just come in from the last training of the day?" Tess asked, with obvious false sweetness.

He scowled at her. "Aye, but now I've got to go out and train again. Do ye have a problem with that?"

He pointed at Brigid then to Tess and Martha. "Keep her abed until supper."

With that, he strode from the room without so much as a goodbye for any of them.

"I thought if ye were awake ye may be weak from yer sickness and supper is nae for another three bells." Tess held out the trencher to her, and as Brigid took it and settled it into her lap, she tried to think how to ask the things she wanted to about Cormac. She opened her mouth to ask her questions, closed it, and looked down at the food before her.

With a snort Tess said, "Just ask me. If I do nae wish to tell ye, I'll nae."

Brigid glanced up in surprise to find Tess and Martha both smirking at her. She smiled at them. "I see ye two have become friends already."

They grinned at each other. "Aye," they said in unison.

"I was wondering about Elsie and how she died."

"I thought ye might be," Tess said, a twinkle in her eye.

"Did ye?" Brigid asked, frowning. "Why did ye think that?"

Martha snickered. "Ye're attraction to the laird is nae exactly undetectable."

"Martha!" Brigid cried out, heat sweeping across her face, neck, and down her chest.

"She's right," Tess said, with a wave of her hand, "but do nae fear. 'Tis only noticeable to one who pays verra close attention."

"Or two," Martha added. When Brigid gave her a questioning look, Martha added, "I care for ye, so I pay close attention to ye and how things make ye feel."

"And I care for Cormac, so I do the same," Tess added. "Even if he is a grown man and wishes me to stop."

Brigid smirked at that and offered Martha a pointed look to which Martha simply shrugged.

"Someday, lass, when ye have children, ye'll understand that ye do nae quit trying to mother them simply because they grow older."

Brigid reached forward and grabbed Martha's hand, giving it a squeeze. "I'm lucky to have ye, Martha."

"Aye," Martha said, "ye are, and I'm lucky to have ye,

too."

"He's attracted to ye, too, incidentally, though ye need to ken that getting him to accept it, is another matter entirely," Tess said.

Brigid thought immediately of the kiss and what he said to her after. "I'm somewhat aware," she offered.

Tess sat on the edge of the bed. "I'll tell ye what I ken and what I think, but Cormac has nae offered his inner feelings to me. He keeps those close."

Martha went around to the other side of the bed and sat on the edge, so Brigid had both women sitting on either side of her. It gave her such a warm feeling that she smiled. "This is the closest to a family talk I've ever come," she said, only realizing she'd said it aloud when Martha picked up her hand and squeezed it. Brigid's embarrassment at having said such a thing for others to hear heated her further.

"I ken yer nae my family," she rushed out.

"Hush now, lass," Tess said. "Ye are part of the clan now, as is Martha, so we are as family."

Tears pressed at Brigid's eyelids, but she blinked them away.

"What do ye ken of Elsie's death?" Tess asked.

"Nay much. Just that she died the same day Maisie was ravished, which was also the day Cormac bested Ramsay at the Donald tourney."

"Aye," Tess agreed. "He did, and yer brother—"

"Stepbrother," Brigid corrected.

"Aye, stepbrother," Tess agreed. "He accused Cormac of cheating, which he did nae. He was simply better."

"Ramsay spent endless hours training to please my da, I think, but there was nae anything one could do to totally please my da. It was a fruitless endeavor at best but made even more so by the fact that Ramsay was nae a natural swordsman."

"Aye," Martha agreed. "He is awkward in his handling of the sword."

"If he was nae trained from a young age, it would nae ever come as natural to him as someone like Cormac. His da put a sword in his hand before Cormac was out of his nappies."

"I do nae think Ramsay handled a sword until his mother wed my da. His mother was a servant at the Donald Castle—"

"Elsie, Britta, and Aila's home?" Tess asked.

"I had nae thought upon that fact," Brigid said, "but aye."

"I supposed it's nae of import," Tess said. "It's just an odd coincidence."

Brigid shrugged. "Aye. Shall I continue?"

Tess waved a hand in encouragement.

"Ramsay did nae ken his father," Brigid offered. She'd always felt sorry for him because of that, and it had in a sense made her understand what drove him—the desire to be someone of importance and not thought of simply as a bastard, but that did not excuse his actions.

Tess clucked her tongue. "We are nae simple creatures, us humans. We desire belonging, and often in our quest to achieve it, we destroy connections instead of building them."

Brigid nodded as Martha made a sound of concurrence.

Tess said, "Yer stepbrother charged at Cormac, and—"

"I ken this part. Cormac swept his feet out from under him."

"Aye, and Maisie and Elsie were there and laughed at him. Cormac sent them to the cottage, likely in an effort to get the foolish lasses away, because he kenned they were further embarrassing Ramsay."

"Cormac has a kind heart," Brigid said.

"Aye," Tess agreed, "but he'll nae take ye saying so as a compliment. He was taught that lairds are tough and do nae show emotion."

"As is the way of foolish men," Martha said.

"Cormac had to attend a meeting with the king, and while there, smoke was spotted rising in the air. He realized it was coming from the direction of the cottage where Maisie and Elsie were. He ran there, found Maisie outside in a state of half undress, badly beaten, and babbling. The cottage was on fire, and when he asked Maisie where Elsie was, she pointed to the cottage. He ran into the burning cottage and pulled Elsie out."

The last sentence was filled with horror and sorrow, and Brigid had to swallow past the lump in her throat and inhale a long, slow breath to quell her own horror and nausea.

"Was she dead?"

A dark look crossed Tess's face and she shuddered. "Nay, nae yet. She was burned badly and clinging to life."

Chills swept over Brigid, and she could see out of the corner of her eye Martha's grimace. Her hand had fluttered to her neck as if to ward off the mere thought of what it must have been like. Brigid's mouth was suddenly so dry that she was unsure she could form words. Tess seemed to understand this. She filled a goblet with mead and handed it to Brigid who reached for it with a shaking hand. After she had taken a long drink, she set the goblet down.

"Ye were there?"

"Aye. Me, Cormac, Ross, Camden, Quinn, and Britta, Elsie's cousin."

"I've nae met Britta yet."

Tess made a face. "She's nae my favorite." She shrugged. "Anyway, Elsie—" Tess paused and rubbed her upper arms as if to ward off a chill. "She was trying to hang on to life, but the burns, well, she was nae going to be able to survive, and we all saw it. He saw it."

Brigid did not need to ask who 'he' was.

Tears trickled from Tess's eyes. "He told her she could go. She started wheezing and moaning, struggling with the letting go, ye see. And he vowed to her he'd nae forget her, nae ever replace her."

Brigid nodded, surprised when warm tears tracked down her own face.

"So, lass, I see his attraction to ye, and I can see him denying it, and he will fight it. He'll fight it with all he has because he's confusing moving on with forgetting. He can love another and still have a place in his heart where his love is for her and nae forget her. Ye do nae ken him but a bit right now."

"Aye," Brigid responded, blinking in surprise at how hoarse her voice was. "Ye're right."

Tess wiped her tears away and smiled. "Would ye like to ken him better?"

There was no point in denying it, so Brigid nodded.

"Well, then," Tess said, patting Brigid on the shoulder, "ye will, and if ye find yer heart wants him, then I suppose ye'll have to fight for him, but I do believe, if ye find ye're a match, he'd be worth it. He's a true and good man."

"Aye," Brigid agreed. "He does seem to be."

She pushed her trencher to the side, her hunger gone with the story of how Elsie died. When she started to rise, both Martha and Tess protested, and she could tell by the determined look in their eyes that neither woman had any intention of letting her get out of bed this day. But she had other plans. She meant to go see Maisie. She was curious if Ross MacLeod had made any progress with the lass. She knew what had happened to Maisie was Ramsay's fault, and yet guilt did niggle at her by mere association with him, and she wanted to aid Maisie. If she could do so, maybe the people here would be more accepting of her, and maybe if they were more accepting, then Cormac would at least not have that guilt to deal with, and then maybe—

She stopped her wayward thoughts. She needed to take one step at time. She desired the man, and she thought she liked him, but she could not say for certain yet. She gave a large, pretend yawn, and then scooted down her bed to lie down. Looking from one woman to the other, she sent a silent prayer of forgiveness for lying up to God.

"I'm awfully tired. I think I'll take a nap, if ye two do nae mind?"

"Do ye nae wish for a bite?" Martha asked, looking concerned.

"I wish a nap afore supper," she said.

"Do ye want us to stay with ye?" Tess asked, picking up the trencher.

"Nay, I think I'll sleep better alone. Why do nae one of ye come to fetch me for supper?"

"Ye can come work in the healing room with me," Tess said to Martha. Martha nodded enthusiastically as she'd always had a curious mind.

Once the women departed, Brigid lay there a good long while, giving them a chance to make their way down the passage and to whatever task might occupy them, then she rose, went to the door, and peeked out to ensure no one was in the corridor. When this was confirmed, she glanced around the room, hoping to see her gown there, but there was no such luck. She frowned at that. Likely, they had not left her a gown on purpose. That was fine. She didn't need a gown to go three doors down to Maisie's bedchamber. She'd simply have to ensure she stayed in the room and ran into no one. How hard could that be?

Chapter Fourteen

A moment later, she knocked on Maisie's door, not surprised when the woman did not answer it. She cracked the door open and there sat Maisie in the same chair as last time, looking straight at the door.

"Ye're still alive I see," the woman said, her tone unfriendly, but at least she'd spoken.

Brigid slipped into the room and when Maisie's eyes widened at Brigid's half undressed state, she thought it a good sign that at least the woman was now speaking and taking note of her surroundings.

"Did ye hope Aila and Britta would kill me?"

"Aye," Maisie said, not blinking.

Brigid inhaled a long breath as she walked toward Maisie while sweeping her gaze around the room to ensure there was nothing in there the woman could use to injure her with. She'd gotten Maisie out of her bedchamber and to the great hall last night by refusing to quit talking, and she planned to drive Maisie out of her room again today. The more she was around people, the better.

She pulled up the only other chair in the room so that it was directly in front of Maisie. "Have ye spoken with Ross?" Brigid asked, opting to use the man's given Christian name as it was more personal, and she wanted Maisie to be reminded of personal connections.

The woman simply stared at her, though now with

narrowed eyes.

"I was glad to see he came straight away when bid. He must love ye verra much."

More staring, but now Maisie's nostrils flared.

"And to nae be betrothed to another woman after a year shows devotion, do ye nae think?"

"I think," Maisie said, offering a cold-eyed smile, "that I despise ye."

Despite the rude words, Brigid counted it as a victory. Feeling something was better than feeling nothing.

"I imagine he has tried to talk to ye?"

Maisie's expression became a mask of stone, but her hands in her lap twined together tightly. Brigid simply needed to keep pushing the woman.

"It could help ye," she said slowly, "to talk about it."

The woman's expression went from a mask to contempt. Brigid racked her mind and thought mayhap she should share a bit of her pain from her past. It did not compare to Maisie's experience, but perhaps knowing personal details of Brigid's life would make Maisie feel more comfortable.

"My mother died right after I was born." Golden brown eyes bore into Brigid, but she continued. "My companion Martha is like a mother to me, but my da was nae ever kind or loving. Neither was my only other family—my stepbrother." She thought perhaps it was best she did not yet speak Ramsay's name.

"I kenned since a verra young age that my da had wanted a son, nae me. Martha, my companion, told me so after my da told me one day to nae talk unless spoken to and to nae be seen unless asked to do so."

She looked down and traced the outline of her scars on her wrist. "My da and my stepbrother both put me in the dungeon with the rats when I forgot and spoke without being asked to or spoke too truthfully when given permission to speak. I was verra sad about it, and that's when Martha told me what she knew about my da wanting a boy."

Maisie began humming to herself, but Brigid was determined to keep going.

"We both assumed it was because he was disappointed that he did nae have a son to inherit, but I found out verra recently that my da did nae ever tell me I had inherited a castle from my mother when she died."

The information got no reaction from Maisie, which was disappointing, but Brigid continued. "It's called Clooney Castle, and it's a strategic stronghold used to protect one of the king's castles against Viking Raids, therefore the king is beholden to the owner of it."

Maisie snorted, which was better than nothing.

"My stepbrother was going to force me to wed Sinclair Ferguson."

Maisie shoved out of her chair at that, causing Brigid to do the same. But the woman moved fast. She was out of the door before Brigid could even ask her to stop. By the time Brigid caught up with her, Maisie was half-way down the corridor and going into another bedchamber. Brigid charged in behind her, certain this was some sort of breakthrough. Brigid stopped a few steps into the room and inhaled a sharp breath.

The large room held a massive bed, an enormous upright chest, and a washstand, but other than that the furniture it was spartan. There was nowhere to sit, except the bed. On the walls, multi-colored tapestries hung, along with a flag which Brigid immediately recognized as the MacLean battle flag. Weapons hung upon the walls for easy and immediate access. That, and the great size of the room, must mean this was Cormac's bedchamber.

There was no time to give it much thought beyond that because Maisie was grunting and shoving at the chest, clearly trying to move it from the wall. Feeling she had no choice but to aid the woman—she had caused this reaction, after all—Brigid strode over to the chest and, positioning herself on the other side, helped pull it from the wall. She gasped when it moved enough to realize there was a secret passage behind it.

Maisie plunged into the darkness and Brigid was forced to follow or leave the woman to go alone, which, considering everything, seemed a horrible idea.

Brigid heard footsteps in front of her but was unable to see even her hands in front of her face. "Maisie!"

The footsteps away became faster. The blasted woman was running from her.

Brigid cautiously forged ahead. She longed to return to Cormac's chamber where there was light and not this stygian darkness. After two turns, she realized she dare not lose track of Maisie or risk becoming lost in the tunnel. She concentrated on the sound of footsteps just ahead, holding back fear which would cripple her. Her feet scuffed cold dirt and cobwebs brushed her face. She lightly traced the stone to her right to help maintain a sense of up and down—and to keep from running into the wall in the dark.

The warm, close air was difficult to breathe, and she wrinkled her nose as the dank air filled her throat and lungs.

Suddenly, her feet slipped on wet stone and her hands met open air. With trepidation, she tapped the ground ahead of her with one foot. Stairs.

"Maisie!" she called, but still the woman did not respond.

The steps ended, but the ground continued to slope. The temperature dropped and the air grew lighter, fresher, smelling of the sea. A moment later, Brigid heard the swish of the waves from the loch.

Ahead of her, the darkness departed, slashed by brilliant moonlight. Maisie was outlined for one moment before she disappeared into a thick forest where the trees rose tall and strong to the night sky.

Brigid stepped out of the tunnel and looked back to see the MacLean stronghold towering high above on the rocks. The tunnel had run underground down the hill to the forest. It was, she realized with a shiver from the cool wind, a secret escape route. She shoved branches aside on the overgrown route, then started down a path that had logs fallen across it and hard, knotted, roots running over the dirt. Her stomach pinched as she ran, until finally she had to stop and double over to catch her breath. When her breathing became even once again, she stood, and not a hundred feet ahead, on the far bank of the stream, stood Maisie.

Fear lodged in Brigid's throat, but she pushed herself forward through the thick brush toward the water that glistened under the moon beams. She clambered over a log only to land in a thorn bush whose branches tangled with her sleeve. She yanked her sleeve loose, but the thorns cut across her cheek, leaving a stinging trail that warmed as blood welled to the surface. Leaves crunched under her bare feet, branches poked her, twigs snapped, and rocks stabbed at her skin, making her wince. Yet she kept going.

She had started this, and she could not turn back now. Maisie had brought her here for a reason, and her gut told her it was not to try to harm her. She moved to the edge of the dark murky water and looked between where she was and where Maisie stood on the other side. Maisie had to have crossed the water by walking across the fallen log. The mere thought of doing that make Brigid's stomach flip. Not for all the gold in Scotland did she want to risk falling into the water again.

"Maisie, what is this place?"

The woman did not answer. She wrapped her arms around her waist and began to keen loudly. Brigid moved toward the log. Sweat dampened her brow, gathered under her arms, and trickled down her back.

"Maisie, please come back across!"

Something in the trees startled at her shout, and she could have sworn she heard a growl. She glanced around the dark woods, searching for the source of the noise but did not see wolves or any other threatening creatures of the night.

"Maisie, I do nae wish to cross. Ye ken I can nae swim. If I were to slip—"

A distinct growl reached her. Brigid glanced up sharply and met two glowing eyes directly behind Maisie. The white of a predator's teeth flashed against the dark night.

"Maisie! Come across!" she screamed, but the woman rocked and keened, rocked and keened.

"There's a wolf behind ye!" Brigid yelled, fear and hope-lessness rising to almost choke her. She stepped onto the slick log and her stomach plummeted, but she could not go back.

One pair of eyes became two, and then three.

She placed one foot in front of the other and then took another step. She looked straight ahead, fearful that if she looked down, she would fall. She reached the other side, her heart pounding so hard she was certain it would thump right through her chest.

The growling vibrated the air, and behind Maisie on a ledge stood three wolves with teeth bared. Brigid moved slowly toward Maisie who was still rocking and keening, and with half her attention on the wolves and half on Maisie, she touched the woman on the forearm. Maisie looked up then, blinking as if coming out of a trance, and Brigid almost cried out with relief.

"Behind ye are three wolves," Brigid whispered. Maisie's eyes went wide, but Brigid shook her head and made a very low *shushing* noise. "The worst thing ye can do is run or scream." She remembered how Ramsay had taught her that when they were much younger. It was one of the few kind moments he had ever shown her. Wolves had appeared in the woods on an outing with him, and he had backed her ever so slowly out the way the two of them had come, holding her hand and talking to her.

"Take my hand," she commanded, trying to keep her voice low but her tone authoritative. It must have worked, because Maisie took Brigid by the hand, and Brigid nearly startled at how clammy and cold the woman's skin was. Maisie was scared near to death, and Brigid did not think it was of the wolves but her memories of the night she'd been attacked.

She backed them slowly toward the fallen log, afraid to even turn to look where to step lest the wolves sprang at them and caught them unaware. She gave a quick glance behind her when her foot reached the soft earth of the stream bank. She stepped onto the log, curling her toes as best she could around the slippery wood to grip it. Four steps in, Maisie joined her.

The wind picked up, tossing her hair around her face and her skirts against her ankles, but she moved one foot behind the other without faltering. If they could get to the other side, she'd feel a bit better.

They took another step, and another, neither talking, the whistle of the wind and beating of her heart in her ears all consuming. Then a boom reverberated in the air followed by a brilliant flash of bright silver and blue light so close that both she and Maisie screamed. The wolves pounced from their position and stalked toward the log. And in that moment, Maisie jerked, lost her footing, and fell, taking Brigid with her. She plummeted through the air and plunged into the dark, icy water, sinking once again like a stone.

Chapter Fifteen

"Is yer plan to train all day every day to avoid Brigid?" Camden asked, between bites of meat.

Cormac took a drink of his wine, allowed the liquid to warm a path down his throat and settle into his belly before he answered.

"I am nae avoiding her," he lied. The guilt had been especially bad today because he had been unable to get thoughts of the lass out of his head, but he did not plan to keep avoiding her. She was here to stay as part of his clan, and he had to learn to be around her and control his desire for her. That, he'd do, bit by bit.

Wanting to end the conversation, Cormac turned from Camden toward Ross who sat to the right of him on the other side of Maisie's seat.

"Did ye speak with Maisie today?"

The man shoved a hunk of bread in his mouth and between chewing it, said, "I tried. I went into her bedchamber with Tess, but she refused to even look up from her hands, and then I went to her bedchamber afore supper to see if I could escort her down to the great hall, but the door was wide open, and she was nae in there."

"She's likely with Tess then," Cormac replied, even as a warning voice whispered in his head.

"Nay," Ross said, pointing toward the great hall door. "Tess is there now, and Maisie is nae with her."

Cormac looked to the entrance of the great hall and Tess was indeed entering with Martha by her side. They walked at a clipped pace that first alerted him something was amiss. As they got closer, he saw the genuine concern in Tess's eyes. Martha strode at Tess's heels, wringing her hands.

Cormac stood. "What has happened?"

"We can nae find Maisie or Brigid," Tess said to which Martha nodded.

"I told ye nae to allow Brigid to leave her room!" he bellowed. He shoved his way down the dais with Camden and Ross on his heels.

He was starting toward the great hall door when Tess called out to him. "We already checked Brigid's room and Maisie's."

"Camden," he bit out, "have Quinn gather a contingent of a dozen men. Scan the gardens and the inner courtyard. Tess, gather the upstairs servants, and check the castle rooms."

He exited the great hall and made his way down the corridor, telling each servant he passed to keep an eye out for Brigid or Maisie and, if spotted, to bring them to the great hall. Then he took the stairs three at a time and went to Maisie's room to see if there was any clue as to where the women might be. Martha entered the room, huffing and puffing just as he was about to leave.

"There's nae anything here," he growled.

The woman nodded. "Aye. I ken already. Ye'll nae find anything in Brigid's bedchamber, either. We looked thoroughly. She would nae have gone far; I do nae imagine."

"Why is that?" he asked.

"She did nae have a gown. We did nae leave one purposely, so that she'd nae leave her room."

That didn't make him feel any better.

"Ye take the left side of the corridor, and I'll take the right," he said.

He didn't wait for her to answer. He went in the first bedchamber, scanned the room, found it empty, and left. He did the same for the next four bedchambers, and each was empty. Everyone was at supper. Each time he came out of a room, Martha did the same with a little shake of her head. When he got to his room, he threw the door open and came to a shuddering halt. Icy fear twisted inside of him. He strode across the room to his chest which was pulled away from the wall to reveal the secret escape passage that had not been used since the castle was attacked when his da was a child.

"My lord?"

He ignored Martha as unanswered questions pelted him. Had Sinclair or Ramsay somehow gotten past his guards, the gates, and found their way in? No. Had Maisie gotten hold of a weapon and forced Brigid out of the castle with her? Possibly, but to what purpose? He started for the passage, but Martha grabbed at his elbow from behind.

He turned toward the older woman, her eyes filled with worry, her lips pinched, her forehead wrinkled in true concern.

"It will be fine," he assured her, though he had no notion if it would. Elsie's image filled his head then, and he flinched with the memory of her death. "This leads to the woods. Go find Tess or Camden or Quinn, tell them what's occurred, and they'll bring help if it's needed."

"I'll go with ye. I—"

"Nay," he said. He squeezed her shoulder. "Ye'll slow me down. I need ye to find one of them. They'll sound the horn and send men. Aye?"

"Aye," she said, the word filled with raw emotion.

He gave her one last squeeze before turning away and delving into the dark passageway. The stale air was hot and sticky, the ground bumpy beneath his feet, but as he ran, he noted the lack of cobwebs that should have littered the tunnel in the years of unuse. The women, or at least one of them, had come this way. The passage sloped down, the temperature dropping as it did, but he knew it was because it was winding him down toward the woods. He ran until he burst from the passage and faced the thick woods.

Bright moonlight illuminated the trees, but he had no notion which way to go.

A scream came from the forest. He stilled, and it came again.

"Help, help! Please!"

Without hesitation, he took off straight into the woods, toward the sound of his sister's voice. The path was overgrown, and as he started down it, it seemed familiar, but he could not fathom why. As he shoved branches out of the way and ran across twisted roots and logs, he came to the opening that led to the waterway, and he stopped to listen as a memory hit him. This place looked similar to the area where Elsie had died and Maisie had been ravished, and that similarity set a chill in his body.

"Help!" Maisie cried out again. He scanned the woods, did not see her, and she cried out once more. "Cormac! Cormac! Here. I'm here! In the water!"

His shot his gaze to the water, and there, barely visible, was his sister clinging to a branch near the embankment of the fast-moving waterway that led to the loch. With all the rain they'd had in the last sennight the water moved at an unusually clipped pace. He removed his sword from its sheath in case he had to dive into the water to rescue her, then started across the fallen log that led to the side of the embankment she was nearest. The log was slippery and he almost lost his balance, but he made it across, scrambled through thick brush, and slid down the muddy embankment toward her.

He dropped to his belly and took a firm hold of the thick branch to his left then extended his hand to her. "Can ye give me one hand?"

She hesitated but a moment before nodding, released the branch she was clinging to with her right hand, and held it out to him. Just as he grabbed her forearm, the water jerked her off the branch, and she was pulled down stream. Bracing himself against the current, he tugged her toward him until she was halfway on the embankment.

"Push with yer feet," he commanded, and she obeyed without question. When her free hand reached the dirt, he released the branch he held, grabbed her, and yanked her to safety. She landed beside him, belly down, her face turned to his. In the moonlight, he could see the fear etched on her face and in her eyes.

"There were wolves," she whispered, and then her eyes widened. She scrambled to her knees as she turned toward the water.

"I've killed her!" she screamed, and he didn't need to ask who the 'she' was. The icy fear that had built in his chest felt as if it broke within him into shards that shot through his veins. It was panic. He knew it.

"Tell me," he demanded. He leapt to his feet, scanning the dark moving water.

"I slipped off the branch. She was . . . she was trying to aid me. I slipped and I fell in, and I took her in with me. She can nae . . . she can nae swim!" Maisie wailed, but it was at his back. He was already diving into the water.

It sucked him in with the force of the current, and the cold took his breath for a moment, rendering him almost unable to move. He was a very strong swimmer though, and found his way to the surface in seconds, swimming downstream with the flow. But would Brigid have? It was doubtful that she could have done so, given she could not even swim. He'd failed her. He'd failed her just like he'd failed Elsie. Misery filled his lungs as he gulped in a mouthful of water, coughed, and spit it out. He was slammed into a rock that cut his arm, and then another which scraped his leg. He knew this would dump him into the main loch in front of the castle, so he rode the course, his helplessness growing with the knowledge that there was nothing he could do.

The water turned to the right and left, then right again, and that was when he saw her, clinging to a rock in the middle of the water flowing rapidly around her. It was her hair, so pale in all the darkness, that he spotted. He swam in powerful strokes against the force of the water trying to shove him downstream. He was almost upon her when she lifted her head from the rock and sobbed at the sight of him. He came up behind her, grabbing above the nook she clung to, and he circled his arm around her waist.

"Do ye trust me?" he asked, though he knew he had no right to.

But she nodded, sobbing quietly, and said, "Aye."

"Then ye need to let go. This will dump us in the calm part of the loch, and I'll flip ye on yer back, so that I'm under ye, and aim us feet first down the water. That way," he said, having to raise his voice over the gushing sound of water, "if we hit anything, it will be with our feet and nae our heads."

"I'm scairt," she said.

"I have ye. I vow it. I'll nae fail ye."

Her hand came to his forearm he'd positioned just under her breasts. "When should I let go?"

"Now!" he commanded. She did and he shoved them away from the rock. He held her to his chest and fought to keep himself on his back and their feet pointed downstream. Water filled his nose, his eyes, his mouth, but he spit it out, gulped breaths of air, and repeated the process. He couldn't speak to her in his own struggle, couldn't ask her if she was half-drowned, but she was still braced against him, so she was alive, and that was what mattered.

His muscles burned from his efforts, and just when doubt of how long he could keep them afloat crept into his thoughts, they were dumped into calmness, quietness, and stillness of the main loch.

Within a few breaths, his feet touched ground, and he brought her upright and facing him. He didn't think but simply reacted to the intense need to ensure she was not injured. He cupped her face as her hands came to his shoulders.

"Are ye injured?"

"Nay," she said, her voice hoarse likely from inhaling water. "I've a few cuts and scrapes, and I do nae doubt I'll have bruises, but I'm alive."

Her last three words unleashed a torrent of emotion in him. She was alive. He'd saved her—by the Grace of God, he'd saved her. Why her and not Elsie he didn't know. Guilt washed over him for his failure with Elsie, for his yearning for this woman before him, when he'd vowed to never yearn for another woman again. He'd vowed never to forget Elsie, never to replace her, and all he could think about was Brigid. He hated himself in that moment for his weakness, but a measure of doubt was there too. He was not dead; he was alive, but he was not really living. He knew it, but the only thing, the only one who had made him feel joy again, was the woman before him whom his sister hated and who by simply shining so bright herself threatened to darken his memories of Elsie forever. Didn't she?

"Thank ye," she whispered, snapping his attention to her once more. He could feel the violent shaking of her body, and so he encircled her in his arms, meaning only to give her comfort, but when her hand came to his heart, and her breasts pressed against his chest, all he could think upon was how he wanted her lips under his once more. He tried to fight the want, the desire, but when he glanced down at her to find her staring up at him with obvious longing, his self-restraint vanished. Her hands delved into his hair, and he was lost to the longing, driven by an urgency to touch her that was almost frenzied.

He pulled her closer to him, melding their bodies as one, as he nipped and tugged at her lips, parting them and sliding his tongue into her mouth. She groaned, and the need he heard, and the desire of her response made him tremble with his own wanting. He slipped his hands down her spine, locking her in place, not wanting to let her go. He kissed her lips, then her neck, then back up to her face, her nose, her neck again.

Her hands roamed the expanse of his back, his arse, and back up to his waist, where she twined her arms around him and returned his frenzied kisses with her own. She was a ride through the forest in utter abandon. Whereas his desire for Elsie had been a calm but steady thing, his attraction to Brigid was wild and uncontrollable.

He tried to slow the kiss, to bring the moment back

under his control. He wanted to memorize the way her lips felt so soft under his, the taste of honey in her mouth, the smell of the water in her hair and upon her skin. He moved his mouth over hers, devouring the softness and wanting to consume so much more than just her lips. Everything but her slipped away. His guilt, the night, the worry, and fear.

Finally, he reined his passions back, his body painfully hardened.

"I see ye two are alive."

Camden's voice was like a hot poker to Cormac's brain. He broke the lingering kiss with Brigid immediately and the world came crashing back down on him. He dropped his hands and stepped back a space as guilt consumed him whole. He had forgotten his vow, his family allegiance, and Elsie completely in those few moments with Brigid in his arms.

Brigid's fingertips fluttered to her lips, and a hurt look crossed her face, but it was she who faced Camden. Cormac was locked in place as a war between guilt and want raged within him.

"We're fine," Brigid answered. "How is Maisie?"

Camden tilted his chin over his shoulder. "She went back to the castle with Ross and Tess."

Cormac tore his gaze from Brigid to focus on his brother for a moment and found Martha and Quinn also standing there.

"Was she still talking?"

Camden shook his head. "Nae other than to tell us ye jumped into the water to try and find Brigid."

"She's got a lot of fear locked up in her," Martha said.

"Aye," Brigid agreed, drawing his attention back to her, "but I think she's on the verge of trying to release it. I want to talk to her when we get back to the castle."

"Nay," he replied, protectiveness swelling. "This is the third time she has either put ye in danger herself or stood by while someone else did. Nae anymore."

When Brigid set a hand to his arm, his temper, which had begun to boil, calmed a bit, surprising him that she could have that effect on him—a curious counter-effect of her mere presence filling him with desire.

"She did nae put me in danger," Brigid said quietly. "I followed her from her bedchamber to yers, and out of the tunnel to the woods. I crossed the log of my own accord, and she did nae intentionally pull me into the water. Wolves were there, and we crossed backward over the log. She slipped, and aye, I went down then, but it was nae purposeful on her part. I want to go talk to her. There's a reason she went to the water."

He nodded. "Aye, I think so, too. The spot looks much like the one near the cottage where she was attacked, and Elsie was killed. Come on then," he said, taking her hand before he could re-think his action. But then when her fingers intertwined with his, he did not pull back.

He started to lead her out of the water as his thoughts turned and a question formed in his head—was it possible to be with Brigid and nae forget Elsie as he had vowed? Could he hold Elsie in his heart forever and make room for Brigid?

Chapter Sixteen

*A*s Brigid entered the castle, Cormac at her side and his hand still securely holding hers, a strange feeling filled her belly as if a hundred butterflies had taken up residence. Her heart began to race. Her skin flushed with heat, then she shivered, suddenly cold.

He paused and turned to her; eyes narrowed with concern. "Are ye well?"

Was she? She'd been banged up, taken in mouthfuls of water, nearly drowned, and all of this after being ill from the poisoned meat and wine, but when his concerned look became one of fear and he raised his hand to her face and cupped her cheek, she knew it was none of that affecting her now. It was him. She could still feel his lips on hers, his hands in her hair, his drugging kisses. He had risked his life to save her not once, not twice, but three times. He had told her they could not be friends, that he wanted her, and that he had been mistaken and they could be friends. She knew now he had made a vow to never love another, that likely he would never give himself a chance to love her, and yet she was falling for him. Could she stop it?

"Lass, do I need to carry ye?"

Her heart swelled at the concern in his voice. No, she didn't think she could stop falling in love and that frightened her terribly. She longed to be loved, to have a family, to feel as if she belonged, so it was terribly foolish to have hope that she could have these things with a man who was trying to deny any feelings for her, wasn't it? But he did have feelings of desire and concern if nothing else. And yet, her heart told her he felt more, and that's why she had hope.

She took a deep breath and made a decision—she would rather be a fool and have hope than be closed off to the chance that he might eventually allow her into his heart. And if she discovered he wouldn't? Well, she would have to face that when the time came. *If* the time came. Yes, she would remain hopeful.

"Brigid?"

"I'm fine," she said. "'Tis just the enormity of all that has occurred hit me."

His gaze fell to her lips for a moment before he raised it to her eyes once again, and the tenderness there was heart-rending. He cared. She knew it, but whether he would accept it, allow it to become more, was something only time would tell.

With a nod, he led her into the castle and up the stairs, with Martha and Camden following behind. At Maisie's bedchamber door, she paused and turned to him.

"I'd like to go in alone."

He looked as if he was going to protest, but after a moment, he nodded. "If ye need me—"

"I ken ye will be right here," she said, her chest expanding with yet more hope. She knew he meant here and now, outside of this door, and yet it felt like so much more.

If she could get Maisie to talk, if she could help the woman, perhaps that would be a step toward healing both Maisie and Cormac. With that thought in her head, she entered the room and her hope dwindled just a bit when Ross and Tess shook their head at her. Maisie faced the window with her back to all of them.

Tess crossed to the door where Brigid still stood. "She's nae said a word," Tess whispered.

"Maisie," Brigid called out.

The woman whirled around, astonishment on her face.

"Why ye?" Maisie croaked. Brigid frowned. "Why ye?" Maisie repeated.

"What do ye mean, *why me?*" Brigid asked.

"Why ye?" Maisie demanded louder.

Brigid shook her head, not understanding.

"Why ye? Why ye?" Maisie screamed, and then she barreled toward Brigid so suddenly that she yelped in surprise. The door behind her flew open just as Maisie reached her. Tess grabbed at Brigid as Maisie raised her hands as if to hit her. Brigid ducked and Cormac moved in front of her, catching his sister by her wrists. Tears streamed down her face as Maisie tried to get out of his grip, but he held on as she screamed.

"Why her? Why her?"

Brigid could do no more than stand there, rooted to her spot with astonishment and despair.

"Why her?" Maisie demanded once more.

"I do nae ken why her," Cormac said, and Brigid realized by his tormented tone that he understood what Maisie was talking about, but Brigid still didn't.

"Why did God let her live?"

It struck Brigid then as Cormac shook his head helplessly, and the knowledge nearly crushed her. Maisie wanted to know why God had taken Elsie but spared Brigid. The hope she had nurtured not long ago seemed to slip through her fingers as she watched Cormac and Maisie cling to each other in their sea of grief and despair.

She stepped around them and departed the room to find Martha waiting for her in the corridor. Martha took her hand and gave it a squeeze. Tears blurred her vision. She released Martha's hand and walked quickly past Camden, looking down so he would not see her tears, and made her way to her bedchamber. There she flung herself on her bed and let the tears flow.

She wasn't sure if she was just sobbing for herself due to the loneliness, the lack of love from her father and the cruelty from Ramsay she had endured, or if she was also crying for what had happened to Maisie and Elsie. Maybe she was so distraught because she was exhausted? No, that wasn't true. It was her. It was Maisie, and it was Elsie, whom she had never even met, but it was also Cormac. He had not meant to give her hope for them, but she'd felt it, and now it seemed foolish in the extreme.

Martha ran a soothing hand over the top of Brigid's head as she had often done when Brigid was sad as a child, making calming sounds as Brigid cried. Her nose became stuffed, the tears started to lessen, and she began to hiccup. The tears finally slowed to no more than sniffles. Martha held a rag before her. She sat up, accepted the offering, and blotted her nose and eyes. Martha watched, a wealth of sympathy in her gaze.

After a long moment, Martha said, "Now that ye've gotten that out of ye, ye are nae allowed to feel sorry for yerself or believe that ye are nae worthy of his love."

Brigid's mouth fell open. Martha always had been very perceptive, but love? "I do nae love him."

Not yet.

Martha stared at her expectantly and Brigid gave her a rueful smile. "Aye, I think I could, but 'tis hopeless. Ye saw him."

"Aye. Comforting his sister."

"Aye, about the woman he loved and still loves."

Martha shrugged. "The heart is big enough to love more than one person in a lifetime."

"His sister hates me," Brigid mumbled.

Martha frowned at her. "Ye can sit around making excuses or ye can make a plan."

"What sort of plan could I possibly make?"

"Brigid Campbell, I did nae raise ye to be a quitter. Ye want to aid the lass, aye?"

Brigid nodded.

"And ye want a chance to see what may occur between ye and Laird MacLean, aye?"

"Aye." Brigid knew Martha was the one person she could admit this to.

"Well then," Martha said, patting her on the knee, "ye must break through to the lass first."

"How am I supposed to do that?" Brigid demanded. "I've been trying."

"Well, do ye ken when ye were a wee lass, and ye decided ye were afraid of the dark?"

"Aye. I'd nae sleep in my bedchamber alone, and I refused to go outside at night."

"I was patient at first."

"I've been patient!" Brigid protested.

"I did nae say ye had nae," Martha replied. "But there is a time when ye must take a firm hand and abandon the gentle one."

Brigid frowned. "How will I ken when to do that?"

"Ye'll ken it," Martha replied. "Just listen to yer gut."

Brigid spent the next sennight trying to draw Maisie out once again, but the woman seemed to have retreated farther inside herself than she had before. And it wasn't only that Maisie would not speak to *her*. She had gone back to ignoring everyone. And Maisie wasn't the only one who had retreated. Brigid rarely saw Cormac, and when she did, he was aloof and kept a physical distance between them as if it were possibly dangerous to get too close to her.

When his clansmen and women started to warm up to her, she hoped he might as well, but the nicer his clan was to her, the more withdrawn he seemed to become. Aila and another kitchen helper brought her fresh gowns that several MacLean women who were near her size had generously donated. She wore one to dinner one night that she thought looked nice on her. As she entered the Great Hall, she nearly collided with Aila and a woman with long dark hair that reached to her bottom.

Aila waved a hand at Britta. "Brigid, this is Britta."

Aila gave Britta a pointed look, and Brigid knew Aila was trying to prod her friend to apologize for plotting to poison her. Aila had already apologized, but she'd yet to get an apology or introduction to Britta, who had oddly been absent from her duties upstairs every time Brigid had gone looking for her to meet her. As Brigid stared at the woman, she was struck with the feeling she'd seen her before.

"I hope ye two are nae rushing from the great hall on my account," Brigid joked, thinking to lighten the moment and let Britta know she wasn't going to demand an apology.

"Nay," Aila said and elbowed Britta.

Britta jerked her head up, but still did not meet Brigid's gaze, instead looking past her.

"I'm sorry for my part in poisoning ye. And thank ye for yer understanding." She curtsied and raced off before Brigid could respond.

Aila sighed. "She'll come around."

"I hope so," Brigid said. "Where are ye going?"

"Two of the women in the kitchen took ill, so Britta and I are aiding with the serving tonight."

"Do ye need an extra pair of hands?" Brigid asked.

"Nay. 'Tis kind of ye to offer but go in and enjoy yer supper."

"Well, if ye need me. . . ."

"I ken where to find ye," Aila replied with a smile.

Brigid made her way quickly to the dais. Camden swept his gaze over her as she sat.

"Cormac, does nae Brigid look lovely in the green gown?"

Cormac turned from speaking to Ross to focus on her, and she could see the appreciation in his eyes. "Aye, lass. Ye look lovely."

"Elsie's favorite color was green," Maisie said.

The table fell into an awkward silence at the first words the woman had spoken since the night in her bedchamber.

"'Tis my favorite color as well," Tess chimed in.

Brigid was certain Tess was trying to make her feel less uncomfortable.

Supper passed with Tess, Camden, Ross, and Martha doing most of the talking, while Brigid and Cormac stayed mostly silent, unless someone asked one of them a specific question.

Maisie did not speak again until a sweet pie was served that Brigid had made. Tess had told her it was Cormac's favorite and she waited as he tasted it, hoping he'd say something. He took a bite, a pleased smile on his face.

"Brigid made it!" Tess said. "She joined us in the kitchen today."

"Elsie made the best baked goods I ever tasted," Maisie said. Spite punctuated each word.

Brigid's cheeks warmed and Cormac's smile faltered then disappeared.

"Aye," he said, shoving his pie away from him. "She was an excellent baker."

Brigid had the uncharitable thought that she wanted to ring Maisie's neck, but she knew the woman was just trying to ensure her friend's memory was not replaced. Brigid didn't want to replace Elsie; she just wanted a chance. Martha gave her a pointed look, and Brigid decided perhaps it was time to put understanding away, as Martha had suggested.

She leaned forward and looked Maisie square in the eye. "I'm glad ye have finally found a topic ye are willing to converse upon," she said as sweet as she could.

Ross spit his wine out, Camden started to chuckle, and Cormac stared at her with clear surprise. Maisie rose with her goblet in her hand, her face flushed, and slung the contents of her goblet at Brigid. Wine splashed into her eyes. She gasped and closed her eyes against the sting.

"Maisie, for God's sake!" Cormac roared.

Immediately, the hall fell silent.

Brigid wiped the wine from her eyes and opened them. She stood, temper boiling, grasped Maisie by the hand, and yanked the slighter woman forward.

"Ye need a washing and now so do I, so to the bath we go."

It just so happened that the wooden washtub in her room was still filled with water. Albeit dirty water, but not nearly as dirty as Maisie was now, or Brigid for that matter.

Out of the corner of her eye, she saw Ross rise and Cormac shake his head. It made her feel good that Cormac was supporting her in this.

Maisie tried to dig in her heels, but the woman vastly

underestimated how angry Brigid was. Hand gripped tight, Brigid marched Maisie down the middle of the silent row to the door of the great hall, keenly aware that all eyes were on her. She half-expected someone else who despised her for simply being a Campbell to intervene, but to her surprise, she received looks of encouragement from the MacLeans.

Once through the door, Maisie began to scream. "I hate ye!"

Brigid pulled her toward the stairs, breaking a sweat as she went. "I do nae like ye much either at the moment!"

"I'm nae going up those steps!" Maisie yelled.

Brigid eyed the stairwell. There was no way she'd get the woman up them unwilling. Tugging her down the corridor was one thing, but a flight of stairs was a different matter completely.

"Ye'll go up those stairs with her," a voice came from behind them, "or I'll carry ye up myself, and we both ken ye do nae want me touching ye."

Brigid glanced over her shoulder to find Ross MacLeod standing there with Cormac and Camden by his side. When she looked to Maisie, the woman's jaw had slipped open, and she looked so upset by the prospect of her former betrothed touching her that Brigid momentarily felt sorry for the woman, but not so much so that she was going to recant her threat.

Maisie hunched her shoulders forward like a defeated animal and walked slowly to the stairs, abandoning her fight with Brigid. As they took the steps, putting distance between them and the men below, Brigid said, "we are going to have a talk."

"Ye can nae make me talk to ye!" Maisie growled.

Brigid hadn't truly expected an answer, but Maisie's

response both shocked and amused her. She was, in fact, talking in spite of herself. Brigid paused when they reached the top of the stairs.

"I do nae wish to make ye, Maisie, but ye need to talk to someone. Though I have nae had happen to me what ye did, I *have* been tied up, left in a dungeon with rats, and left to go hungry by my stepbrother, so I do share a hatred of him with ye."

She gave Maisie's hand a tug and they continued down the hallway.

Beside her, Maisie sucked in a sharp breath. "'Tis nae only him I hate," she whispered.

"Me?" Brigid asked. She opened her bedchamber door and released Maisie. She was pleased when the woman walked into the bedchamber without having to be dragged.

"Nay," Maisie said on a sigh and wrapped her arms around herself. "I do nae hate ye, though I do honestly hate the thought of Elsie being forgotten because of ye."

Brigid frowned. "Why do ye think Elsie would be forgotten because of me?"

"Cormac is falling for ye."

"I think ye need to tell Cormac that. He does nae seem to ken it," Brigid retorted. She crossed the room to the washtub and knelt. Cupping a handful of water, she splashed it on her face to rinse off the remnants of the wine.

"He kens it," Maisie said. Brigid heard the woman's footsteps, then she felt the brush of Maisie's arm and leg as the woman knelt beside her. Maisie's hand touched hers, startling Brigid, and cloth was pressed into Brigid's hand. "For yer eyes."

"Thank ye," Brigid murmured and wiped the water from her eyes. She opened them and met Maisie's intense gaze.

"Tell me what happened."

Maisie nodded, but she put her hands into the water, cupped them, and splashed water on her face. Brigid returned the cloth to Maisie, and the woman wiped her face. The cloth left streaks of white skin showing underneath the grime that had collected upon the woman's face for God knew how long.

"I wish a bath," Maisie said, staring wistfully at the water.

"'Tis cold. Yer first proper one in such a long time should be warm. Wait here."

She rose and crossed to the chamber door. Opening it, she found Cormac and Camden sitting side by side against the wall across from Maisie's chamber. She grinned at the two men. This was family. This was devotion and love, and this, this was what she wanted. She did not, she realized, want to settle for less.

"Yer sister wishes a bath. Could one of ye fetch—"

"Aye," they both said, jumping up to fulfill the request. They looked at each other and laughed. "We'll bring hot water right away."

"Thank ye," she said, and started to turn away when someone set a hand to her shoulder. She glanced behind her to find Cormac's face very close.

"Thank ye, Brigid. For yer patience, yer caring, and nae giving up."

His warm breath washed over her cheek and neck and set gooseflesh racing down the entire length of her body. She swallowed. This night was not about her feelings for Cormac.

"Ye're welcome," she said, struggling to get the words out in a reasonable tone. "'Twas nae a thing."

When he pressed a kiss to her cheek, she sucked in a

surprised breath. "'Tis everything to me."

He released her then, and she turned in the doorway, grasping the door to push it closed. She glanced up for one last look. Cormac strode side by side down the passageway with his brother. He stopped at the head of the stairs and glanced toward her. Even from such a distance, he was so disturbing to her in every way that her heart flipped, her body heated, and a flutter commenced in her belly. She let out a little sigh and stepped back to shut the door, keenly aware of his gaze on her, as if to ensure she was safely in the room.

"Can ye aid me with the laces of my gown?" Maisie asked.

Brigid crossed the room, made a motion for the woman to turn around, and immediately saw the problem. The laces were crusted with dried dirt, and nearly impossible to get undone.

"Brace yerself."

Gripping the soiled laces in both hands, she gave a tug. She worried the motion might trigger a bad memory in Maisie, but the woman did not make a sound.

"There," Brigid replied, stepping back to inspect her work as she unraveled the last of the laces.

Maisie disappeared behind the dressing screen and when she did not come back out, Brigid got a bit worried.

"Are ye well?"

"Aye. I just want to stay here until the water is in the room."

A knock came at the door. She frowned. It seemed too soon for Cormac and Camden to be back with warmed water. Nevertheless, she crossed the room and opened the door, and there they stood, each holding buckets of steaming water. Her heart did a little flip when Cormac smiled at her.

"Tess was a step ahead of us. She'd thought Maisie might want a bath."

Brigid nodded but cast a worried look at the screen where she knew Maisie hovered, and when she looked back to Cormac, he gave her a nod of understanding.

"We'll be quick," he assured her.

She stepped aside and watched as they poured the steaming buckets of water into the washtub. Once they had departed the room, Maisie stepped out, her underclothing still on like a thin layer of protection against her memories.

Brigid understood immediately. "I'll sit behind the clothing screen while ye bathe."

A relieved look settled on Maisie's face, and Brigid went behind the screen, and, with no place to sit, made herself as comfortable as possible on the floor.

After a moment, water splashed, and then more water splashing rang in the room. Brigid whiled away the time as best she could. Then Maisie spoke.

"Elsie went to get water."

Brigid opened her heavy eyelids and sat up from her position against the wall. She gave a hearty yawn. "Are ye saying she was nae there when. . . ."

"She was nae. Ramsay came right after she left, but before . . . before he left me, she came back."

Brigid frowned. "And . . . and did she try to stop him?"

"Nay. She was running."

Maisie's voice sounded very nearby. Brigid stood. "Is it okay to come out?"

"Aye," Masie replied.

Brigid stepped carefully around the screen. Maisie stood near the tub, cheeks rosy from being freshly scrubbed, eyes bright, lips pink, and her hair slicked back from her face. She looked truly alive for the first time since Brigid had met her.

"I'm tired," Maisie said, the weariness apparent in her tone. She stepped behind the dressing screen and was back out in a moment with her nightclothes on.

"Maisie, what was Elsie running from?"

Fear flickered in Maisie's eyes. "Sinclair Ferguson."

Brigid's eyebrows dipped to match her frown. "Sinclair?" She cast her memory back to the tourney and did recall him being there. "Why was Elsie running from him?"

"She was screaming." Maisie glanced over Brigid's shoulder as if looking at the scene that day. She turned and walked to her bed where she sat against her pillows, knees pulled to her chest.

Brigid crossed the room and sat beside her. "She was screaming and calling him a murderer. She said he'd killed his wife Mary at the stream. She ran straight past me at first. I was . . . I was dazed, ye see." Her cheeks grew red. "I was on the ground. From . . . from—"

"'Tis fine," Brigid assured her. "I understand."

Maisie nodded with a look of relief. She nibbled on her lip for a moment before continuing. "Sinclair came running after her, chasing her. I—" She covered her hands with her face. "I do nae ken what happened exactly after that. Yer brother, he . . . he knocked me out. When I awoke, the cottage was on fire and Cormac was there, holding her, crying. I . . . I was in Ross's arms."

"Why did ye quit talking for so long?"

Maisie rubbed her hands over her arms. "I surrendered, and I was ashamed," she said, in a voice so low that Brigid had to strain to hear her.

"What do ye mean ye surrendered?"

"I was afraid he'd kill me, and I did nae want to die, so I quit fighting him," Maisie admitted, tears filling her eyes and overflowing down her cheeks.

Brigid quickly wiped them away, her chest burning with fierce anger. She wanted to kill Ramsay and Sinclair.

"Ye did what ye needed to survive. That is nae giving up. Ye are here. Ye are a fighter. Ye do nae have anything to be ashamed about. My stepbrother does. Sinclair does. They will pay for their sins. I vow it. Ye do nae need to be afraid they will reach ye."

Maisie laughed. "I'm nae afraid they'll reach me. My brothers would nae ever allow it."

To have such faith in someone to keep ye safe, even after all Maisie had been through, was very telling of the sort of men she thought her brothers were.

"What of Ross? Ye do nae have faith in him to keep ye safe?"

"I do, but I . . . I can nae imagine allowing him or anyone ever to touch me in the way a husband and wife do."

Brigid nodded. "I can understand that. But perhaps ye should at least tell him the truth and see what he has to say."

"Mayhap," she said, not sounding convinced. She yawned and looked ready to fall asleep and Brigid was very tired herself.

"Do ye wish to go to sleep?"

"Aye, but will ye stay with me for a bit?"

The request surprised and touched Brigid. "Aye," she replied. She aided Maisie in getting under her coverlet then she sat beside her on the bed. Maisie took Brigid's hand, surprising her yet again.

"I'm sorry," she whispered. "I would nae have let ye drown. I was about to swim back to ye that first time in the loch."

"I believe ye," Brigid replied, and she did. There was no

falseness in the woman's tone.

"And I kenned the poison Britta and Aila gave ye would only make ye sick. Still, it was horrid of me nae to say anything. I'll talk to them both."

"Nay," Brigid said. "Please do nae. Aila is already being nicer, and Britta will come around. I wish to win her over on my own."

Maisie smiled approvingly at her. "Just like a true Mac-Lean."

Brigid blinked in surprise. "I'm nae a MacLean."

"An honorary one then, until. . . ."

"Shush!" Brigid hissed, and they both dissolved into fits of laughter. Once the laughter died, Brigid said, "yer brother made a vow to nae ever love another woman again."

"Oh," Maisie said, her eyelids fluttering shut. "That will make things harder. He takes his vows seriously. But ye can reach him just like ye reached me."

Brigid was thinking about that statement when Maisie cocked one eye open. "If ye want to. If ye think you can love him."

"I am nae sure yet," Brigid said. "I think I maybe could, but I also think it's maybe foolish of me to open my heart to a man who has said he'll nae be opening his again."

"'Tis nae a better time to be a fool than when ye are being a fool for love."

"Who said that?" Brigid asked.

"Cormac," Maisie said, with a wink.

Chapter Seventeen

*H*e shouldn't have been listening at the door, but he'd mistaken their laughter for a yelp, and after everything that had happened, he had been concerned Maisie might be trying to harm Brigid again.

Cormac could not tear his gaze from Brigid. She sat on the bed facing Maisie, his sister's hand clutched in her own. Her pale hair hung down her back. She was so selfless. She'd risked her life twice for Maisie, and she had forgiven Maisie for the boat incident and her part in the poisoning. And now, Brigid had concern not for herself, but Maisie. Brigid was a woman he could love—if he could ever let himself love again. The problem was he didn't know that he could.

He could not dismiss the words he'd heard her say from his mind. She thought maybe she could love him. It filled him with warmth and happiness. There was no doubt about it. But it set a knot in his chest and gut, too. Maisie, it seemed, had come to terms with Brigid, so there was not that barrier stopping him, but what of his vow? He stared at the door thinking on why he'd made it. He'd wanted Elsie to pass in peace, and he'd wanted to assure her he'd never forget her. Could he love Brigid and keep his promise to not forget Elsie? He didn't know, but he knew he wanted to try, and if he found he couldn't, well, he'd simply have to turn away from Brigid once and for all.

"If ye want to retire for the night," Camden said, "I'll wait for Brigid. I'll be happy to escort her to her bedchamber."

Cormac turned toward his brother to tell him to keep his hands and gaze off Brigid and found Camden smirking at him. "What, brother? Is it nae still good with ye if I pursue her?"

The heat in Cormac's face spread to his neck. He knew from his brother's grin that he'd never intended to pursue Brigid. He'd simply been trying to get Cormac to act, even if it was out of jealousy.

"I can nae say what I want."

"Oh, I think ye *can* say," Camden replied. "If ye recall I saw the two of ye with yer lips locked while standing in the water."

"I recall," Cormac growled.

"Do nae worry," Camden said, waving a dismissive hand at him. "I was only teasing ye about the lass, and even if I had notions to pursue her, I do nae think she'd care. Ye're a lucky, arse. Do nae end up simply an arse."

"Cormac."

He wasn't sure if it was his name being called that woke him or the tap against his shoulder, but he opened his eyes to find Brigid kneeling in front of him.

She peered at him with a concerned gaze. "Have ye been sitting here all night?"

"All night?" he asked, repeating her words as if he were not in possession of his wits.

She smiled and his chest tightened at the lovely sight.

"Aye, by the sunlight streaming into yer sister's room

that woke me, I feel safe to say it's most definitely morning."

"Then, aye," he said, hauling himself to his feet. He held out his hand to assist her and she accepted his help.

They stood face to face, only a sliver of space between them. She tilted her head back to look at him. Her forehead creased as if she struggled with what to say. That was fine by him. He took the moment to drink in her beauty. Even with dark smudges under her eyes, a cut on her right cheek, and her hair a halo of sleepy tangles, she was the loveliest creature he'd ever seen. And it once again filled him with guilt that he thought so, which made him frown.

The crease in her forehead deepened, and she let out a long sigh, and he knew that what she saw on his face upset her.

"I may hurt ye if I try to let ye in," he said, deciding on the spot to be truthful. It seemed the best course of action.

Her eyes widened. "Because of yer vow nae to love another?"

"How did ye ken that?" he asked in surprise.

"Tess."

He should have known. "Aye, because of that. If ye do nae wish my attentions because of where I find myself . . . ."

She turned the bonniest shade of pink. "I wish them, for now, if ye wish to give them."

"I wish to give them," he admitted. "But I can nae make promises—"

She pressed a finger to his lips. "I'm nae asking ye to, Cormac. Currently, we are just two people seeing if we'd even suit, aye?"

"Aye," he replied, his gaze falling to her mouth. He wanted to kiss her again.

Slowly, the corners of her mouth turned up in a smile.

"If ye wish to kiss me—"

He didn't need any more invitation than that. His hands tangled in her hair, bringing his lips to hers in a flash. He backed her against the wall with the force of his kiss, but she returned it in kind, surprising him when she nipped his lower lip before parting her own to allow him entry into her mouth.

He delved inside, their tongues touching, his body hardening. Then a throat cleared, sending him stepping back. Tess and Martha stood behind them, scowls on their faces. He disregarded their silent disapproval and returned his attention to Brigid. She looked even bonnier than she had a moment earlier with her lips pink and swollen from their brief encounter, and her green eyes shone bright with unmistakable desire.

Her breath came as hard as his, which told him she wanted him as much as he did her. He wished to do far more sinful things than kiss the lass, but he wouldn't unless he could promise her a future. She deserved that and so much more.

"I take it, I do nae need to remind ye that Brigid here is a proper lass?" Martha bit out.

"Martha!" Brigid gasped, her pretty pink cheeks flaming scarlet.

"Do nae *Martha* her," Tess grumbled. "Unless there's been an offer of marriage that we do nae ken of—"

"That will be enough, Tess," Cormac said. "Ye ken verra well there's nae been an offer of marriage." He winced at how clipped his words sounded and how Brigid flinched at what he said. "I'm sorry, lass. I mean to say—"

She held up a hand. "Ye do nae need to apologize for speaking the truth. I appreciate the honesty. Now, listen to me. I discovered something of import last night when I spoke with Maisie that ye need to ken."

He nodded, torn between frustration and relief at her change of subject.

"Sinclair was at the cottage where Maisie was attacked."

"Are ye saying Sinclair also ravished my sister?" Cormac asked, his hands balling into fists.

"Nay, nay." Brigid stepped close and set a hand to his chest, a move which calmed him immensely. "Maisie says Sinclair chased Elsie to the cottage. That Elsie had gone for water—that's when Ramsay attacked Maisie. Sinclair chased Elsie back to the cottage. She was screaming that Sinclair had killed his wife . . . ."

"Mary," Cormac said.

Brigid nodded. "Aye. I heard she fell from a horse and died."

"'Twas what I heard as well."

"I think Sinclair has been wedding women who had property that he'd inherit and control himself if they died before an heir was born. That is how my property is."

"The castle ye mentioned?" he said, his anger so hot it scorched his veins.

She nodded. "Aye. The castle is mine and controlled by who I wed, but only until my heir comes of age to inherit. Then, if the child is male, he inherits it, and it stays with that family, but if the bairn is female, she inherits it and passes it along to her heir. If I were to die without an heir though—"

"Then Sinclair would ensure the castle became his," Cormac finished. "Did Maisie see Sinclair kill Elsie?"

"Nay. Ramsay knocked her out, and when she came to, the cottage was on fire, and all she saw was ye . . . ." Her words trailed off, but she didn't need to say more for him to see the scene in his mind, and the vivid picture was another reminder of his vow.

She stared at him for a long moment with a sad, knowing gaze, and he got the distinct impression she understood the pain he was in. He hated that because he knew his torment, his indecision, and his hesitation caused her suffering. But he didn't know how to change that.

"Do ye ken if any of Sinclair's wives had property?" she asked.

He could see her mind working, but he did not know to what purpose.

"Nay. Why?"

"Because if they did, we can take that information to the king, along with what yer sister told me, so that Sinclair is punished at least for Mary's death."

"I'm nae certain the king would take my sister's word."

"I think he'd take mine," she said.

"Yers? I do nae follow."

"I was up half the night thinking about what Maisie told me. I tried to think why Ramsay would keep the secret that Sinclair was there as well, and that Elsie said Sinclair killed Mary. And I came up with only one possible answer."

"Sinclair kens Ramsay ravished Maisie."

"They both have something they can hold over each other."

"Aye," she said again. "Thus, they struck a bargain to keep each other's secrets, and I think, well, I think they intended to seal the bargain with Ramsay wedding me to Sinclair."

He was going to kill her brother. And then Sinclair. It didn't even have to be in that order, as long as both men died.

"Killing them," she said with perfect insight to his thoughts, "will only hurt ye. It will nae bring Elsie back or wipe away what happened to Maisie, and it would deprive her family of ye, as the king would surely punish ye for the deeds."

"Aye!" Tess agreed heartily.

"Nae to mention ye'd have two black marks upon yer soul," Martha added. "And I think two will make it awfully hard to avoid eternal damnation."

He snorted. "Is that so? I'm nae certain I care."

"Well, ye should," Brigid said in a matter-of-fact tone. "Ye'll be reunited with Elsie in Heaven, so remember that."

His lips parted in astonishment at her selfless consideration of that fact. He was touched to the core. He wanted to gather her into his arms and kiss her again, but with Martha and Tess standing here, he refrained. Not to mention, they were right. He should not be kissing Brigid in public, or private, until he was certain they wanted and could have a future.

He cleared his throat. "I do nae see how yer word could sway the king. Ye did nae see Ramsay ravish Maisie, and ye did nae see Sinclair kill Elsie."

"Nay, but I think I could get a confession from Ramsay."

"Nay," he erupted. "I'll nae allow ye to risk yerself like that."

"'Tis nae yer choice to make," she said, her chin notching up. "'Tis mine."

"As yer laird, 'tis my choice." When she opened her mouth as if to argue he pressed his finger to her lips. "I said nay, and that is the end of the discussion."

She narrowed her eyes, and then surprised him by slowly nodding her acquiescence. He didn't trust her easy agreement one bit. With that in mind, he said, "And if ye talk my clot-heided brother into taking ye back to yer brother or Sinclair, do nae mistake me, I may rescue the two of ye, but I will send Camden from the clan for that disobedience, and I'll nae let him return."

Brigid's eyes widened in shock. "Ye would nae dare!"

"I would," he assured her. To keep her safe, he'd dare that and much more.

"If this is the sort of officious man ye are, then ye can just keep away from me!" With that, she swiveled away from him and stormed toward the stairs.

"Where are ye going? he demanded, his desire to ensure no harm came to her rising.

"To the loch, ye big Scot clot-heid. And do nae ye dare follow me."

Chapter Eighteen

"*I* told ye nae to follow me," Brigid huffed as she marched straight into the water. She got no further than up to her ankles in the loch before Cormac grabbed her by the wrist and stopped her forward progress.

"And I told ye, ye would nae be going to the loch without me," he replied and swung her around to face him. They were so close she could smell his ire, and the heat of it washed over her.

"I do nae need ye to watch me like a bairn every time I come near the water," she huffed, still vexed with the man for dismissing her plan. He couldn't know it, of course, but when the idea had come to her, it had given her such hope that if she could get a confession from Ramsay, and see that Ramsay and Sinclair paid for their evil deeds, then maybe that would help not only Maisie in putting the past behind her, but it would aid Cormac too.

But there was no hope for that now, because the man was mule-headed and a dictator, and—

Why did he have to have such a fine strong jawline, and such intense eyes, and lips that felt so good upon hers?

Her body leaned toward him of its own volition.

"Brigid."

Brigid startled at the blatant need weighting his husky voice, shocked to find her eyes closed and her face tilted up to his for a kiss.

"Brigid," he said again, but this time the need was replaced with resignation that washed over her like icy water to instantly cool her own kindled desire. "I can nae . . . I mean to say, we can nae kiss."

He took a step away from her.

Away. From. Her.

Her mortification could not have been more complete.

"I do nae ken if I can ever offer ye marriage, so I can nae allow ye or me to compromise yer good name again."

She had been wrong. Her mortification certainly could be more complete. She wished fervently the water would suck her under and make her disappear, but of course she stood there ankle deep, feet freezing and cheeks, face, and chest burning. So, they would not be kissing again, unless he decided there was a place in his heart for her.

"Maybe I'll decide I do nae want a place in yer heart," she blurted, feeling even more foolish for letting her pride guide her tongue.

"Mayhap ye will," he said on a long inhale.

"Please leave," she bit out. She turned from him to stare out at the shimmering blue loch waters and even bluer sky. She'd come to the loch longing to get clean and feel the sun on her face. Now, she mostly just longed to be alone.

"I can nae leave ye down here by the water by yerself."

She was beyond reason with her sudden anger. At him. At herself. At the ghost of a woman who was robbing her of her chance to get to know a man who was currently vexing her to no end, who she may or may not despise once she really knew him, but by the gods she wanted the chance, just not in this particular moment!

"Well?" she demanded, swinging round to face him once more. "How can I get ye to leave me be? I want to stand here alone, stare out at the water, have the sun on my face, and mayhap even wash my body."

His look went from one of astonishment to unmistakable desire. She saw the moment he braced himself against his feelings for her. His jaw tensed, his nostrils flared, and the vein in his temple by his right eye beat a furious rhythm.

"Ye would have to ken how to swim before I let ye alone at the loch."

"Fine!" she huffed.

His brow furrowed. "Fine?"

She threw up her hands in utter frustration. "Teach me to swim!"

He stared for a long moment, complete surprise on his face. "Ye can nae learn to swim in one day, Brigid."

"I can try. So, either ye try to teach me or send someone else to do so. Mayhap yer brother would be willing. He's much nicer than ye!"

She had intentionally used Camden's name because they were brothers and she assumed they were competitive, but the way his eyes narrowed to dangerous slits made her realize instantly she had hit on a tense suggestion.

"I'll teach ye myself, or I'll try to, but ye must listen to everything I say."

"Yer bidding is my command," she said, sweet as honey but gave him a look she hoped was sharp as a well-honed blade. When he gave a half laugh, half snort, she knew her look had hit her mark.

She watched as he made his way the short distance out of the water to rid himself of his sword and a dagger, and then, to her surprise, he stripped down to nothing but his braies. Her mouth went dry at the sight of his muscular back, broad shoulders, and strong arms. When he turned back to her, his black hair glinting with the sun behind him, gaze bright with his frustration, and his chest bared to her in all its well-honed muscular perfection, her breasts grew heavy, and an ache tightened her core. She knew nothing would dull it save his touch, but she'd eat fire before she asked for that again.

"Take yer gown off," he said, looking physically pained at having to say those words. She nearly laughed at his discomfort. *Nearly.*

He waved a hand. "Ye can nae learn to swim with heavy skirts weighting ye down."

"I would nae want to compromise yer honor, so I'll just keep my heavy skirts on," she retorted, her voice dripping with sarcasm.

"Brigid," he said, the word clipped with obvious frustration. "Either take off yer gown so I can teach yer stubborn self to swim, or ye will leave the water with me. And if ye'll nae leave willingly, I'll throw ye over my shoulder and carry ye up and through the castle to the embarrassment of ye."

"Ye would nae," she said, spitting mad. "Ye would nae risk my reputation."

"I would to keep ye safe. I'd risk yer reputation to save yer life." And because he sounded like the hounds of hell upon his heels themselves would not bend his will, she acquiesced.

A few moments later, she found herself belly deep in the water with Cormac by her side showing her how to arc her arms over her head, cup her hands, and glide them through the water, which, according to Cormac, was supposed to move her body forward.

Once she mastered that, he slid his arm under her belly, and before she knew his intent, he lifted her off her feet and with his knee under her legs, brought them up behind her. She immediately stiffened and started to grab at him as panic gripped her.

"Take a deep breath, fight yer fear, and kick yer legs."

"Fight yer fear," she muttered, but kicked her legs furiously to get her anger at him out of her body. Magically, it worked, but the harder she kicked, the more her body moved, and the unintended result was that her breasts kept rubbing against his arm and the last of her anger gave way to a frustrating yearning and tingling, which she struggled to ignore.

"Good," he said. "Ye're doing an excellent job. Now, I want ye to stroke yer arms like I taught ye while kicking yer legs."

"Like this?" she asked, doing as he bid.

"Aye! Verra good."

She grinned, pleased with herself.

"Now, as ye kick yer legs and stroke yer arms, I want ye to turn yer head to take a breath. This is how ye'll get the air ye need."

Once more, she did as he bid her, and he praised her again. She didn't want his praise to mean so much to her, but it did.

"I think ye should take a break," he said.

"Nay!" she protested, wanting to master swimming. It was no longer simply a way to be alone. It was symbolic of so much more. Conquering her fear of water was the key to conquering his fear of opening up to her.

"Again."

And so she proceeded to kick, stroke, and breathe, again and again, until she was panting with the effort.

"Now we break," he demanded, and his unbending tone told her he would not give in this time, so she reluctantly nodded. He set her on her feet, and they stood in the cold water, her heavy breathing filling the silence.

After a few moments, her breaths slowed until only

silence sat between them. He pushed a strand of hair off her cheek to tuck it behind her ear. His brows drew together in an agonized expression, as if touching her pained him. She understood, she thought, because she felt a pain too, deep within her, and it was the pain of unfulfilled wanting.

"How did ye come to be so outspoken?" he asked, his question surprising her and making her laugh.

"I do nae ken," she said honestly. "I was nae ever this way until I got here."

"Nay ever?"

She thought about that for a long moment. "Well, nay. I did have a few times where I spoke my mind, but I paid the price for it." When he gave her a questioning look, she continued. "My da smacked me across the face once in front of a table of men for giving my opinion on a scrimmage he was involved in."

He cupped her face with such tenderness her breath caught in her throat. "I wish I'd been there. I would have protected ye from him."

He said it with such intensity that she knew he meant it, and his words made her feel safe, just as his actions had since she'd come to his home. Mayhap that's why she felt she could speak her mind.

"What other things do ye think made ye hold yer opinions?"

"Well, my da told me when I was younger that I was nae meant to be seen or heard, and that I was only good for what I could someday bring him with a union, and if I did fail to obey, as early as six summers, he would lock me in the dungeon. I learned quickly to keep my silence and Ramsay was the same as my da."

"I will make Ramsay pay for what he did to ye," Cormac said, his voice chilling in its lethalness.

"I already told ye the best, safest way of truly getting Ramsay to pay."

"One can nae always be safe in their choices, Brigid."

She had to press her lips together against pointing out that his statement contradicted his actions. He was trying to only make safe choices for them. Choices that would guard her reputation, and, she suspected, guard his heart, but now was not the time or place to mention such a thing.

So instead, she chose a less prickly topic. "I'm ready to try swimming on my own again."

She thought he might protest. The sun that had been directly over their heads when they had started, had now descended in the sky, so she knew they had been at the loch for some time. He gave her a thoughtful look then nodded. This time, after he had her on her belly and she began to kick her legs and move her arms through the water, he let her go with the command to swim.

She sank like a stone.

He immediately pulled her to the surface, coughing water, sputtering, and blinking the drops out of her eyes. And they did it again, and again, until her arms and legs ached, and her throat and nose hurt from all the water she'd sucked in, inhaled, and coughed back up. She sank yet again, and he pulled her to the surface once more.

"I give up. I can nae do it."

She started to stand up, but he grabbed her legs and pulled them behind her once more, sliding his hand under her belly as he spoke.

"Do nae ever give up on something ye want with all yer heart and soul. Again."

She knew he had not meant to give her hope with those words, but she could not help but take it. If it should be that she wanted him with all her heart and soul, she would push forward through doubt and only give up when she was certain there was no hope left. He had a vow, and now this, this was hers.

Chapter Nineteen

"Where are ye going?" Camden asked a fortnight later over the ringing of the supper bell.

Cormac paused in front of the handmade linen paper map before them where they had created all the locations of Sinclair's deceased wives. They planned to visit each home to discover if Brigid's theory was correct, and if Sinclair Ferguson had indeed been choosing wives to wed to collect their inheritances after he killed them.

The other part of the map was an intricate drawing of Brigid's home. Brigid's idea to elicit a confession from Ramsay had been a good one, but she had been wrong in thinking Cormac would ever let her risk herself to get it. This part was a bit trickier, and they had not worked out how or where they would get the confession from Ramsay, but they would. What he did know was that the confession needed to be in front of a neutral party who also happened to hold sway with the king, and Ross MacLeod had given him the idea just last night who they could call upon. The man Ross had apprenticed with, who was now a close friend and mentor, was also a close friend and mentor of the king—Robert IV, Count of Dreux. The missive from Ross to Dreux, requesting him to come to their aid and explaining why, had been sent last night.

"Cormac, did ye hear me?"

Before Cormac could answer his brother, a knock came

at the solar door.

"Enter," he bid, and the door opened to reveal Tess, who held up a folded missive with an emblem he immediately recognized as belonging to the king.

"This was just delivered for ye by two of the king's men. They asked to see ye, but I fibbed and told them ye were away from the castle for a fortnight to give ye more time to answer should ye need it."

Unease unfurled in his belly as he strode to Tess and took the missive from her. "Ye're certain it was the king's men?"

She shrugged. "As certain as one can be. They had his coat of arms emblazoned on their cloaks, and they have his seal upon the missive they left for ye."

He brought the missive up to examine it and ran a finger over the wax. "Aye, it does appear to be the king's, and ye're correct that ye can only be so certain."

She pursed her lips. "I do nae need ye to tell me I'm correct, Cormac."

He chuckled at that, glad for the lighthearted moment. "Ye get surlier each day."

She cocked her eyebrows. "I'm surly because I'm watching ye waste precious time ye could be happy."

He knew what she meant, and he did not want to have the discussion again. She had approached him four different times to tell him he could love one woman while nae forgetting another. Logically, he knew he could, but something was holding him back, and he did not know what. It was not Brigid herself. Every moment in that astonishing woman's company made him admire her with all his being and want her with it, too. If he could love again, it would surely be her. So, he ignored Tess's hint at what she wanted to speak on yet again.

"Thank ye for bringing me the missive. Will ye tell Brigid I'll meet her at the loch instead of coming to get her in her bedchamber?"

"Ye do nae have time for a swim lesson!" Tess exclaimed. "The horn for dinner has already rung!"

"I'm aware," he replied, "but I vowed to meet her every day until she swam on her own, and I'll nae break that vow."

"Ye and yer vows," Tess grumbled, turning away from him and toward the door. "I'll tell her," she tossed over her shoulder, "but ye need to quit giving vows without thinking them through properly."

"Tess," he said, instilling a warning note in his tone.

"Aye, aye. I'll nae say another word."

After she departed the room, Camden looked as if he was about to pick up where Tess left off, so Cormac waved the missive to distract him.

"Can we concentrate on this for the time being?"

"That was nae stated as a question," Camden said, his tone dry, his look even more so.

"How verra astute ye are, brother," Cormac replied. He looked down at the missive and opened it, relieved to have the natural distraction, but the relief did not last long.

"What's wrong?" Camden asked, and Cormac supposed the worry must show on his face.

He met his brother's concerned gaze. "Ramsay lodged a complaint and request with the king that we aided his rebellious, ungrateful stepsister—"

"Are those the king's words?"

"Aye," Cormac said, and the unease that had earlier unfurled now laid siege to his insides. His pulse spiked, his belly hollowed, and his throat closed a bit.

"What else does it say?"

"That Brigid ran from her wedding because she is spoilt, and that we aided her in a misguided attempt to fulfill vengeance upon Ramsay for an act he did not commit. And he requested the king demand we return her, which the king agrees with."

Camden's mouth took on an unpleasant twist which mirrored the way Cormac felt. "How long until we are supposed to return her?"

"A sennight. The king has decreed that we each come without warriors to Iona Abbey—"

"A neutral location," Camden inserted.

"Aye," Cormac agreed. "Except, of course, I am to have Brigid to return to Ramsay. The king also states that any harm either of us does to the other will be punishable by death."

Camden arched his eyebrows. "Well, at least the king included 'harm done' in that."

Cormac made a derisive noise from deep within his chest. "Alexander is young and foolish. He's swayed by Ramsay's silver tongue, but I do nae doubt he will become a better king with age."

"I doubt it," Camden said. "I assume ye are nae going to do as bid?"

"Of course, nae," Cormac said. "I'll go, but with Dreux." He flashed a smile. "He's nae one of my warriors after all, and he should have arrived here by then. Ramsay has unknowingly given me the perfect opportunity to meet with him and get the confession we need. Once I've obtained it, Dreux and I can take it—and hopefully Ramsay—to the king."

"Ye ken he'll nae meet ye alone just as ye do nae plan to meet him alone."

Cormac nodded. "Undoubtedly, he'll have guards stationed along the way, but so will I. And now I'm off to meet Brigid."

He was halfway through the solar door when Camden said, "Tess is right, ye ken."

"Camden," Cormac replied, instilling the same warning note in his tone with his brother that he had with Tess.

"I'm nae as easily deterred as Tess, brother, but I think ye're using yer vow to Elsie as an excuse nae to face what's really holding ye back."

"Oh, aye?" Cormac snapped. "And what is that?"

"I do nae ken," Camden said. "Only ye can figure that out, but I suggest ye do so soon, before ye inflict such a hurt on the lass that she closes herself to ye."

Irritated, Cormac stormed out of his solar and nearly barreled into his sister who, he realized with a glace down the hall, was fleeing from Ross. He caught Maisie by the elbow and steadied her.

"Please," she said, imploring him. "Make Ross leave our home."

"I can nae do that, Maisie. He's here to aid me with something," he said, purposely being vague because he did not want Maisie or Brigid to learn of the plan and foolishly risk themselves in a misguided effort to try to assist them.

"Then make him stay away from me," she begged.

He heard the desperation in her voice, and though he knew Ross was only trying to speak to Maisie because the man cared greatly for her, Cormac shook his head at the man. Ross grimaced, but immediately turned around and headed back the way he had come, shoulders hunched in defeat.

"Maisie, I ken ye were hurt verra badly, and it will take time to get over it, but eventually ye'll have to put the past behind ye if ye wish to move forward with the future. If ye do nae, ye'll be stuck in yer misery for the rest of yer life, and that is nae a way to live."

Maisie shoved away from him, her gaze derisive. "Ye're one to talk. I see ye at dinner staring moonily at Brigid, but I also ken verra well that ye are holding yerself back, nae allowing yerself to move forward because—"

"I made a vow," he interrupted. "'Tis different."

Maisie made a derisive noise. "Yer vow is nae what's holding ye back. 'Tis fear."

"Aye," he agreed. "Fear that I'll forget Elsie."

"Mayhap a little, but I'd wager 'tis more fear that if ye let yerself, ye will fall in love again, and *that* is what scares ye. Ye loved, and ye lost, and ye do nae wish to feel that pain again."

He started to disagree, but he realized with shock that he wasn't entirely certain that his sister was incorrect. God's blood. All this time that he'd been holding back had it been fear of falling again, losing again, hurting again, more than fear of forgetting?

Maisie's look grew soft, and she surprised him by hugging him. "'Tis all right, brother. I understand the fear."

He couldn't allow that. He couldn't set an example of avoiding really living again to avoid pain and loss. He set her gently from him. "I will try if ye will try."

She pressed her lips together, but she didn't deny him. Finally, she inhaled a deep breath. "Together?"

"Aye," he agreed. He wasn't certain where to begin, but realized, there was no doubt he had to try.

The question of whether he'd been avoiding truly living to escape loss and pain stayed with him out of the castle and as he made his way down the stairs toward the loch. Halfway down, he spotted Brigid, floating in the middle of the water. His stomach dropped, and panic gripped him. He ran down the remaining stairs, and when he hit the ground at the base of the steps, he discarded his weapons and stripped down to his braies.

What the devil was she thinking? She could float now, yes, but floating and swimming were two different things! Hadn't he instructed her to only go waist deep when he was not with her? He ran into the water then dove in, swimming like his life depended on it, because God's blood, it felt like it did. As he swam toward her, images of her dead and floating face down came to him, so that by the time he reached her, he was livid.

"What the hell are ye doing?" he roared.

She blinked at him, and then her eyes narrowed dangerously. "Swimming," she bit out. "What the hell are ye doing?"

"I told ye nae to go more than waist deep!" he thundered. "Ye could drown."

"Nay, I do nae think I will because I finally have it!" she exclaimed, all her anger replaced by excitement.

Think? She did not 'think' she could drown. The woman did not take proper precautions with her life!

He opened his mouth to tell her so, but she rolled over, her hands cupping the water as he'd taught her. "Watch me, Cormac!"

And then she swam away from him. The urge to stop her, to grasp her and hold her in his arms was so strong, that he knew his sister was right. He was afraid to love her and lose her, and he didn't know if he could conquer that fear. But as he watched her, such pride swelled and such desire, that when she swam back toward him, he didn't say anything at first. Instead, he caught her by the arm when she was near and drew her even closer.

Water clung to her eyelashes and her nose, and her skin

had a sun-kissed glow to it, making her so lovely his chest ached.

"That was amazing," he said, his voice husky. "And ye are incredible in yer determination and fearlessness. I'm proud of ye. I—"

"Oh!" She cried out and doubled forward, her chin dipping into the water. "I've a cramp in my foot."

He swooped in immediately and flipped her onto her back to swim her onto shore.

"Cormac!" she protested. "I can swim it!"

"Nay," he replied, his mind fixed on what could have happened to her if he had not been there. By the time they reached the shore, he was imagining her drowned once more. He swept her into his arms and carried her out of the water.

He placed her on her feet, and she spun about, her brows drawn together, lips pressed tight, and a dangerous glint in her eyes. "Ye *can nae* be there to rescue me every time I'm swimming!"

"That's exactly what I'm worried about!" he thundered.

Chapter Twenty

*B*rigid teetered between astonishment and frustration at this man who commanded attention when he entered a room, who was brave, strong, and compelling. But he was also afraid to lose someone again.

And she was in love with him.

Lord above, how had that happened? *She loved him.* She was in love with him. He had not taken her heart, she had given it freely and perhaps foolishly, but she could not take it back now. She only prayed he did not break it.

At a loss for what to say, she did the only thing she could think of.

She kissed him.

A moment later, she pulled back and whispered, "Thank ye for caring enough to worry about me."

He stared at her as if memorizing every detail of her face. It made her heart flip. She watched with delight as his bold gaze melted into yearning.

"I do care," he said, his voice hoarse. "I want ye to ken that I do."

His words were like a salve on the wound to her heart. She been longing to hear him say the words that he cared for her. He'd given signs, all sorts of them, but the words had been absent.

"I do nae believe I could live through the pain of such loss again," he said.

Those words were not as welcome as the others.

"I see," she said slowly. Was he telling her that he'd decided he did not want to open up to her?

"Nay," he said. "Ye do nae see. I'm mucking up what I'm trying to say. I . . . I desire ye."

She bit her lip, braving a small smile. "Aye." She cleared her throat, hearing laughter there, and it would not do to laugh at his agitation with having such a personal conversation. "I ken ye do. Desire is good," she said, "but—"

"'Tis nae enough."

"Nay," she agreed. "It is nae."

"I admire ye, too," he said, and by the way he shoved his hand through his hair, she knew he understood that was not what she was looking for. "And I think ye're intelligent, and caring, and loyal, and by God, all I have been able to think about for the last sennight is how I want to kiss ye again."

"So, kiss me," she said, throwing caution completely to the wind because, in her opinion, it had no place in the turbulent waters of love.

One hand came to her neck and the other her hair, and then he tilted her head back and claimed her mouth with a kiss that spoke of his hunger for her. He sucked at her lips, pulling at first the upper then the lower. He drew the tip of his tongue against the swollen flesh then parted her lips, sending his tongue inside to twirl with hers in a perfect dance of passion.

He pulled away, trailing kisses across her cheek to her ear. "Ye smell like heaven. I do nae think I've ever smelled anything as good."

"Nae even fresh baked bread?" she teased.

"Nay. 'Tis nae even close."

He clasped her body tight to his. The hard length of his

manhood pressed against her belly and awoke the ache only
he had ever caused to pulse to life deep inside. They stood,
hearts pounding, breaths laboring. She wished he'd kiss her
again.

He took a half step back but rocked forward again as if
reluctant to leave her. "I want to stay here all night with ye,
but we best get to supper. If I were nae laird—"

"I understand yer duty," she assured him and did her
best to hide her disappointment.

"I want to try to let ye in," he blurted, surprising her.
Her heart soared at his words. "I can nae promise what will
happen, but I do wish to try."

"Can I ask why the change of heart?"

He cupped her cheek with his large hand. "Ye, and
some words of wisdom from Maisie."

"Truth?"

"Aye." He took her hand in his and drew her with him
toward the seawall stairs. He held her hand tight all the way
up the stairs and into the outer courtyard, but when they
got to the inner courtyard, he released her hand. She took a
sharp breath against her disappointment. But she would not
wallow in it. He had taken the first step to let her in and that
was everything. She'd simply have to see what time brought
from him, and pray it was the love she longed for.

Supper went by in a blur, lost as she was in what he'd
told her, and lost a little in worry that even though he
wanted to try to let her in, he'd not be able to. But she could
not dwell on that, and when he asked her to dance after
supper, she was thrilled, having hoped for the last sennight
that he would. She'd grown weary of sitting in tense silence,
forcing herself to ignore his presence while watching other
couples dance.

He didn't lead her to the dance floor by taking her hand,

which would have been, to her mind, like his announcing he was courting her, instead he set a light hand to the small of her back. It was not the same, but the small, protective gesture thrilled her, nonetheless. And he didn't just have one dance with her—they remained on the floor until her feet ached, and when she could dance no more, the bards came out to tell stories.

Cormac led her to a table where Quinn and his wife and three other couples sat. Quinn offered a friendly smile and Aila did as well.

When Brigid sat, Aila leaned close and whispered, "I did nae ever get a chance to thank ye properly for arguing to Cormac to nae punish us too harshly. I appreciate yer understanding. I ken how ye aided Maisie, and she said that if ye and her brother were to wed, she felt confident ye'd try to keep Elsie's memory alive."

"Of course, I would," Brigid assured the woman.

"How goes it with Cormac?" Aila whispered.

Brigid stole a glance at his profile from under her lashes. He was talking to Quinn, but she could tell by the look upon Cormac's face that his mind was elsewhere. Was it with her, Elsie, her brother, the king? She wished she knew. One of the things she hoped for in marriage was a true partnership in which they shared their problems with each other.

"'Tis too early to tell," she finally whispered back.

She settled into her seat to listen to the bard's stories, and though they were interesting, she was tired from swimming and dancing and struggled to keep her eyes open.

"Do ye sing?" Aila's voice drew Brigid from a light doze. She blinked away the sleep and sat up straighter.

"Aye, but nae—"

"Brigid and I will sing!" Aila called out. She grabbed Brigid by the hand and hauled her to her feet. Heat immediately flushed her face as Aila drug her to the fireplace where two other women stood. She had been almost asleep and had not even realized the bard had stopped his stories and the women had begun singing.

"Aila," she hissed in the woman's ear. "I do nae wish to sing in front of a crowd."

Aila glanced at her. "Are ye shy?"

She nodded, except that wasn't quite true. The last time she'd sung in the great hall at her home, she'd been ten summers, and her father had made fun of her singing. She'd not sung in front of anyone since.

"Oh, I'm sorry. I did nae ken. I'll fix it." She turned her attention to the other women. "Brigid does nae feel well, so she's off to bed."

She knew Aila was well intentioned, but the woman's blurted lie forced Brigid to go along with it, and though she was tired and would not mind her bed, she had hoped to have a moment alone with Cormac. To her regret that moment was lost to her now. She turned toward the great hall door and made her way through, but she got no more than four steps before the swish and creak of the door opening behind her alerted her to someone's presence.

"Brigid!"

She halted and faced Cormac, a smile lifting the corners of her mouth.

"Ye're ill?" he asked.

She bit her lip and shook her head. "Well, nay exactly."

He frowned as he walked toward her, stopping so close she was warmed by the heat radiating off him. He quirked his eyebrows questioningly, and she laughed. "I do nae like to sing in front of people, and Aila thought to give me a way to nae have to."

"Ah," he said, nodding. "Why do ye nae sing in front of people? Do ye sound like a frog?"

Heat burned her face and neck. "I did nae use to think I did."

His brows dipped together. "Ye did nae use to?"

She quickly told him the story about her father making fun of her singing and how she had not sung in front of anyone again. A dark cloud of anger settled on his face.

He shook his head. "I did nae ken it was possible to detest a dead man, but I do detest yer da."

"I appreciate yer anger on my behalf," she said, meaning it.

He studied her for a long moment. "Sing for me, and I'll give ye the truth of it."

"What?" she gasped. "Here?"

He nodded.

"Now?"

He nodded again.

"I could nae possibly," she protested.

"Why?"

"Well, if I'm horrid and someone hears me, I'd be mortified beyond recognition."

He grasped her hand. "Come with me."

"Where are we going?" she asked, laughing, as he led her down the corridor at such a rapid pace, she had to double her steps to keep up with his long strides.

"Somewhere nae anyone will hear ye," he replied and led her out of the castle, into the twilight of the inner courtyard, and then down a path to a breathtaking garden.

"This is lovely!" she exclaimed. "Who keeps this?"

He turned to her, the moonlight shining behind him,

and he offered her a tender smile and a sensuous look. "I do."

"Ye?" she asked, shocked.

"Aye." He shifted his weight, then ran his hand through his hair, a very picture of indecision.

"How did ye learn to garden like this? Tess?"

"Nay. Elsie."

A tiny bit of jealousy stung her heart, but she shoved it aside. Elsie had been part of his life, and she always would be the part of his past that shaped him for his future. But if things went as she hoped, she would be his future that would complement his past.

"Will ye tell me how ye and Elsie came together?" she asked, thinking it was important to know.

"Aye, I'll tell ye. Sit with me?"

She nodded, and he led her to a bench that sat under a flowered arch. Above them was nothing but purple and golden sky, and a few stars that had already made an appearance. They sat, and though he did not take her hand again, their legs pressed thigh to thigh and their arms nestled against each other.

"Elsie was my sister's best friend and her da was my da's closest ally. I knew her since the day she was born. For a long time, I did nae think of her as anything but Maisie's silly friend. They giggled all the time when they were together, and I thought her feather brained and a child."

"But then she grew up," Brigid asserted, assuming he'd been struck by her beauty.

"She did, but I still did nae see her as anything more than Maisie's friend. My attraction to her was a verra slow build. Nae—." He gave her a rueful look. "Nay like it is for ye."

She nodded, encouraging him to go on.

"She came to spend a summer at Duart Castle when she was seventeen summers, and at the end of that time, I was to escort her home with Maisie. Maisie got sick, and Elsie and I got caught in a terrible storm. We spent two days hovering under a tree telling each other all our likes, and our dislikes, fears, hopes, and well—"

"Ye lost yer heart to her."

"Aye," he said.

She wanted him to lose his heart to her as he had Elsie, as Brigid had to him, but she didn't know what more to do.

"Will ye sing for me now?"

Heat immediately seared her cheeks again, but she nodded and sang a song about lost love that Martha used to sing to her. When she finished, he clapped his hands in appreciation, then cupped her face and gave her a searing kiss.

"Ye have a voice to make the angels weep. Ye should sing for the clan."

She shook her head. "Nay. I . . . I could nae."

He set his hand over hers and looked her in the eyes. "Ye need to conquer this fear."

She wanted to point out to him that he needed to conquer his own, but she didn't think it would be so helpful.

"I'll come out here with ye every night until ye feel comfortable enough to sing to the clan," he added.

"Mayhap," she said, but then an idea struck her. He had shared gardening with Elsie, mayhap he could share singing with her?

"Do ye sing?"

"Aye, but nae in front of my clan. To myself only."

She scowled at him. "We'll learn a song together."

When he opened his mouth to protest, she interrupted.

"It seems I'm nae the only one who needs to conquer my fear."

And she was not talking about the singing.

Chapter Twenty-One

*H*e had led her to the garden every night for seven nights straight, aware all the while, that soon he would leave to meet her brother. Each night, he discovered something new about her, something extraordinary, something that pulled him closer to her, and sometimes he would catch her with a look of hope or yearning, and he knew what she wanted. He wanted to be able to give in to her completely and let her in, but still he held back, aware it was fear now, but not able to totally banish it to the darkness from which it had come.

They had practiced their song for seven nights. It was the same one she had sung to him on the first night of lost love, and when the bards finished, they took to the center of the great hall and sang. Brigid sang the female parts, and he sang the male ones. Silence reigned when the song ended, but then the room erupted with thunderous applause.

Her smile was radiant, her joy so lovely and heartwarming. Doubt crept in again, stealing his breath to consider what life would be like if he never saw her smile again. It would crush him, and she was not even his wife. He had not given her a single word of love. If he did, if he allowed her further in, and he lost her, it would kill him.

She frowned suddenly, and he knew she'd seen the worry on his face. After accepting words of approval from practically everyone in the entire clan, he led her to the garden to say goodbye.

He could not put off his journey to the homes of Sinclair's dead wives even one more day or he'd miss meeting with Ramsay at the abbey.

Under the moonlight with a cool breeze blowing, she turned her face up to him, and he could not resist the desire to kiss her. Maybe it was because he would be leaving her tomorrow for a sennight, or maybe it was because there was so much weighing on his mind, but he felt almost desperate to claim her. He put a hand to her waist and drew her to him as he touched his lips to hers. Her arms slid about his waist, her hand dipping low to his arse to cup him there.

She'd never been so bold with him, and her actions snapped the thin tether holding his control. He backed her against the garden wall and hoisted her legs around his waist. In the next breath, he tugged down her boddice, as she moaned and writhed under his touch. Her breast sprang loose, full, and high, and the loveliest damn sight he'd ever beheld. He ran the pad of his thumb over her hard bud and she cried out, arching herself toward him.

"More!" she demanded, and by God he was helpless to do anything but give her what she wanted.

The way she responded to him nearly drove him mad. With his body strumming and blood rushing through his veins, he had the vague notion that he should stop, but he dismissed it almost immediately. He wanted her. Every part of her. He wanted to touch her. Caress her. Worship at the altar of this goddess in his arms. He wanted to hold on to the moment. This feeling.

And her.

He brought his mouth to her breast and circled her nipple with his tongue. Fire shot through him. She gasped, he hardened more, and behind him, someone coughed. He bolted upright, yanked up her gown, and shoved her behind him in one swift movement.

There stood Aila and Britta, mouths open and eyes wide.

"I beg pardon, laird," Aila said, darting her gaze between his face and Brigid behind him. "Quinn sent me to find ye. He says to tell ye Dreux has arrived at the castle."

He nodded, unable to find words for a moment. Aila would not say anything, but Britta might, and beyond that, he'd compromised Brigid's honor exactly as he had said he would not. He cleared his throat and shoved a hand through his hair.

"I'll be in momentarily. Will ye tell Quinn to notify Ross and Camden, and have all of them, including Dreux, meet me in the solar?"

"Aye, laird," Aila said, and Britta, who finally managed to clamp her jaw shut, nodded.

Once the women were gone, Brigid stepped from behind him, her face scarlet.

"I'm sorry," he said, the words inadequate for the situation he'd put them both in. They had to wed now, and it wasn't that he hadn't been considering it, but he had held back, because he still did not know if he could ever fully let her in. She deserved more than that, and yet imagining her with someone else was untenable.

"We'll wed when I return from my travels," he said, thinking it through aloud, but when her eyes narrowed, he knew right away he had gone about the asking the wrong way.

"What I mean to say is, will ye wed me?"

That wasn't what Cormac had meant to say at all. The uneasy look upon his face was proof of the truth. Brigid's heart skipped a beat and she had to force herself to swallow and ask the question she was certain she did not want to hear the answer to.

"Why do ye want to marry me?"

"I compromised ye," he answered immediately. "And we were caught. We must wed."

A band tightened around her chest with such great force that she vowed the protective casing around her heart cracked. She would never forget this moment. It would be seared into her memory as the most dreadful of her life.

His hair curled at his neck in a manner that looked adorably boyish. The moon glowed in the sky. The way he stood, with his legs braced apart, emphasized the power of his thighs.

But his tight-lipped smile was bleak, and his right hand was fisted. He did not want to wed her, because he wasn't certain he would ever let himself love her. It was both praiseworthy of him and like a dagger in her heart.

"Do ye love me?" She hated that her voice shook when she asked the question, but there was no hope for that.

"I—" He shifted from foot to foot, shoved a hand through his hair, then let out a ragged sigh that filled her with misery so heavy her legs nearly buckled from the weight. "'Tis nae a simple thing, Brigid."

She knew it made sense to him, but her heart rejected the logic, and anger pulsed to life. "'Tis simpler than ye ken," she said, poking him in the chest so hard a pain shot through her index finger. "Ye give yer heart! Contrary to what ye said, I can nae take it. Elsie did nae *take* it! We can fill it with things, emotions ye can nae deny, but *ye* have to make the choice to give it."

She turned away from him as tears blurred her eyes, and when his fingers grazed her shoulder, she shrugged him off and swung back toward him to poke him in the chest once more.

"Ye filled me with hope, happiness, a feeling of worthiness, and home—"

He opened his mouth, and she held up her hand to silence him.

"Home is a feeling! 'Tis called belonging. Ye made me feel I belong here, possibly with ye, and aye, ye filled my heart with love. I love ye."

"Brigid—"

"I wish I did nae!" she bit out. "I wish I did nae, because despite all my trying to reach ye, all my hope, I have come to realize ye can nae love me in return. Ye're too scairt, or cold on the inside, or dead, I do nae ken!"

Her head was thundering, her mind spinning, her heart splintering. She had to get away from him. "I do nae ken," she said again, this time quieter. "What I do ken is that I will nae wed ye. I will nae wed a man who does nae love me. I deserve more. I want more."

Before he could say a word, she turned and ran, down the garden path, through the outer courtyard, then the inner one, and into the castle, passing gaping servants as she went. She did not stop until she got to her bedchamber. There she flung herself on her bed and let the tears flow freely.

All her life all she had wanted was to be loved, protected, needed, and included in a family. He had brought her into his home but not his heart.

She had, she realized, expected Cormac to try to convince her to change her mind, and though she knew she wouldn't, it hurt her even more that he had kept his distance. Three days! She had not seen him in three days, and she refused to ask anyone what he was doing. No one mentioned him or spoke to her of his proposal, so she suspected he had not told anyone. Not even Aila or Britta said anything directly to her, though she did get sidelong looks from both women.

Martha asked her several times if something was amiss, but she denied it each time. She went from being angry, to miserable, to angry again, but then she settled firmly into misery.

At supper on the fourth night, when he didn't appear yet again, she could not take the not knowing anymore. She turned to Camden and leaned close to him in the hopes that no one else would hear. "Is yer brother ill?"

Camden set down his goblet and gave her a puzzled look. "Nae that I'm aware of."

"Nae that ye're aware of?" she fumed, trying to keep the frustration out of her voice.

"Well, aye. Given he's nae at Duart, I suppose he could be ill and I'd nae ken."

Now it was her turn to frown. "He's nae at Duart?"

"Are ye going to keep repeating everything I say?" Camden teased, but she was in no mood to be provoked.

"Camden," she said, her dark warning tone sounding much like the one she'd heard Cormac use multiple times. She blinked in surprise and so did Camden. "I'm nae in the mood to be trifled with."

He smirked. "Nay? 'Twas hard to tell," he said, sarcasm underlying each word. "Ye and Cormac are quite the pair."

"We are nae a pair!" she growled.

He snorted. "Well, ye act the same. He was surlier than

ye are when he left three nights ago."

"Where did he go?" she demanded, abandoning her resolve not to ask about him.

"I can nae say," he hedged.

"Ye've a tongue do ye nae?" she growled. "Ye can form words, so ye *can* say."

"Nay." He shook his head. "Cormac will kill me if I do."

"I'll kill ye if ye do nae."

"Like I said," Camden replied, picking up his goblet and tipping the rim to her in a mock salute, "ye two are a perfect match."

"We are nae a match," she huffed under her breath, her rebellious emotions getting the best of her tongue. "Yer brother does nae believe in me."

He gave her a sidelong glance of utter disbelief. "Love makes people blind," Camden muttered. "I do nae ever wish any part of it."

"I am nae blind! I can see he does nae believe in me, and he certainly does nae love me!" She'd meant to keep her voice down, but she'd raised it over the thundering of her heart, and now the dais was quiet and everyone upon it stared at her.

"He believes in ye," Camden said, his tone now the quiet one. "He does nae believe in himself."

"And he loves ye," Maisie added, leaning forward to look at her with earnest eyes. "He just has nae accepted it yet."

"Aye," Tess agreed from her right. She turned and met Tess's gaze. "He will, lass. He's verra close."

"How do ye ken that to be true?" she whispered as tears blurred her vision.

Suddenly Maisie was beside her, squeezing her shoulder. "Because of how hard he's fighting to deny it. His love for ye is pushing at the walls he created and soon, it will crack them. Just hold on."

"I want to," she whispered. "But—"

"Nay, 'buts'," Tess said to which everyone, including Martha, gave a hardy 'aye'.

"If ye feel hopeless, turn to us," Maisie said, "We are family." Brigid frowned. "We are yer family. Nae in name yet, but in the heart."

"In loyalty," Camden added.

"Where it counts," Tess said.

They were right. They were her family now. Even if Cormac never tore down his walls, his clan was her family, his siblings were her family, just as Martha was. Family, she understood, was not always the one you were born into. It could be the one you made, and she chose to make hers here, with her new friends and Martha—and hopefully Cormac.

"Where is he?" she asked.

"Aye, Camden," Martha said. "Where did he really go? I do nae believe for a moment that he, Ross, and Dreux went to see about new vessels."

"They did nae," Camden said, his gaze meeting Brigid's. "They went to visit each of Sinclair's former wives' homes to see if yer theory was correct about him. Once they get the proof they need, they are to meet with yer stepbrother—"

"What?" she gasped. "Ramsay is nae to be trusted!"

"Do nae fret," Camden replied. "Cormac kens this, and the meeting is by the king's order."

"King's order or nae," Brigid replied, "I promise ye, Ramsay has something brewing. Did he take warriors with him?"

"A dozen."

She thought about all her brother's men at his disposal and Sinclair's too. "'Tis nae enough. Ye must go to where he is to meet Ramsay with at least five score."

Camden stared at her in silence for a moment. Finally, he nodded. "I agree. But that means I need to take the men this night, so we can hide ourselves. The king ordered them both to come alone, except for ye."

"Me?" A soft gasp escaped her. "Is he supposed to be returning me to my stepbrother by the king's order?"

"Aye," Camden said. "But he will nae. He has chosen to defy the king rather than give ye up, and if that is nae love, I do nae ken what is."

She couldn't speak. Could hardly breathe. Her chest was filled to overflowing, and it was with hope. Glorious hope. He did love her. Now, all he had to do was admit it.

The remainder of the night was a swirl of men preparing to ride out and possibly go to battle, and she, as well as Martha, Tess, Maisie, and the wives and loved ones of the warriors, aiding them.

When all was ready, Camden stood before them with Quinn at his side. "Listen to Quinn," Camden ordered. Maisie and Brigid nodded dutifully. "There are plenty of men to hold the keep against attack as long as the enemy is held to the outer courtyard, and Quinn kens well how to do this."

Camden eyed each of them. "Listen to Quinn," he repeated.

"We will," they said in unison. Brigid gave a little shiver as the hairs on the back of her neck prickled.

"Camden," she called as he mounted his horse.

He looked down at her. "Aye?"

"Tell Cormac . . . well . . . tell him, I love him." Her cheeks burned at saying the words aloud, but she was glad she had.

She walked around for two days in a haze of worry and anticipation, and it seemed to her everyone else did too. The men were on edge, especially Quinn, who doubled the guards in the keep and on the rampart. The only person who did nae seem particularly affected was Britta who still had not warmed up to Brigid.

Britta hummed a merry tune while everyone else was breaking their fast on the third day after Camden left, and that night, she was the only one who wanted to dance and sing after supper.

When Brigid at last went to bed, she could not sleep. Something niggled at her, but try as she might, she could not place her finger on what was bothering her. With everything going on, it could have been a dozen different things. She tossed and turned for what felt like forever, and finally her eyes closed, and she drifted off to sleep.

"Go back to the tent, daughter," her father commanded when she had finished her supper. She wanted to protest, this was her first tourney she'd been allowed to attend, after all, but she knew better than to voice her opinion.

She nodded, rose, made her way past Laird Donald on the dais and the man who had won the tournament, Laird MacLean. The great hall was crowded, the inner courtyard even more so, and she felt turned around by the throng of people. She thought she was heading in the direction of the tent she was assigned, but when she reached the end of the path and found herself at the entrance to a lovely garden, she realized she was most definitely going the wrong way.

She was about to turn around when she saw a flash of skin and then heard giggling. She squinted to get a better view, and the full moon and torches aided her to see two figures locked together closer than she'd ever seen a man and a woman. The woman had hair as black as night that hung down her back—her bare back— and her arse was bare too. She was, in fact, not clothed at all. The man held one of her legs up, and it was wrapped around his waist. They were both groaning and smiling, and suddenly he shifted, turning his head, so she could see his profile—Ramsay! She bit her lip, her gaze falling to the woman with the shimmering hair and heart-shaped face. Either the woman did nae truly know Ramsay and the horrid sort of man he really was, or the woman was a fool—or perhaps she did nae care.

Brigid was startled awake by the sound of horns. It took her a moment to realize they were the war horns, and her heart tripled its beat as she stumbled out of bed. She ran to the door to the courtyard, and in the bright moonlight, she saw fire blazing in the outer courtyard. Suddenly, the gates to the inner courtyard opened, and a warrior, holding a torch, charged in with a sea of men behind him. She gasped at the sight of her stepbrother and the memory that hit her from her dream.

Ramsay had been with Britta. Britta was the woman he'd been with in the garden at the Donald tourney. That was why the woman had always looked vaguely familiar to Brigid.

Her door was thrown open and Martha stood there, wide-eyed and shaking. "Tess sent me to fetch ye. Quinn has been poisoned. The warriors are scrambling, and yer brother is at the doors to the castle. Come!" Martha strode across the room and grabbed her by the hand. "Tess says for us to take the secret passage away."

Brigid jerked her hand out of Martha's hold. "He's here for me," she said. "And I'm nae about to let my family die to save myself."

Chapter Twenty-Two

*T*he sun was nearly gone in the sky as Cormac rode hard toward Iona Abbey with Ross and Dreux flanking him. He hoped Ramsay was still there and he'd not have to give pursuit after the man if he'd decided Cormac was not coming to the meeting. It had taken longer than he'd anticipated for them to make their way to the strongholds of all three of Sinclair's past wives, but Brigid's theory was confirmed. The women had all had inheritances with stipulations like Brigid's. Now, he needed to somehow get Ramsay to confess in front of Dreux about his and Ramsay's deeds. Then he would drag the man to face the king, who would hopefully rule that both men would face death. That's what they deserved, and if the king would not serve justice, the fathers of Sinclair's deceased wives would undoubtedly fight to do so. As to Ramsay, he would meet justice one way or the other.

As he rode, Brigid's image once again filled his head as it had nearly every moment since she'd walked away from him. She loved him. And he'd hurt her because he was the biggest damn fool that had ever lived. It had taken her walking away from him, telling him she would not wed him because she deserved more, for him to realize she was absolutely right.

The first day on the journey as he rode alone with his thoughts, all were of her and what their life could be together. And when he thought of his life if he did not risk himself again, it was lonely and empty. He needed her.

No one could take your heart. They filled it with emotions that gave you hope, warmth, belonging, and security, as Brigid had said, and then you had to decide to take the risk and give that person your full heart, your love, in return. He'd been afraid of the possibility of loving her and losing her, but if he denied his love for her, he would certainly lose her. He'd wanted to turn around and go home, forget the mission, and fall at her feet to beg her forgiveness and a second chance, but the mission would hopefully make their future more secure.

As he crested the hill and came upon the road that led to the Abbey, he pulled on Ailbert's reins, shocked to see his warriors milling about mid-way upon the road and along the top of the embankment that slanted down to the road, and even at the abbey itself. His men on the road parted, and Camden rode hard toward him. Warning spasms of alarm erupted through Cormac.

Beside him, Ross said, "Something is gravely amiss."

"Aye," Cormac agreed as Camden reached them.

"Before ye yell at me," Camden said, as he stopped his horse, "we've been here for two days, hidden."

Cormac frowned. "Why?"

"Brigid said Ramsay would have something brewing, and I agreed."

Cormac's right temple began to throb. "Did I nae tell ye to nae tell Brigid?"

"Aye, but I told her, and she says to tell ye that she loves ye."

His chest tightened at that. "Am I to take it Ramsay did nae appear?"

At Camden's nod, an oddly primitive warning sounded

in Cormac's ears.

"He did nae," Camden said, "I do nae understand it. Why would Ramsay appeal to the king, and then miss his opportunity to get Brigid back?"

The answer came to Cormac like an arrow in the gut. It took his breath, jolted his heart, and sent his muscles rippling with awareness. He wheeled Ailbert around.

"This was a ploy," he bit out, certain all the way to his bones that this was true. As he lifted his reins to signal Ailbert to gallop, a horse came down the lane toward them. He knew. He knew when he saw it was Quinn who approached that Brigid was gone.

There was a look upon his face of sadness, regret, shame at having failed. Quinn stopped before him, his destrier foaming at the mouth from how hard Quinn had ridden him. Cormac's ears buzzed with questions, so that he only caught some of Quinn's words.

Ramsay at the castle.

What if he never saw her again?

A hundred men with him.

What if she was wed to Sinclair by the time he reached her?

She surrendered herself to Ramsay to save anyone else from being hurt.

Thirty men dead. Fires in the stables.

What if she was dead? What if she was violated? What if she didn't know he loved her? That he wanted to give her all his love? All of his heart? Forever.

Britta had poisoned Quinn.

Britta was in love with Ramsay.

Britta did not believe Ramsay had ravished Maisie.

Brigid.

Brigid had recalled seeing Britta and Ramsay naked in the garden at the Donald tourney.

Brigid had dreamed it.

He couldn't breathe. He couldn't breathe thinking he'd failed her. Might have lost her. No. No. He would reach her. He would save her. He would love her until his dying breath. He let out an animal cry, and then he rode. He rode toward home as if his life depended on it.

Because it did.

It took a day to gather his troops and three more for warriors from the MacLeod Clan and the Donald Clan to join him. It felt like a thousand lifetimes. Sleep was scarce in those days. Instead, his mind replayed the moments since he'd met her. Her taking the arrow for him to protect him the day they'd snatched her from her home. Her lying to protect Maisie after Maisie had tried to drown her. The first time his lips touched her sweet, soft ones after the incident in the loch. Her sweet taste of honey, and a smile that warmed him through. The way she nibbled on her lip when she was about to lie. Her determination to learn to swim. Her contagious excitement when she did. His hands in her silky hair, and on her soft body. Her little moans of pleasure that came deep from her throat. Her big heart and even bigger laugh that came from her belly. The way she danced with pure grace, and how she felt as if she belonged in his arms. Her slender fingers entwined with his.

The memories kept coming, and they were both comforting and torturous. He could not live without her. He did not want to. While he waited for all the warriors to gather, he sent Camden to the king to discover if the king had written the missive Cormac had received. In the meantime, as he waited for Camden to return, he dealt with Britta. They gathered in the Great Hall with the full council present, and a new chair for Maisie, who had asked to be part of the council.

Britta entered the Great Hall with ropes around her wrists and ankles and Quinn on one side of her with Aila on the other. He wasn't surprised to see Aila by her cousin. Even though Britta had poisoned Quinn, she had taken a care to only give him enough to make him sleep. But she had done so with the purpose of creating chaos in the chain of command when Ramsay showed up. They had, it had been discovered, been communicating for a year with missives.

"Britta, ye ken, do ye nae, that ye stand accused of the crime of intent to hurt a clan member and treason against the clan itself?" Cormac asked.

Britta nodded. "Aye, laird, I do. I did poison Quinn, but I did nae have any intention of the clan being put in jeopardy."

Cormac had purposely not allowed the hearing to be an open one, but there were ten guards in the back on the Great Hall and one of them called out, "Bah! Liar!"

Cormac raised a hand for silence, then met Britta's gaze. "What did ye intend?" he asked, having already heard what she told Aila, but he wanted to hear it for himself before he set down his judgement.

Britta wrung her hands. "Ramsay told me to poison Quinn simply so it would make retrieving his stepsister easier. I did nae have any notion that he was going to set fires to our land," she wailed. "And I could nae really see the harm of him taking her back. Ye did nae want her here except to use Maisie's hatred of her to bring Maisie back to life. It worked, so what harm in sending the woman back?"

She paused, smiled thinly and said, "I ken ye lust after her, but ye would nae ever take her as a wife, so sending her back was better for her."

He blinked in surprised at Britta's words. This was his

fault in a sense. Had he admitted his feelings, he and Brigid would now be wed, and she would be safe by his side. He gritted his teeth and leaned forward, resting his forearms on the dais.

"I want her here. I love her. And I intend to wed her if she'll have me. And the harm of sending her back is that Ramsay is evil."

"Nay!" Britta cried out. "He is a good man." Her gaze flew to Maisie. "I'm sorry, but he could nae have done what ye think. It was someone else. Nae him. Yer mind . . . yer mind played tricks on ye."

Maisie slapped her hand to the dais as she stood. She marched down the dais and to Britta, stopping in front of the woman.

"My mind is nae playing tricks on me. I recall the day with perfect clarity and what happened. I wish I did nae. I wish I could forget it."

Maisie shuddered. "Ye—" She pointed a finger at Britta. "Ye're a blind fool. Ramsay kenned Sinclair killed Elsie, and he has kept that secret!"

"What?" Britta gasped.

"Aye," Maisie snarled. "The man ye chose to be loyal to is a dishonorable, lying, savage. He tied Brigid in a dungeon with rats whenever she displeased him, and he would nae let her out!"

Cormac's hands curled into fists. He'd had no idea of that. Was she in a dungeon now? Waiting to be wed to a murderer? Were rats crawling on her? By God, he would kill Ramsay when he got his hands on him. He didn't care what the king said. He'd go to war for Brigid. He'd go to a hundred wars for her.

"Enough!" he bellowed, wanting this to be over. He could not wait another day for Camden to return. He didn't give a damn at this point what consequences attacking Ramsay's castle brought from the king. He had to get to Brigid. "Ye're banished from here forever, and if ye return, ye will be hanged."

"I can go?" Britta asked, astonishment on her face.

Cormac had a moment of pity for the woman. He knew immediately where she thought to go. "Do nae go there," he warned her. "He's nae who ye believe him to be."

She was already turning to march away when the Great Hall door slung open, and Camden flew in, waving a missive in the air. "'Twas nae from the king!" he exclaimed.

"What?" Cormac roared, rising from his seat.

"Ramsay stole the king's seal when he was at court," Camden said. "The king was so livid he sent troops to aid ye in attacking the castle. His only request is that we keep Ramsay alive to send him to the king for punishment."

"What of Sinclair?" Cormac asked, already making his way down the dais.

"Sinclair is dead," Camden said. "The king received word while I was there. It seems he had an accident while hunting with the MacKenzie Clan."

Lara MacKenzie had been Sinclair's second wife. Only child of Laird MacKenzie. Beloved daughter.

Cormac nodded. "Justice has been served."

He thought immediately of Elsie. A pain cut through his chest, but he was certain she could now rest in peace.

"Aye," Camden agreed.

"Let's go get Brigid."

"And vengeance," Camden added.

Cormac paused and turned to Camden with a sudden realization. "Vengeance I can live without if I must, but Brigid—" He shook his head. "I can nae live without her."

Chapter Twenty-Three

*T*he dungeon was every bit as horrid as Brigid remembered. The only saving grace was that this time, her wrists were not tied. But the rats still came out at night, scampering and trying to bite. Mercifully, she had hidden a large stick in her skirts in expectation of finding herself in here again, but when she batted at the fifth rat that had come for her tonight, the stick finally snapped into three pieces. Tears flooded her eyes and she scrambled toward the cell door to scream again for release.

"Please!" she cried out. "Please, let me out of here!"

No voices came. No one to save her. Nothing but darkness and silence, save the scratching sound of the rats. She kicked out every time something brushed her foot. She clenched her fists so tight her nails dug into her palms, leaving pain beneath neat, red, half-moons where they broke the skin.

She opened her fists and sobbed, thinking of Cormac. Where was he? She had been positive he would come for her. Had she been wrong? No, no! She could not give in to despair. He loved her. He loved her, and he would save her, whether he ever admitted the love aloud or not. Still, tears streamed down her face as doubt hammered at her.

And then something strange seemed to move through the silence. A vibration like a rumbling. Was it storming? She stilled and listened, and the vibration grew so loud that it rumbled in her chest and under her feet. Cormac! It had to be Cormac! Hope pumped through her veins as she gripped the bars of her cage.

Footsteps pounded down the hallway. She strained to see in the darkness when a torch bloomed ahead. "Cormac!" she shouted, shaking with relief until Ramsay appeared on the stairs.

"He's here," Ramsay said, his voice flat. "But he'll nae be taken ye alive."

Fear slithered through her as Ramsay opened the cell, and she scuttled backward to avoid him. He closed the distance and grabbed her arm.

"Ye do nae want to kill me!" she said, frantic. "Ye want to wed me to Sinclair."

"Aye, I did," Ramsay said, clamping her wrist in a hurtful grasp as he dragged her from the cell. "But Sinclair is dead, and MacLean is here with the king's men, attacking my home. Do ye ken what that means?" Ramsay snarled, jerking her around to face him.

She nodded. "Aye. The king believes ye ravished Maisie."

"The king would nae turn from me for that, ye fool!" Ramsay said. "She's a woman. Ye're a woman. Women have little importance to leaders like us."

"Ye need to believe that," she realized. "Ye need to have power over women, to feel power over someone, because ye were made to feel helpless nearly yer whole life."

"Shut up," he snarled and yanked her up the stairs into the night of the courtyard. But it didn't appear to be night so many torches burned on the other side of the moat to light the darkness. Cormac was here, and he'd brought hundreds of men with him by the looks of it. She swept her gaze over the sea of men and saw multiple banners flying.

"If ye kill me, he will surely kill ye," she said. "But if ye spare me—"

"Spare ye?" he sneered, dragging her toward the rampart stairs. "Why would I spare ye? There was nae anyone who spared me! I was beaten at the Donald Castle as a child, and then I was beaten here by yer father. I was belittled at every turn! Ye're wedding to Sinclair was my chance to have true power," he roared, tugging her up the last steps to bring them both to the thin platform of the rampart. They were high above Cormac and his men now. The wind blew hard, and fear gnawed at her.

"Do ye remember when I tried to drown ye?" he asked.

She nodded.

"I thought it a mercy. Honestly, I did. The way yer da treated ye and me—well, death seemed a kindness." He halted abruptly and faced her, one fist pounding his chest for emphasis.

"I could nae do it!" He shouted at her, at the wind, at the sea of men below. "I was weak! I was weak just like yer da said, and I need to be strong. I need to show everyone they can nae defeat me. I need to show them what happens if they try."

He grasped her to him and hugged her fiercely. "Do nae fear, Brigid. Drowning is quick."

She knew what he intended a breath before he shoved her from the parapet. She fell into the water below, the impact jarring and painful. She shot to the bottom with the force of her fall. Her feet touched slime, and for one moment, panic rose and she feared she would drown. It was cold. It was dark. She could not remember how to swim, but then she saw Cormac in her mind, showing her the strokes, telling her what to do, and she knew she could reach the surface, and even if she could not, he'd come for her. He'd save her.

She shoved off from the bottom and kicked her legs, pulling at the water with her arms. As she broke the surface, a hand grabbed her and tugged her into strong arms.

"Ye remembered how to swim."

The fear and the relief in Cormac's voice tore at her.

She faced him as she treaded water. "I remembered, but even if I hadn't, I knew ye'd come for me."

He smiled and she could just make out the tenderness in his gaze as he nodded.

"Because I love ye."

"Aye," she agreed, hearing the words so sweet that tears filled her eyes.

"I love ye," he said, giving her a brief kiss. "I love ye. I give ye my heart. My body. My soul. I surrender to ye completely."

"That's all I ever wanted," she said, and he brushed his lips to hers once more.

⚜

After sending Ramsay, guarded by a dozen MacLean warriors, on the road to the king to receive his punishment, it took two days to return home, and night fell as they approached Duart Castle. Brigid assumed they'd all immediately find their beds, but after Cormac helped her dismount, he took her by the hand, all his men still around them in the courtyard.

"Marry me."

She'd wondered when he'd ask her again. She'd had no doubt that he would, and that certainty of his love was the most comforting thing she'd ever felt.

She nodded. "Aye. I will."

"I mean tonight," he said, smiling ruefully.

She frowned. "Tonight?" He nodded. "But I'm dusty from the road and bruised from the fall into the loch, and I've nae had a proper washing, and—"

He pressed a finger to her lips and leaned forward, his lips by her right ear. "I want ye in my bed this night. I want to make ye mine completely. I do nae want to wait another day. I want to wed ye and make ye my wife. I do nae care if ye are travel-worn, dirty, bruised, smelly—"

"Do I smell?" she asked, wrinkling her nose.

"Aye," he said, kissing her. "'Tis why I'll bathe ye as soon as we gain the bedchamber as husband and wife. I'll wash yer hair, and then yer body, and—"

"Ye should have started with that!" she said on a laugh, grabbed his hand, and said, "Come on then, let's get married!"

Not long after, they stood in the small chapel crowded with Maisie and Ross, who Brigid noted to her delight were holding hands, and Martha and Tess, who grinned and dabbed at tears, as well as Cameron, Quinn, and Aila. A knot formed in Brigid's chest and her throat thickened as she stood in front of the priest with Cormac. She glanced over her shoulder and a sigh of contentment escaped her. She was wedding the man she loved, surrounded by their family. She had finally found a home, a place to belong.

The vows went by quickly, and when they were over, Cormac gave her a kiss that was most inappropriate to deliver in public, but no more scandalous than any he'd given her previously. Still, when he pulled away from her, she was breathless and her cheeks flamed. Before she could get over that embarrassment, he swept her off her feet and into his arms, and as she nestled there, he turned them both to the crowd.

"Ye'll have to celebrate without us. My wife and I have our own private celebration planned."

"Cormac!" she gasped, but her protest was drowned out by cheers of approval.

He wasted no time exiting the chapel and making his way to their bedchamber, all the while telling her what he wanted to do to her, and each revelation made the ache inside of her a little more piercing.

By the time they reached the bedchamber and he set her to her feet, she didn't know which one of them was more crazed for the other. They came together in a rush, body to body, hands everywhere, lips pressed firmly together, and clothes miraculously discarded on the floor in a puddle until they were both bare as the day they were born. She stood on tiptoe to kiss him again, but he held her back with his hands on her shoulders.

"I need a minute to just drink ye in."

She nodded, doing the same with him. He was carved perfectly, all muscle and sinewy strength, dusted in all the right places with a light feathering of hair. He raised a hand to cup her face, kissed her gently, then slid his fingers down her neck and between her breasts. He cupped the right breast, then brought his other hand up to caress the left. His touch to her heavy, tingling breasts shot a fierce yearning through her and she moaned.

"Cormac," she said, "the bath can wait."

"Nay." He shook his head. "I want to wash ye, touch ye, care for ye and show ye the tenderness for ye that's inside of me."

It was the most perfect thing he could have said. She nodded, and he took her hand and led her to the tub of steaming water that had been put in their room while they were in the chapel. He took care to help her, steadying her as she stepped in, and the moment the warm water washed over her, she did have to admit it felt like heaven. She gave a sigh as she settled into the tub, and then he stepped in. He barely fit and water sloshed over the edges, but they both just laughed.

It took some maneuvering, but he settled himself behind her so that his thighs were on either side of her. He circled his arms around, she leaned her head back against his chest and closed her eyes, and he rested his chin on top of her head. She had never felt more loved in her life.

"When ye fell," he said, his voice catching, "all I could think was I could nae lose ye."

"Well, ye did nae," she said. She opened her eyes and settled her hands atop his thighs. "But if ye had, ye would survive."

"Aye," he said, "I would, but I'd nae want to."

"Ye would get over that, because ye'd have to," she said, running her hands as high up his thighs as their bodies pressed so close together would allow.

"Why would I have to?" he asked, his voice husky. He released his hold on her to move his hands under her arms, and then to her shocked delight, his fingers splayed across her belly and then trailed between her slightly parted thighs. He opened them a bit more with a gentle nudge, then with a touch that left her quivering, he slid his hands to her light curls that covered her womanhood.

"Ye have nae answered me," he whispered, his breath fanning her cheek and neck.

"I can barely think when ye touch me like that," she gasped.

He chuckled. "In a moment, ye'll really ken what it is to nae be able to think when ye are touched here." His fingers rubbed a spot that was magic. It shot pure pleasure from it to every part of her body and made her yearn for more.

"Answer me or I'll stop," he teased.

"Ye would have to go on because our family needs ye."

"Our family," he said, the pleasure the words brought him obvious in his tone. "I love that verra much." He ran his fingers over her nub once more. She arched backward into him with delight. He brought one hand to her right breast, and as his left hand rubbed gently at her nub, his thumb and index finger circled her nipple.

"My God!" she cried out. "This is the best feeling ever."

"'Tis just the beginning," he said, bringing his mouth to her ear to nibble first there and then at her neck as his hands worked their sorcery. The stroking of his fingers sent pleasure jolts through her that built the tension within her. She thrashed her head as her heart hammered, and her breath came in short gasps. She was going to die of need.

"Please!" she begged. "Give me what I need!"

"I am," he chuckled, "but ye have to let go. Surrender to me. Trust me to lead ye where ye need to be."

She closed her eyes and let go to the warmth, to the pressure of his fingers between her legs, to the slide of them around her sensitive nipple, to his heartbeat against her back, his scent of woods and sweat, springy chest hairs tickling her back, thighs molded to hers, and the sensation of his expert touch. The force in her built until she felt as tight as a bow, and then released in a wash of hot pulses that claimed her entire body. They went on and on, making her inside clench in spasms, until she felt as useless as a newborn bairn.

They sat there for a long stretch of time, both panting as the water cooled. He then picked up the soap sitting on the side of the washbasin and dunked it under the water before running it over her stomach, her arms, and her breasts. His hands caressed her with such tender, sweet care that her throat ached. He ran his thumb around each nipple, slippery from the soap, and her desire sprang back to life.

"Cormac," she panted.

"Aye, I ken."

She knew he did. He was hard as stone against her buttocks. "Let me just wash yer hair."

"Forget my hair," she said, and pushed away to twist toward him. "I want to feel ye inside of me."

"Good God, woman. That is the best sentence I've ever heard in my life." He had them both up and out of the water in a flash, and he wrapped her in a drying cloth before sweeping her off her feet and carrying her to the bed. He lay her gently down, and then got a cloth for himself and dried quickly off. When he came back to the bed, she lay aside her cloth, opened her knees, and crooked her finger at him.

His weight pushed the bed down with a creak but then he settled between her thighs and shocked her by bringing his face down to her most private part. And then he worked magic of another nature with his tongue instead of his fingers, and she started to splinter yet again, but this time, this time, she grasped him by the shoulders, holding herself together at the seams, heart racing, breath short, and tugged him up.

"Take me!"

He rose and the look he gave her was one of pure love, pure need, pure surrender. He positioned himself between her thighs, slid his hand under her arse, and said, "It will take a moment of adjustment, but then—"

"I trust ye," she assured him.

He slid into her in one long, deep stroke. She gasped, felt herself stretch, but they stilled together, his body atop hers, his flesh molding with hers, their love and desire binding them. He arched an eyebrow at her and she nodded, and he began to move in slow strokes. The pain faded and the pleasure resurfaced, building in intensity with each slide of his body into hers. Soon she writhed beneath him, eager to touch his skin, his hair, kiss him, and lift her hips to meet each of his now vigorous thrusts.

That thrilling tension built again, but now she soared higher and higher until she shattered into a million glowing stars. As warmth washed over her, she cried out, and he did too, stilling atop her. A moment later he collapsed to the bed, careful to shield her and bring her into the protective circle of his arm.

A deep feeling of peace filled her as she lay there with him, too consumed with emotion—to speak for a great while. Her heart was bursting with love as he brought his hand to her back to trace a path back and forth across the sensitive skin.

"I have nae ever had such pleasure giving to another, lass."

She grinned. "I've nae ever had such pleasure in the receiving." She propped herself up on her elbow and looked toward him to find him staring at her, a serious look on his face.

"What are ye thinking?"

His slow smile tipped up the corners of his mouth to reveal his dimples she loved so much. "I'm thinking I wish I'd surrendered to ye the day I met ye. We could have been doing this all along."

She laughed and kissed him atop his heart that still beat rapidly. "We've a lifetime together to do this," she assured him.

"Aye," he replied, pressing a kiss to her shoulder and then her forehead. "We certainly do."

She pressed her cheek back to his heart, the steady sure thump of it comforting to her, and her body relaxed completely as she surrendered herself to the happiness that surrounded her, the love between them, and the feeling of home that had long escaped her but now was hers for the taking.

Epilogue

A Year Later

The warriors of Clooney Castle were a rough and rowdy bunch, but Brigid had no doubt they would come to heel. The Clooney warriors had been left to their own devices for far too long by her father and Ramsay, and they were in desperate need of someone to believe in who would believe in them as well.

"Ye're certain this is what ye wish?" Cormac asked her one more time.

Brigid nodded. She'd never been more certain in her life, except for her love for her husband, and her family, and the bairn growing in her belly.

"If ye are nae the new laird," one of the warriors called out, "then who is?"

The crowd roared their approval of the question.

Brigid looked to Maisie who stood by Ross, and Ross took his wife's hand in his left one as he held up his right.

"I'm the new laird of Clooney Castle, and I'm Ross MacLeod."

"We ken who ye are, Wolf!" someone cried out from the crowd. "How did ye come to be our laird?"

Ross grinned at Maisie, and she grinned back then turned to look at Brigid.

"Thank ye," she whispered before focusing on the crowd before her once more.

"Ross had the good fortune of my loving him," Maisie said, her voice strong, sure, and healed. "And I had the good fortune of my brother loving and wedding Brigid Campbell, now Brigid MacLean. It was her castle by inheritance, as ye well know, and with the king's permission, she transferred it to me."

Cormac squeezed Brigid's hand and leaned close to her to whisper in her ear. "Ye are the most selfless woman I ken. Ye did a good thing giving my sister this castle to start new again."

"She'd already started anew," Brigid assured him. "I gave her no less than she deserved for nae surrendering to the darkness that wanted to consume her. She will build this castle, with Ross's help, into the strongest fortress in the Highlands, and with it, she will continue to rebuild herself and make our family stronger."

"I love ye, Brigid MacLean."

"And I love ye, husband."

I hope you enjoyed reading Brigid and Cormac's story and will consider leaving a review! I appreciate your help in spreading the word about my books, including letting your friends know. Reviews help other readers find my books. Please leave one on your favorite site!

If you love sweeping epic romance that takes you on a rollicking adventure through the highlands, then you should try out **When a Laird Loves a Lady**, which is book one in my *Highlander Vows: Entangled Hearts* series. You can read a bit about book 1 below.

Not even her careful preparations could prepare her for the barbarian who rescues her. Don't miss the USA Today bestselling *Highlander Vows: Entangled Hearts* series, starting with the critically acclaimed When a Laird Loves a Lady. Faking her death would be simple, it was escaping her home that would be difficult.

READ WHEN A LAIRD LOVES A LADY, NOW –>

Keep In Touch

Get Julie Johnstone's Newsletter
https://juliejohnstoneauthor.com

Join her Reading Group
facebook.com/groups/1500294650186536

Like her Facebook Page
facebook.com/authorjuliejohnstone

Stalk her Instagram
instagram.com/authorjuliejohnstone

Hang out with her on Goodreads
goodreads.com/author/show/2354638.Julie_Johnstone

Hear about her sales via Bookbub
bookbub.com/authors/julie-johnstone

Follow her Amazon Page
amazon.com/Julie-Johnstone/e/B0062AW98S

Excerpt of When a Laird Loves a Lady

One

England, 1357

Faking her death would be simple. It was escaping her home that would be difficult. Marion de Lacy stared hard into the slowly darkening sky, thinking about the plan she intended to put into action tomorrow—if all went well—but growing uneasiness tightened her belly. From where she stood in the bailey, she counted the guards up in the tower. It was not her imagination: Father had tripled the knights keeping guard at all times, as if he was expecting trouble.

Taking a deep breath of the damp air, she pulled her mother's cloak tighter around her to ward off the twilight chill. A lump lodged in her throat as the wool scratched her neck. In the many years since her mother had been gone, Marion had both hated and loved this cloak for the death and life it represented. Her mother's freesia scent had long since faded from the garment, yet simply calling up a memory of her mother wearing it gave Marion comfort.

She rubbed her fingers against the rough material. When she fled, she couldn't chance taking anything with her but the clothes on her body and this cloak. Her death had to appear accidental, and the cloak that everyone knew she prized would ensure her freedom. Finding it tangled in the branches at the edge of the sea cliff ought to be just the thing to convince her father and William Froste that she'd drowned. After all, neither man thought she could swim. They didn't truly care about her anyway. Her marriage to the blackhearted knight was only about what her hand could give the two men. Her father, Baron de Lacy, wanted more power, and Froste wanted her family's prized land. A match made in Heaven, if only the match didn't involve her...but it did.

Father would set the hounds of Hell themselves to track her down if he had the slightest suspicion that she was still alive. She was an inestimable possession to be given to secure Froste's unwavering allegiance and, therefore, that of the renowned ferocious knights who served him. Whatever small sliver of hope she had that her father would grant her mercy and not marry her to Froste had been destroyed by the lashing she'd received when she'd pleaded for him to do so.

The moon crested above the watchtower, reminding her why she was out here so close to mealtime: to meet Angus. The Scotsman may have been her father's stable master, but he was *her* ally, and when he'd proposed she flee England for Scotland, she'd readily consented.

Marion looked to the west, the direction from which Angus would return from Newcastle. He should be back any minute now from meeting his cousin and clansman Neil, who was to escort her to Scotland. She prayed all was set and that Angus's kin was ready to depart. With her wedding to Froste to take place in six days, she wanted to be far away before there was even the slightest chance he'd be making his way here. And since he was set to arrive the night before the wedding, leaving tomorrow promised she'd not encounter him.

A sense of urgency enveloped her, and Marion forced herself to stroll across the bailey toward the gatehouse that led to the tunnel preceding the drawbridge. She couldn't risk raising suspicion from the tower guards. At the gatehouse, she nodded to Albert, one of the knights who operated the drawbridge mechanism. He was young and rarely questioned her excursions to pick flowers or find herbs.

"Off to get some medicine?" he inquired.

"Yes," she lied with a smile and a little pang of guilt. But this was survival, she reminded herself as she entered the tunnel. When she exited the heavy wooden door that led to freedom, she wasn't surprised to find Peter and Andrew not yet up in the twin towers that flanked the entrance to the drawbridge. It was, after all, time for the changing of the guard.

They smiled at her as they put on their helmets and demi-gauntlets. They were an imposing presence to any who crossed the drawbridge and dared to approach the castle gate. Both men were tall and looked particularly daunting in their full armor, which Father insisted upon at all times. The men were certainly a fortress in their own right.

She nodded to them. "I'll not be long. I want to gather some more flowers for the supper table." Her voice didn't even wobble with the lie.

Peter grinned at her, his kind brown eyes crinkling at the edges. "Will you pick me one of those pale winter flowers for my wife again, Marion?"

She returned his smile. "It took away her anger as I said it would, didn't it?"

"It did," he replied. "You always know just how to help with her."

"I'll get a pink one if I can find it. The colors are becoming scarcer as the weather cools."

Andrew, the younger of the two knights, smiled, displaying a set of straight teeth. He held up his covered arm. "My cut is almost healed."

Marion nodded. "I told you! Now maybe you'll listen to me sooner next time you're wounded in training."

He gave a soft laugh. "I will. Should I put more of your paste on tonight?"

"Yes, keep using it. I'll have to gather some more yarrow, if I can find any, and mix up another batch of the medicine for you." And she'd have to do it before she escaped. "I better get going if I'm going to find those things." She knew she should not have agreed to search for the flowers and offered to find the yarrow when she still had to speak to Angus and return to the castle in time for supper, but both men had been kind to her when many had not. It was her way of thanking them.

After Peter lowered the bridge and opened the door, she departed the castle grounds, considering her plan once more. Had she forgotten anything? She didn't think so. She was simply going to walk straight out of her father's castle and never come back. Tomorrow, she'd announce she was going out to collect more winter blooms, and then, instead, she would go down to the edge of the cliff overlooking the sea. She would slip off her cloak and leave it for a search party to find. Her breath caught deep in her chest at the simple yet dangerous plot. The last detail to see to was Angus.

She stared down the long dirt path that led to the sea and stilled, listening for hoofbeats. A slight vibration of the ground tingled her feet, and her heart sped in hopeful anticipation that it was Angus coming down the dirt road on his horse. When the crafty stable master appeared with a grin spread across his face, the worry that was squeezing her heart loosened. For the first time since he had ridden out that morning, she took a proper breath. He stopped his stallion alongside her and dismounted.

She tilted her head back to look up at him as he towered over her. An errant thought struck. "Angus, are all Scots as tall as you?"

"Nay, but ye ken Scots are bigger than all the wee Englishmen." Suppressed laughter filled his deep voice. "So even the ones nae as tall as me are giants compared te the scrawny men here."

"You're teasing me," she replied, even as she arched her eyebrows in uncertainty.

"A wee bit," he agreed and tousled her hair. The laughter vanished from his eyes as he rubbed a hand over his square jaw and then stared down his bumpy nose at her, fixing what he called his "lecturing look" on her. "We've nae much time. Neil is in Newcastle just as he's supposed te be, but there's been a slight change."

She frowned. "For the last month, every time I wanted to simply make haste and flee, you refused my suggestion, and now you say there's a slight change?"

His ruddy complexion darkened. She'd pricked that MacLeod temper her mother had always said Angus's clan was known for throughout the Isle of Skye, where they lived in the farthest reaches of Scotland. Marion could remember her mother chuckling and teasing Angus about how no one knew the MacLeod temperament better than their neighboring clan, the MacDonalds of Sleat, to which her mother had been born. The two clans had a history of feuding.

Angus cleared his throat and recaptured Marion's attention. Without warning, his hand closed over her shoulder, and he squeezed gently. "I'm sorry te say it so plain, but ye must die at once."

Her eyes widened as dread settled in the pit of her stomach. "What? Why?" The sudden fear she felt was unreasonable. She knew he didn't mean she was really going to die, but her palms were sweating and her lungs had tightened all the same. She sucked in air and wiped her damp hands down the length of her cotton skirts. Suddenly, the idea of going to a foreign land and living with her mother's clan, people she'd never met, made her apprehensive.

She didn't even know if the MacDonalds—her uncle, in particular, who was now the laird—would accept her or not. She was half-English, after all, and Angus had told her that when a Scot considered her English bloodline and the fact that she'd been raised there, they would most likely brand her fully English, which was not a good thing in a Scottish mind. And if her uncle was anything like her grandfather had been, the man was not going to be very reasonable. But she didn't have any other family to turn to who would dare defy her father, and Angus hadn't offered for her to go to his clan, so she'd not asked. He likely didn't want to bring trouble to his clan's doorstep, and she didn't blame him.

Panic bubbled inside her. She needed more time, even if it was only the day she'd thought she had, to gather her courage.

"Why must I flee tonight? I was to teach Eustice how to dress a wound. She might serve as a maid, but then she will be able to help the knights when I'm gone. And her little brother, Bernard, needs a few more lessons before he's mastered writing his name and reading. And Eustice's youngest sister has begged me to speak to Father about allowing her to visit her mother next week."

"Ye kinnae watch out for everyone here anymore, Marion."

She placed her hand over his on her shoulder. "Neither can you."

Their gazes locked in understanding and disagreement.

He slipped his hand from her shoulder, and then crossed his arms over his chest in a gesture that screamed stubborn, unyielding protector. "If I leave at the same time ye feign yer death," he said, changing the subject, "it could stir yer father's suspicion and make him ask questions when none need te be asked. I'll be going home te Scotland soon after ye." Angus reached into a satchel attached to his horse and pulled out a dagger, which he slipped to her. "I had this made for ye."

Marion took the weapon and turned it over, her heart pounding. "It's beautiful." She held it by its black handle while withdrawing it from the sheath and examining it. "It's much sharper than the one I have."

"Aye," he said grimly. "It is. Dunnae forget that just because I taught ye te wield a dagger does nae mean ye can defend yerself from *all* harm. Listen te my cousin and do as he says. Follow his lead."

She gave a tight nod. "I will. But why must I leave now and not tomorrow?"

Concern filled Angus's eyes. "Because I ran into Froste's brother in town and he told me that Froste sent word that he would be arriving in two days."

Marion gasped. "That's earlier than expected."

"Aye," Angus said and took her arm with gentle authority. "So ye must go now. I'd rather be trying te trick only yer father than yer father, Froste, and his savage knights. I want ye long gone and yer death accepted when Froste arrives."

She shivered as her mind began to race with all that could go wrong.

"I see the worry darkening yer green eyes," Angus said, interrupting her thoughts. He whipped off his hat and his hair, still shockingly red in spite of his years, fell down around his shoulders. He only ever wore it that way when he was riding. He said the wind in his hair reminded him of riding his own horse when he was in Scotland. "I was going to talk to ye tonight, but now that I kinnae..." He shifted from foot to foot, as if uncomfortable. "I want te offer ye something. I'd have proposed it sooner, but I did nae want ye te feel ye had te take my offer so as nae te hurt me, but I kinnae hold my tongue, even so."

She furrowed her brow. "What is it?"

"I'd be proud if ye wanted te stay with the MacLeod clan instead of going te the MacDonalds. Then ye'd nae have te leave everyone ye ken behind. Ye'd have me."

A surge of relief filled her. She threw her arms around Angus, and he returned her hug quick and hard before setting her away. Her eyes misted at once. "I had hoped you would ask me," she admitted.

For a moment, he looked astonished, but then he spoke. "Yer mother risked her life te come into MacLeod territory at a time when we were fighting terrible with the MacDonalds, as ye well ken."

Marion nodded. She knew the story of how Angus had ended up here. He'd told her many times. Her mother had been somewhat of a renowned healer from a young age, and when Angus's wife had a hard birthing, her mother had gone to help. The knowledge that his wife and child had died anyway still made Marion want to cry.

"I pledged my life te keep yer mother safe for the kindness she'd done me, which brought me here, but, lass, long ago ye became like a daughter te me, and I pledge the rest of my miserable life te defending ye."

She gripped Angus's hand. "I wish you were my father."

He gave her a proud yet smug look, one she was used to seeing. She chortled to herself. The man did have a terrible streak of pride. She'd have to give Father John another coin for penance for Angus, since the Scot refused to take up the custom himself.

Angus hooked his thumb in his gray tunic. "Ye'll make a fine MacLeod because ye already ken we're the best clan in Scotland."

Mentally, she added another coin to her dues. "Do you think they'll let me become a MacLeod, though, since my mother was the daughter of the previous MacDonald laird and I've an English father?"

"They will," he answered without hesitation, but she heard the slight catch in his voice.

"Angus." She narrowed her eyes. "You said you would never lie to me."

His brows dipped together, and he gave her a long, disgruntled look. "They may be a bit wary," he finally admitted. "But I'll nae let them turn ye away. Dunnae worry," he finished, his Scottish brogue becoming thick with emotion.

She bit her lip. "Yes, but you won't be with me when I first get there. What should I do to make certain that they will let me stay?"

He quirked his mouth as he considered her question. "Ye must first get the laird te like ye. Tell Neil te take ye directly te the MacLeod te get his consent for ye te live there. I kinnae vouch for the man myself as I've never met him, but Neil says he's verra honorable, fierce in battle, patient, and reasonable." Angus cocked his head as if in thought. "Now that I think about it, I'm sure the MacLeod can get ye a husband, and then the clan will more readily accept ye. Aye." He nodded. "Get in the laird's good graces as soon as ye meet him and ask him te find ye a husband." A scowl twisted his lips. "Preferably one who will accept yer acting like a man sometimes."

She frowned at him. "*You* are the one who taught me how to ride bareback, wield a dagger, and shoot an arrow true."

"Aye." He nodded. "I did. But when I started teaching ye, I thought yer mama would be around te add her woman's touch. I did nae ken at the time that she'd pass when ye'd only seen eight summers in yer life."

"You're lying again," Marion said. "You continued those lessons long after Mama's death. You weren't a bit worried how I'd turn out."

"I sure was!" he objected, even as a guilty look crossed his face. "But what could I do? Ye insisted on hunting for the widows so they'd have food in the winter, and ye insisted on going out in the dark te help injured knights when I could nae go with ye. I had te teach ye te hunt and defend yerself. Plus, you were a sad, lonely thing, and I could nae verra well overlook ye when ye came te the stables and asked me te teach ye things."

"Oh, you could have," she replied. "Father overlooked me all the time, but your heart is too big to treat someone like that." She patted him on the chest. "I think you taught me the best things in the world, and it seems to me any man would want his woman to be able to defend herself."

"Shows how much ye ken about men," Angus muttered with a shake of his head. "Men like te think a woman needs *them.*"

"I dunnae need a man," she said in her best Scottish

accent.

He threw up his hands. "Ye do. Ye're just afeared."

The fear was true enough. Part of her longed for love, to feel as if she belonged to a family. For so long she'd wanted those things from her father, but she had never gotten them, no matter what she did. It was difficult to believe it would be any different in the future. She'd rather not be disappointed.

Angus tilted his head, looking at her uncertainly. "Ye want a wee bairn some day, dunnae ye?"

"Well, yes," she admitted and peered down at the ground, feeling foolish.

"Then ye need a man," he crowed.

She drew her gaze up to his. "Not just any man. I want a man who will truly love me."

He waved a hand dismissively. Marriages of convenience were a part of life, she knew, but she would not marry unless she was in love and her potential husband loved her in return. She would support herself if she needed to.

"The other big problem with a husband for ye," he continued, purposely avoiding, she suspected, her mention of the word *love*, "as I see it, is yer tender heart."

"What's wrong with a tender heart?" She raised her brow in question.

"'Tis more likely te get broken, aye?" His response was matter-of-fact.

"Nay. 'Tis more likely to have compassion," she replied with a grin.

"We're both right," he announced. "Yer mama had a tender heart like ye. 'Tis why yer father's black heart hurt her so. I dunnae care te watch the light dim in ye as it did yer mother."

"I don't wish for that fate, either," she replied, trying

hard not to think about how sad and distant her mother had often seemed. "Which is why I will only marry for love. And why I need to get out of England."

"I ken that, lass, truly I do, but ye kinnae go through life alone."

"I don't wish to," she defended. "But if I have to, I have you, so I'll not be alone." With a shudder, her heart denied the possibility that she may never find love, but she squared her shoulders.

"'Tis nae the same as a husband," he said. "I'm old. Ye need a younger man who has the power te defend ye. And if Sir Frosty Pants ever comes after ye, you're going te need a strong man te go against him."

Marion snorted to cover the worry that was creeping in.

Angus moved his mouth to speak, but his reply was drowned by the sound of the supper horn blowing. "God's bones!" Angus muttered when the sound died. "I've flapped my jaw too long. Ye must go now. I'll head te the stables and start the fire as we intended. It'll draw Andrew and Peter away if they are watching ye too closely."

Marion looked over her shoulder at the knights, her stomach turning. She had known the plan since the day they had formed it, but now the reality of it scared her into a cold sweat. She turned back to Angus and gripped her dagger hard. "I'm afraid."

Determination filled his expression, as if his will for her to stay out of harm would make it so. "Ye will stay safe," he commanded. "Make yer way through the path in the woods that I showed ye, straight te Newcastle. I left ye a bag of coins under the first tree ye come te, the one with the rope tied te it. Neil will be waiting for ye by Pilgrim Gate on Pilgrim Street. The two of ye will depart from there."

She worried her lip but nodded all the same.

"Neil has become friends with a friar who can get the two of ye out," Angus went on. "Dunnae talk te anyone, especially any men. Ye should go unnoticed, as ye've never been there and won't likely see anyone ye've ever come in contact with here."

Fear tightened her lungs, but she swallowed. "I didn't even bid anyone farewell." Not that she really could have, nor did she think anyone would miss her other than Angus, and she would be seeing him again. Peter and Andrew *had* been kind to her, but they were her father's men, and she knew it well. She had been taken to the dungeon by the knights several times for punishment for transgressions that ranged from her tone not pleasing her father to his thinking she gave him a disrespectful look. Other times, they'd carried out the duty of tying her to the post for a thrashing when she'd angered her father. They had begged her forgiveness profusely but done their duties all the same. They would likely be somewhat glad they did not have to contend with such things anymore.

Eustice was both kind *and* thankful for Marion teaching her brother how to read, but Eustice lost all color any time someone mentioned the maid going with Marion to Froste's home after Marion was married. She suspected the woman was afraid to go to the home of the infamous "Merciless Knight." Eustice would likely be relieved when Marion disappeared. Not that Marion blamed her.

A small lump lodged in her throat. Would her father even mourn her loss? It wasn't likely, and her stomach knotted at the thought.

"You'll come as soon as you can?" she asked Angus.

"Aye. Dunnae fash yerself."

She forced a smile. "You are already sounding like you're back in Scotland. Don't forget to curb that when speaking with Father."

"I'll remember. Now, make haste te the cliff te leave yer cloak, then head straight for Newcastle."

"I don't want to leave you," she said, ashamed at the sudden rise of cowardliness in her chest and at the way her eyes stung with unshed tears.

"Gather yer courage, lass. I'll be seeing ye soon, and Neil will keep ye safe."

She sniffed. "I'll do the same for Neil."

"I've nay doubt ye'll try," Angus said, sounding proud and wary at the same time.

"I'm not afraid for myself," she told him in a shaky voice. "You're taking a great risk for me. How will I ever make it up to you?"

"Ye already have," Angus said hastily, glancing around and directing a worried look toward the drawbridge. "Ye want te live with my clan, which means I can go te my dying day treating ye as my daughter. Now, dunnae cry when I walk away. I ken how sorely ye'll miss me," he boasted with a wink. "I'll miss ye just as much."

With that, he swung up onto his mount. He had just given the signal for his beast to go when Marion realized she didn't know what Neil looked like.

"Angus!"

He pulled back on the reins and turned toward her. "Aye?"

"I need Neil's description."

Angus's eyes widened. "I'm getting old," he grumbled. "I dunnae believe I forgot such a detail. He's got hair redder than mine, and wears it tied back always. Oh, and he's missing his right ear, thanks te Froste. Took it when Neil came through these parts te see me last year."

"What?" She gaped at him. "You never told me that!"

"I did nae because I knew ye would try te go after Neil and patch him up, and that surely would have cost ye another beating if ye were caught." His gaze bore into her. "Ye're verra courageous. I reckon I had a hand in that 'cause I knew ye needed te be strong te withstand yer father. But dunnae be mindless. Courageous men and women who are mindless get killed. Ye ken?"

She nodded.

"Tread carefully," he warned.

"You too." She said the words to his back, for he was already turned and headed toward the drawbridge.

She made her way slowly to the edge of the steep embankment as tears filled her eyes. She wasn't upset because she was leaving her father—she'd certainly need to say a prayer of forgiveness for that sin tonight—but she couldn't shake the feeling that she'd never see Angus again. It was silly; everything would go as they had planned. Before she could fret further, the blast of the fire horn jerked her into motion. There was no time for any thoughts but those of escape.

About the Author

USA Today and #1 Amazon bestseller Julie Johnstone is the author of historical romance novels set in the Medieval and Regency periods and occasionally modern-day times. Her novels feature fast paced plots filled with political intrigue, intricate world building, and complex characters.

Her books have been dubbed "fabulously entertaining and engaging," making readers cry, laugh, and swoon. Julie is a graduate of The University of Alabama & Springhill College. She lives in Birmingham with her youngest son, her snobby cat, and her perpetually happy dog.

In her spare time she enjoys way too much coffee balanced by super-hot yoga, reading, and traveling.

Sign up for her newsletter here:
www.juliejohnstoneauthor.com

Manufactured by Amazon.ca
Bolton, ON

38420555R00159